LETHAL REPRISAL
CRIMSON POINT PROTECTORS

KAYLEA CROSS

LETHAL REPRISAL

Copyright © 2023 Kaylea Cross

Cover Art: Sweet 'N Spicy Designs
Developmental edits: Kelli Collins
Line Edits: Joan Nichols
Digital Formatting: LK Campbell

This book is a work of fiction. The names, characters, places, and incidents are products of the writer's imagination or have been used fictitiously and are not to be construed as real. Any resemblance to persons, living or dead, actual events, locales or organizations is entirely coincidental.

All rights reserved. With the exception of quotes used in reviews, this book may not be reproduced or used in whole or in part by any means existing without written permission from the author.

ISBN: 9798851801174

AUTHOR'S NOTE

Second chance love stories are one of my favorite romance tropes *ever* (hello, Luke and Emily from the **Suspense Series**!!!), and Warwick's character tugged at my heartstrings, so I loved putting it all together in his and Marley's story. I hope you enjoy it.

Kaylea

ONE

Marley carried one end of the long wedding gown bag up Everleigh's front walkway that her bestie had lined with cute ghosts and spiders, to the doorstep where two jack-o-lanterns stood guard. "This thing weighs a ton for its size."

They were cutting it close. Everleigh's Pararescueman fiancé Grady was due home from his shift at the hospital in about twenty minutes. They had to get the dress hidden before he arrived.

"It's because of all the beading and the train," Everleigh said brightly, her long pale blond hair shining silver in the moonlight as she carried the top of the bag. "And that's also why it cost so much."

"Worth every penny of the price tag. It fits you like a glove and the second you put it on your whole face lit up. I knew within five seconds of seeing you in it that it was The Dress. We could have stopped right then and saved ourselves the next two hours."

"And denied ourselves the mimosas and appetizers they served us later? No way." Everleigh unlocked the townhouse door and stepped inside the bright, clean space. "Still can't believe I don't need to have it altered."

"That just means it was meant to be." Marley slipped her shoes off inside the door, feeling right at home. Spending time with Everleigh was always enjoyable and made her feel more like her old self. The spontaneous, social Marley who was always up for anything and loved to have fun.

That version of herself had all but disappeared over the last year, but there had been signs recently that she was starting to make a comeback. In no small part thanks to Everleigh.

They had become fast friends about five minutes after Everleigh had moved into their former apartment building across town. Turned out Everleigh had been through her own personal hell, and Marley had instantly felt protective of her—even before their psycho neighbor and his terrorist buddies had committed a mass shooting at a concert in early July and nearly killed Ev in the process.

At least the bastard was dead.

"Where are we carting this thing to, anyway?" she asked, shelving those thoughts. Everleigh's strength and resiliency amazed her. Life had repeatedly kicked her friend down and each time, Everleigh had gotten back up and carried on. Now she was about to marry the man of her dreams—an honest-to-God hero who had saved her life. Nobody deserved happiness more than they did.

She reminded herself of that every time thoughts of the upcoming wedding stabbed at her heart and made her think of what might have been.

"I carved out some space in the guestroom closet this morning, just in case I found The Dress at my appointment," Everleigh said.

"Good thinking." They carried it upstairs and tucked it away in its secret hiding spot at the back of the closet, then carefully covered it up to make sure Grady wouldn't see it if he came in here looking for his Air National Guard dress uniform.

Marley moved that and some of his gear to the opposite side of the closet, just in case. "There," she said, standing back to study their efforts in satisfaction. "He won't notice a thing."

Everleigh grinned, her slate-blue eyes sparkling with excitement. "Operation Wedding Gown complete."

She was so cute using military lingo. Being engaged to a PJ and besties with a former Marine had rubbed off on her. "Yes, ma'am." She pulled the closet doors shut. "When do you want to look for my bridesmaid's gown?" She'd taken a quick look at the boutique earlier but hadn't tried anything on because today had been about Everleigh.

"Um, that's *maid of honor* gown, but how does next Sunday work for you?"

"Works fine." Since her job title change and promotion at the seniors care home last month, she now worked regular business hours Monday to Friday and rarely had to go in on weekends anymore, unless there was some kind of special event or emergency. She'd even been able to take part of the afternoon off today to go with Everleigh. "Okay, bring it in." She held out her arms expectantly.

Everleigh flashed her a smile and walked into her embrace. Her friend was a tiny little thing compared to her. Though to be fair, she was six feet tall, so most women were smaller than her. "Thanks for today. I love my dress."

"You're welcome and I'm glad. It's stunning on you. Grady's jaw's gonna hit the floor when he sees you in it." Marley gave her a squeeze and let go. "Speaking of, your man's gonna be home any time now, so go ahead and stay up here to get ready. I'll let myself out."

"Okay. You're the best, Mar."

"It's true, I can't deny it," she teased and headed for the stairs.

Outside on the walkway, she inhaled the cool evening air, taking a big breath of the sweet scent of fallen leaves mixed with damp cedar and pushing aside the sudden wave of loneliness at the thought of spending yet another night alone.

Nope. Chin up. Happy thoughts, count your blessings and all that.

She had a lot to be thankful for. Fall was her favorite season. Here in the Pacific Northwest it was different from back in Kentucky, but she loved it just as much. This place was finally starting to feel like home now.

Back in her car, she drove north up the hills away from Crimson Point, the ocean a vast black expanse lit up by a swath of golden moonlight behind her, struggling against the weight of sadness she'd been fighting all day.

Just a few short months ago, she'd been dreaming about picking a wedding dress of her own. Until she'd received the call that had blown her world apart yet again. She still hadn't recovered from it.

A call came in on the hands-free system just as she turned onto her street and her oldest brother Decker's name popped up on the display, saving her from getting sucked into the sadness and grief she was still struggling to process. "Hey there," she answered, glad to hear his voice.

"Hey. This a bad time?"

"Nope. Just got back from wedding dress shopping with Ev. You got your flights finalized yet?" He'd been called in for an important interview last minute. They'd been willing to do it remotely by secure video chat, but he'd wanted to do it in person. She approved, because it demonstrated how serious he was about the job, and he had one hell of a presence in person that wouldn't come across the same way via video.

She was both excited and nervous about his visit. It had been almost two years since she'd seen him in person and now that he was finally out of the Corps, she was hopeful that they could heal the invisible rift that had stood between them for the past fifteen years and work on having the close relationship she'd always wanted with him.

"Yeah. I fly into Portland around fourteen-hundred-hours on Friday."

Two days from now. "Oh, that's perfect. I get off work at four, so I'll be home by the time you get down here. We can pop down to the waterfront for dinner if you're up to it and I'll show you around."

She'd bought him the softest flannel sheets yesterday in anticipation of his arrival, had already washed them and made up his bed in the guestroom. Tomorrow she'd buy the groceries for his favorite meals and make him homemade biscuits and gravy the morning after he arrived.

She didn't cook much these days and didn't see the point in going to all the trouble when it was only her. It would be great to get back in the kitchen and turn out some home cooking for someone she loved again.

Unbidden, Warwick's face appeared in her mind. His hard features softening in a sexy, knee-weakening smile as he came up behind her at the stove and wrapped his arms around her middle while she made the gravy in her grandmother's cast iron skillet.

"Somethin' smells incredible," he murmured in that deep, delicious northeastern England Geordie accent.

"Sausage gravy."

"No." His lips skimmed the side of her neck. *"It's definitely you, pet."*

"Sounds good," Decker said, yanking her back to the present.

"Great. Hang on, I'm just about to get out of the car, so if I lose you I'll call you back."

She quickly parked along the curb in front of her rental cottage she'd moved into in the summer, set against a forested park in a quiet neighborhood just a few miles from Crimson Point. It didn't have a view, but the price of the rent was right, and she had the whole place to herself. The properties on either side of her were rentals too, but with a different management company.

In fact, the only thing she didn't love about her new neighborhood was the house to the east. Currently it had sketchy tenants she'd made a point of steering clear of.

"Have you heard from the boys recently?" she asked, slinging the straps of her bag over her shoulder as she climbed out of the car. Their younger brothers. Identical twins who had caused their fair share of mayhem when they were younger.

"Not for a few weeks. You?"

A middle-aged woman was walking her goofy golden retriever up the opposite sidewalk. "I talked to them both a few days ago." She locked her car as she strode up the walkway to her front door where the porch light glowed in the darkness, making a mental note to pick up a few Halloween things and some candy in case any trick-or-treaters came next week. Maybe she could even talk Decker into carving a pumpkin or two with her once he got here and settled in a bit. "Neither of them could get leave to come see you but they both said to say hi."

He grunted in acknowledgment. "It's fine. You sure I won't be in the way staying at your place?"

It would be funny if it wasn't so sad. She snorted. "I'm sure." She had nothing going on in her personal life and no one knew about the tragedy that had rocked her world a year ago last June. Not her brothers. Not even Everleigh.

She was still too raw to talk about it, the pain too fresh. But life, in its own cruel way, kept moving on, and she'd been forced to move on with it. After more than a year of feeling empty and lost, she had finally accepted that he was gone. Had put a lot of effort into creating a life for herself here.

"I can still book a rental," Decker offered.

"No way, you're staying with me." Left to his own devices, Decker would revert to his solitary ways and then she would barely see him. They needed the time together. "Don't worry, I promise to give you your space when you need it." Time and distance hadn't done their relationship any favors over the years. It was time for a new strategy and a fresh start, beginning with this long-anticipated visit.

"All right."

"Text me when you land so I know—"

"That my plane didn't crash," he said in a dry tone that made her smile. "I already sent you my flight details, so you can track me yourself."

She entered the code into the lock on the door. "Thank you." She'd adopted a pseudo-mother role for the family at the age of not quite sixteen, had tried her best to be the glue that held the remains of their shattered crew together. It was still an integral part of who she was. "I'm really looking forward to seeing you, Deck."

A beat of silence followed. "Me too," he said and cleared his throat. "See you Friday."

"Yes. Safe tra—" She broke off, glancing over her shoulder when a car suddenly raced up the street behind her. It swerved to miss the retriever that had somehow gotten away from its owner.

Bang, bang!

She instinctively ducked as the gunshots cracked through

the air, swallowed a cry as the bullets punched through her front window just feet to her left. *Jesus*.

"What was that?" Decker demanded in a taut voice. "Marley."

Marley didn't answer, too busy scrambling inside. What the *hell*?

Heart pounding, she flung the door shut and went to her knees behind the narrow section of wall between the door and the ruined window.

"Marley, what—"

"I gotta go," she blurted and ended the call, waiting tensely in place.

She heard the car speed off and disappear down the street. She stayed where she was a few more seconds, listening for the rev of that engine to signal it had come back. When it didn't, she pushed out a breath and crept over to pull the edge of the curtain aside and risk a look outside.

The bullets had punched two holes through the front window about chest height. Beyond her tidy front lawn, the street was quiet and still. No sign of the car coming back.

She rose to her feet, peeking left and right down the street for good measure before dialing 911 to report it. Gun violence was practically unheard of here. That some asshole had just driven by and randomly taken shots at her for kicks was terrifying.

She turned and headed for the kitchen to get some cold water. The call had just connected when her front door suddenly flew open behind her. She whirled around, a scream sticking in her throat as a man rushed in and shut the door behind him.

Shock slammed into her, along with an icy wave of cold that froze her to the marrow of her bones.

"911, what is your emergency?" a woman's disjointed voice said through the phone now dangling at Marley's side.

She stumbled back a step and dropped it with a thud on the hardwood floor in the heavy silence that throbbed in her ears.

Stared in disbelief as a sharp blade of agony sliced through her, certain she was looking at a ghost. Or dreaming.

Because there were no other explanations as to how Warwick James was standing in her living room.

TWO

Warwick didn't move, holding Marley's stunned gaze across the room for a long, tense moment while his heart hammered at his ribs. Coming face-to-face with her after all this time was like a sledgehammer blow to the chest.

The look on her face was gut-wrenching. Shock. Grief.

Damn, he hadn't planned for this to happen. Hadn't meant for her to see him at all when he'd secretly driven over here just to assuage the guilt he'd been carrying for months and reassure himself that she was okay. That she'd been able to move on and be happy without him.

He'd battled back the rush of emotion when he'd seen her pull up ahead of him and walk to her door. But when those shots had been fired in her direction, a switch had flipped inside him. He'd reacted without thinking, automatically abandoning his intent of staying out of sight and going straight into protective mode. Her safety took precedence over everything, including his own, and the need to stay away from her.

Now she stood frozen in place across the room, her face bleached of color except for the smattering of freckles that stood out in sharp relief against her ivory skin. "Wh-what are you—"

"Are you alright?" he demanded, looking her over for any sign of injury. He didn't see any blood, but those bullets had hit way too close to where she'd been standing.

His frantic heartbeat only slowed down when she managed a nod. Glancing to her left, he spotted the two flattened slugs lying on the floor near the living room wall.

Before he could move, her phone started ringing on the floor, shattering the tension between them.

She snatched it up, still staring at him, and answered. "Hello. Yes, I want to report a shooting." She gave her address, explained what had happened, her voice slightly uneven. No doubt from the dual shock of the shots and then him appearing out of nowhere.

"Dark gray Honda sedan," he told her when she paused. "Oregon plates. Starts with seven-six-two." Was it the same car he thought might have been following him earlier?

She frowned at him but repeated it to the operator, still staring at him like she was seeing a ghost.

Warwick tore his gaze from her as she talked and stepped to the damaged window to pull aside the corner of the curtain and look out front. The shooter and vehicle hadn't returned. But that didn't mean they weren't planning on coming back.

The buzz of warning at the base of his spine grew stronger. All night he'd felt like something was off. And the timing of the shooting given everything that had happened was way too suspicious. But he needed more information before he could figure out what was really going on here.

"Was that directed at you?" he asked when she finished the call, still looking across the street. A few people were beginning to trickle out of the small apartment building on the opposite side to see what had happened.

Marley didn't answer.

He turned to face her, still on edge and wishing he had a weapon with him. Gun laws here were so relaxed compared to back home. He wasn't used to carrying anything unless he was on an op. "The shooter. Was he aiming at you?" he said urgently.

She blinked, frowned. "What? No, it—no." Her phone rang again. She ignored it, wrapped her arms around herself and shook her head. "How—"

"You sure?" he insisted, unable to shake that internal warning buzz. The shooter's car looked too similar to the one that might have been following him earlier. He'd taken evasive action to find out, and when it had driven past him without incident, he'd relaxed and dismissed it as being due to the nagging sense of danger he couldn't seem to shake lately.

Until the car had suddenly reappeared behind him again and roared up the street for the passenger to open fire. He'd somehow missed it until then.

Marley still hadn't answered him. He couldn't let this go. "Because he fired in your direction when your back was turned." It made his blood run cold to think of it.

This neighborhood was quiet, the end of the street meeting the edge of the park. It had to be targeted. And those bullets had come chillingly close to hitting Marley.

She stiffened, her gaze sharpening, erasing the glazed, shocked look in her eyes. "You were waiting outside my place?"

"Yes," he said, still coiled up inside. Sitting outside like a damn stalker watching her house because he'd needed to see her just one last time before leaving town. He'd crossed the ocean for that chance. But that wasn't important now. He needed to know exactly why someone had just opened fire in her direction.

"Warwick, what the *hell* is going on," she asked, her voice catching. "You've been alive this entire time and didn't bother telling me?" Mingled fury and pain etched her features.

It was a long story. One he'd never intended for her to know about. "I—"

"They told me you were dead. Dead! And now you just show up out of the blue over a year later and burst in here as if nothing ever happened?"

There was no time for this right now. "That's not—"

"You...*asshole*!" she choked out, tears glimmering in her eyes. She grabbed something from the kitchen counter behind her and flung it at him.

He ducked just in time to avoid the book hitting him square in the face. It smacked into the wall behind him with a slap and fell to the floor. "I'm sorry," he began, not knowing where the hell to start. She didn't seem the least bit upset about the drive-by anymore.

"No," she cried, and chucked a throw pillow from the couch at him. He caught it before it hit him in the chest. "You *selfish*, lying asshole. You disappeared without a word last June, then let me believe you were dead all this time when you were actually alive. Fucking *dead*, Warwick. Do you have any idea what that did to me? How could you do that?" She stopped, put a hand to her mouth and choked back a sob, then bent double and put her hands on her knees as she sucked in shaky breaths.

Before he could move or say anything else, she gagged and raced out of view down the hall.

He winced when he heard the toilet seat hit the tank a moment later, followed by retching sounds. "Christ," he muttered, closing his eyes. What a mess. The anguish on her face, in her voice just now, made it feel like someone had plunged a knife into his chest. He'd needed to make sure she was safe. But in doing so, he'd hurt her more.

He dragged a hand through his hair, started to go after her but stopped himself. He didn't have the right to go to her now, to touch her or hold her or do any of the things he wished he could. And given the current level of unease churning in his gut, what he needed to do right now was make sure her yard was secure.

"I'm gonna go take a look outside," he called to her, not surprised when she didn't answer. What a sodding mess he'd made of this whole thing.

He moved quickly through the kitchen and found the back door. Slipped outside into the backyard. A six-foot privacy fence enclosed the lawn bordered by shrubs and hedges. Beyond it, the forest that marked the edge of the park formed a wall of dark shadows.

Nothing inside the yard look disturbed. He checked the windows along the back of the house. All were closed and locked, no sign of anyone having tried to break in.

He went to the corner of the wooden fence. Grabbed the top of it, swung up and over, dropping lightly onto the grass on the other side. From here he had a clear view of the street out front. Several people were on the opposite sidewalk now, curious onlookers coming out to see what had happened.

Ignoring them, he turned his attention to the house next door. The cottage was similar to Marley's, a one-story post-war build that had been updated and appeared freshly painted. All the windows were dark but in the glow of the streetlamps, he could see beer cans and alcohol bottles strewn around the yard and garbage spilling out of torn bags piled up at the side.

Satisfied the area was secure for now but concerned about what might still be coming, he went back around the front and entered the door.

Marley was perched on the edge of her couch when he came in. Her gaze collided with his the instant he stepped through the door and his chest constricted. She was still pale, her expression now set instead of scared or devastated, arms wrapped around her middle as if to protect herself.

From him. It was like a kick to the gut. But he deserved it.

"So if you didn't die, then what the hell really happened?" she asked in a brittle voice. She looked like another blow might shatter her. "Why didn't you tell me, and where the hell have you been all this time?"

His heart twisted. Even pale and in shock, she was still the most beautiful fucking thing he'd ever seen. "I was tryin' to protect you." And now it seemed like he might have failed at even doing that.

"Protect me? From what?" she scoffed.

"From the truth." He remembered the moment they'd met too clearly. Seeing her at that hotel in Atlanta, the smile she'd flashed him had rooted him to the spot. He'd returned from a meeting that night in late April without a clue that he'd been about to meet the woman who would shift his entire world on its axis.

They'd gone for a drink together, then dinner. Two dates later, things turned intense fast. He'd never been the same since.

But she hadn't known the truth about him. Because he hadn't been able to tell her.

Then he'd been called back to the UK for a mission he couldn't tell her about. Three weeks after that he'd met her at a resort in the Bahamas and spent the best, most unforgettable time of his life with her before being called away on the mission to hunt Isaac Grey. He'd left knowing that she had altered the fabric of his universe. That she owned him heart and soul.

And then his entire life had been blown apart by the explosion that had almost killed him.

"What truth?" she snapped. "Just tell me what the hell happened."

"I can't." He wanted to. Desperately. There was so much he needed to say to her, but he couldn't say any of it now. He didn't have much time. The cops would be here any minute and he couldn't risk being here when they showed up. After what had just happened it was even more important that he keep a low profile.

"Why the hell not?"

"Just can't." But before he left, he fully intended to make sure Marley was safe. "Everything's secure outside. Is there anyone else who you think could have been the intended target?" If they hadn't been targeting her, then there was only one other explanation. And he hoped to God he was wrong. "Mar."

The seconds were ticking by too fast. He wished he could stop time. Wished he could go back and—

Well, he wished a lot of things. But it was too damn late to change any of it now.

"It couldn't have been me." The stark accusation in her stare ate at him. "There's no way anyone would want to shoot me. Either they meant to hit next door or it was totally random, some idiots just wanting to scare someone for kicks."

"What's goin' on next door?"

She huffed in annoyance, raw anger burning in her gaze. "New renters moved in next door a few weeks back. Something's going on over there. People coming and going at all hours. Teenagers and young guys mostly. It might have something to do with what just happened."

"Drugs?" He'd read about a recent uptick in drug activity in the region over the past few months. Traffickers were using small towns along the coast to move their product instead of risking their shipments being seized by security protocols at the large ports in Portland and Seattle.

"Maybe."

The drive-by *could* be drug-related. But there was still the other possibility. One that made his heart pound and his stomach clamp tight, confirming his worst fear.

He went over the sequence of events leading up to this. The angle of the shots in comparison to where he'd been parked at the curb. And the driver had swerved suddenly—at the exact same moment the shots were fired.

So the shooter definitely could have been aiming at him, not Marley. Didn't matter if the attempt had been amateurish. And if he was right, then it meant he'd brought the unknown threat hanging over him to her door.

The warning prickle at the base of his spine shot up his backbone, making the back of his neck crawl. His gut instinct screamed that the gaps in his memory around the time of the explosion and the nagging sense that someone was tracking him recently were connected.

A wave of sick fury washed over him that he'd been selfish enough to come here at all tonight. He'd known it was wrong, known it was a bad idea. If he was right about this, he'd not only brought danger to Marley's doorstep—he'd nearly gotten her killed a few minutes ago.

In the taut silence, Marley's gaze tracked over him, lingering on the scars running down the right side of his face and neck. She shook her head, the sadness in her expression eating at his insides like acid. "What the hell happened, Warwick? Just tell me."

His whole body tensed with the need to haul her into his arms and lock her to him. Bury his face in the silky mass of her auburn hair and just breathe her in the way he'd imagined doing a million times since waking up in the CCU in London. To explain. Beg her forgiveness. Beg her for another chance.

He'd never known he could feel the things he'd felt when he was with her. The things he'd felt *for* her. Had never experienced the kind of warmth and caring and connection he'd found with her. Not from anyone in his whole life.

Now he was finally standing in the same room as her with only fifteen feet between them, and every cell in his body craved her like a drug. Craved her so much he could hardly breathe.

But he couldn't stay. She didn't know about his past. Didn't know anything about his job, what he'd done and been involved in, or that his mere presence might have put her at risk tonight.

The drive-by just proved that she was better off without him in her life. Safer. And now that he'd endangered her by coming here tonight, he would never forgive himself.

The faint wail of a distant siren reached his ears, signaling his time was up.

He stood there for just one moment longer, drinking her in while the invisible blade lodged in his heart twisted. "I'm sorry, I can't," he said hoarsely. "And I have to go." He'd try to come back later if it was safe.

Her head snapped up, bewildered brown eyes flaring in disbelief. "What?"

He felt like he was being torn in two, but he had no choice. He rushed past her for the back door.

She shot off the couch. "Warwick!" Her tone was equal measures incredulity and anger.

He deserved her anger. Every bit of her hatred for the pain he'd caused her. For the additional pain he was about to cause.

Fuck.

"Stay inside and away from the windows until the cops secure the area," he commanded without looking back, and slipped out the back door. After checking the backyard he went through the wooden gate in the fence and ran for the vehicle he'd left parked out front.

The sirens were close as he pulled away from the curb. He scanned the sidewalks on the way by. The people standing around trying to find out what was going on.

Two police cruisers turned the corner just as he reached the stop sign, lights flashing. He kept going, needing to make it look like he was leaving the area.

In case the prickling along his neck was right. And he feared it was.

Flashing red and blue filled the rearview mirror as he left Marley's street behind. But with everything that had happened, their presence wasn't good enough for him.

He would stand guard personally in the shadows. Only once he was certain she was safe and that he hadn't brought danger to her doorstep could he give her the explanation he owed her.

It wasn't enough. Not nearly enough. But sadly, it was all he could give her now.

THREE

Marley stood there staring in disbelief at the back door after it slammed shut behind Warwick, unsure whether she wanted to scream or cry. Maybe both.

She sank back onto the couch in a daze, reeling from everything that had just happened. Fighting the instinctive urge to run after him and demand that he come back to explain himself.

He'd wanted to protect her? From fucking *what*? Nothing would be a good enough reason for him to let her believe he'd died.

Rage began to take over, and it felt a hell of a lot better than the sickening shock and helplessness from before.

She wanted answers. He damn well *owed* her answers. As well as a lengthy and detailed apology—that she would tell him to shove straight up his lying ass.

She put her head in her hands, struggling to process it all. For sixteen months she'd believed him dead. Had mourned for him all alone. Had grieved his loss every single day since, all without knowing what had happened to him, only that he worked for the UK government and had died in an accident.

An explosion no one had ever bothered explaining. And

since they hadn't been married, she'd had no legal standing to demand anything.

The only reason she'd even found out in the first place was because the police had apparently found her number on a phone with his fingerprints. She'd struggled through her grief, the agonizing sadness and loneliness.

And then ten minutes ago he'd walked through her door—only to take off without an explanation. But the scars on his face made her believe the explosion part might have been real enough.

A sharp knock on the door yanked her out of her thoughts. "Ms. Abrams? Police, ma'am."

Muttering a curse, she pulled herself together and went to open the door. Her mind was in constant chaos as she talked to the two officers. Explaining what had happened, with the exception of mentioning Warwick. The way he'd taken off when he'd heard the sirens told her something else was going on.

Was he a criminal or something? Because clearly she hadn't really known him at all.

They took her statement, looked around her property and took pictures of her window and the bullets on the floor.

Bullets that had come way too damn close to hitting her.

She crossed her arms as a shiver rippled through her. She was a former Marine. Could handle herself and didn't spook easily, but she'd never been in combat and certainly hadn't expected to be shot at here on her doorstep. Those assholes could have severely wounded or killed her.

"We're going to have our forensics people come in to document everything," the older officer told her. "It'll take a few hours. Is there somewhere else you can go for tonight?"

"Yes." Everleigh and Grady would put her up for the night. "I'll just go pack a bag."

She walked into her bedroom and opened the closet feeling like she was in a fog. A fog so dense that she jumped slightly when her cell phone rang. She snatched it from the bed, some stupid part of her hoping against hope that it might be Warwick.

Of course it wasn't. It was Decker. He'd been calling repeatedly since she'd hung up on him after the shooting. Wouldn't stop calling until she reassured him she was okay.

She didn't feel like talking to anyone, even him, but she needed to let him know she was all right. "Hey. Sorry, I've been busy here." Her voice sounded surprisingly steady. Inside she felt anything but.

"What the hell happened? I heard shots." His anger and concern vibrated through the line.

"Some idiot did a drive-by and hit my front window when I was at the door." But that hadn't shaken her nearly as much as Warwick's sudden resurrection.

"Did you—"

"The cops are here now. Everything's fine, I promise." She didn't dare mention Warwick. Decker didn't really know about him and if she told him what had happened, he would probably hunt Warwick down and beat him to within an inch of his life for hurting her.

"You don't sound fine," Decker said after a slight pause.

Yeah, well, it had been a hell of a night, and he didn't know the half of it. "I'll be okay." There was no way that shooter could have been targeting her. "Really, but I can't talk right now." She pressed her lips together, blinked fast to hold back tears.

God, she was cracking apart inside, her heart breaking all over again. Why had Warwick let her think he was dead all this time? How could he do that to her. And why had he come here tonight in the first place?

"Yeah, okay," Decker said, softening his tone. "Can I do anything?"

She sucked in a breath. *Don't cry, don't cry...* If she started she might never stop, and she'd already cried enough for him. "No, but I can't wait to see you Friday. Love you," she managed to get in before her throat closed up.

"Love you too. Call me anytime if you want to talk, all right?"

She could count on one hand how many times he'd told her he loved her. Hearing it now just about broke her. "I will. Bye."

Ending the call, she drew in long, unsteady breaths, her vision blurred by a haze of tears. Why had Warwick come to Crimson Point? If he'd wanted to see her, why take off so suddenly without explaining anything? And why didn't he want to be seen by the police?

Her mind came up with all kinds of crazy ideas. From drug runner to some sort of mob involvement. And none of that was helping matters.

She needed sanity right now. Stability.

When she'd calmed down a bit and the tears had finally receded, she dialed Everleigh.

"Are you checking to make sure I didn't crack and show Grady the dress?" Everleigh answered in a teasing tone. "Because I didn't even tell him I'd bought one."

"No, that's...not why I'm calling."

A startled pause met her words. "Mar, what's wrong? Are you okay?"

Marley swallowed, pressed her lips together for a long moment until she could speak without choking up. With anyone else she would have lied and said she was fine. But Everleigh was her best friend and she desperately needed her right now. "You know what? No. No, I'm not okay."

There was a rustling sound in the background. Grady's low

voice murmuring something. "What's going on?" Everleigh demanded.

Marley told her about the shooting and police. "But there's…more. A lot more, and the police have asked if I can go somewhere else for the night. Could I—"

"The spare room's all yours," Everleigh said. "For as long as you need it."

Marley exhaled in a rush. She hated being a burden, was uncomfortable leaning on anyone and hated to be the source of drama, but… "Thank you."

"Sweetie, of course. Do you want me to come get you?"

"No, it's fine, I can drive myself. See you soon."

Everleigh and Grady were both waiting at the door when she got there. Her friend took one look at her and pulled her into a hug, holding her tight. It was wonderful and badly needed, but in that moment Marley would have given just about anything for it to be Warwick's arms around her instead.

"Whatever it is, just tell me," Everleigh said, drawing her inside.

Marley went over to the couch and curled up on one end, hands knotted in her lap. Everleigh sank down on the other end, watching her with worried eyes.

Grady stood behind her, dark brown gaze steady on Marley, his quiet, capable presence comforting. "You okay?"

"Yes." Not really, but doing her best to keep her shit together. "Thanks."

"Then I'll just…" He jerked a thumb over his shoulder. "Holler if you need anything."

Marley waited until he'd left the room before saying anything else to Everleigh. "I don't even know where to start. No, yeah I do." She paused to rub at her eyes before continuing. "Remember the guy I told you I'd been seeing last year before we met?"

Everleigh frowned. "The British guy who broke your heart? That's all you ever told me, that he was English and broke your heart. Every time I tried to get you to talk about him, you closed up."

Because it hurt too damn much. "Warwick. His name's Warwick." Pronounced the English way, the second W silent.

Ev tucked her feet under her, gaze sympathetic. "What happened?"

She blew out a breath. "Remember that work conference I was at in Atlanta late last April?"

"That's where you met him?"

She nodded. "He was in town for meetings. We bumped into each other in the hotel lobby, hit it off and, well, fast forward a few weeks and we met up at a resort in the Bahamas." Best time of her life. The happiest. And oh my God, the sex. Off the charts. He'd thoroughly ruined her for anyone else.

"How long were you together?"

"A few weeks in total, but we were apart for a lot of it because he kept having to go back to the UK for work." Legit work? Or criminal shit?

She tipped her head back to rest against the couch cushion and kept going, letting the memories wash over her. "I can't even describe what it was like with him. I was falling so hard and fast for him, the first time in my life that's ever happened to me."

"So what went wrong?" Ev asked, sounding confused.

She wasn't the only one. "He left again. Got a call one morning in the Bahamas and said he had to go. He was gone within the hour, just like that. No further explanation."

"And that was it?" Disappointment drenched Ev's tone.

"No. He called me a few times over the next couple days. Sounded like he sincerely missed me, promised to come see me in Louisville as soon as his upcoming job was done. Some government thing he wouldn't give me details about." It was all so suspicious now. She swallowed. "Two weeks later I got a call from the police in London saying he was dead."

Everleigh gasped. "*What*? Oh my God, Marley—"

"They told me there'd been an explosion. There was no funeral. No other information because we weren't related or married. He was just…gone."

"Why the hell did you never tell me any of this?" Everleigh said, looking stricken. "God, I had no idea, I'm so sorry."

"Don't be." She shook her head at herself. "It wasn't because I didn't trust you. I was in shock, you know? And… well, after everything you'd been through, I thought it seemed stupid and selfish to dump all that on you too." Everleigh had lost her husband and their baby within the span of three hellish months.

Everleigh's eyes filled with tears. "It's not stupid or selfish," she said, wiping at her eyes, and Marley felt like shit for hiding everything from her. "God, I feel horrible for making you feel like you couldn't confide in me."

"No, don't," she insisted, sitting up to grab Everleigh's hands and squeeze them. "You're the best friend I've ever had, and I love you to death. This is on me. I'm…not good at leaning on others, I guess."

Everleigh shot her an annoyed look. "You guess?"

"Okay, I know it. Anyway, that's why I was kind of withdrawn back then."

"And no wonder." She eyed her in concern. "But you're doing better now?"

"I thought I was. Until he showed up tonight."

Her friend's eyes flew wide in disbelief. "*What*?"

"Five seconds after those shots went off, he came through my front door."

Ev pulled a hand free and covered her mouth with it, gaping at her in horror. "No."

"Yeah. I couldn't believe it. He started asking questions about the shooting, kind of took over. Didn't say a word about where he'd been or what had happened. Before I knew it the police were coming. As soon as we heard the sirens, for a second he looked at me like his heart was being ripped out, then this eerie kind of mask dropped into place. He said he had to go, then took off."

"Why? And did you go after him?"

"No goddamn clue. And no, because I felt like I'd been sucker punched and wasn't going to chase after him if he didn't want to stay."

"Oh, Mar." Everleigh slumped back into the cushions, watching her with a mystified expression Marley felt all the way to her soul. "What the *hell*."

"I know. He looks different now. His face is scarred on one side. So maybe he really was wounded in an explosion."

"Oh, man…"

She pushed out a breath, not wanting to dwell on it anymore. "Anyway, I was losing my mind and then my brother called—he's coming in on Friday, by the way—and then I called you." She squeezed the hand she was still holding. "Thanks for letting me stay here tonight. I really didn't want to be alone."

Everleigh gave her a sympathetic smile. "Of course. I'm here for you anytime."

They lapsed into silence after that and she was relieved that Everleigh didn't press her for more details, didn't try to change the subject or distract her. Just sat with her while she struggled to process everything that had happened. Trying to make sense of it. Thinking of the tragedies that had shaped her life.

Her heart had already been shattered twice before. She

absolutely wouldn't forgive Warwick James for doing it a third time.

SHE WAS LONG GONE.

Warwick expelled a breath as he peered through the trees lining the edge of the park behind Marley's property and into her backyard beyond the fence. It was after midnight. Her car wasn't parked out front. All the windows were dark. There was crime scene tape across her front door and the window had been boarded up.

The neighborhood was still and quiet. Nothing suspicious happening, and there had been no sign of the shooter or anyone else checking out Marley's place.

Had she gone to a hotel? A friend's place?

It made sense that she wouldn't want to stay here after what had happened, and in all honesty, she might be safer elsewhere for now. He hoped she had someone she trusted to be with. Someone who cared about her to support her after the shock he'd delivered. But dammit, he wished it were him.

Everything in him ached to hold her. To try to explain everything as best he could. He couldn't leave her in the dark anymore. That would be beyond cruel after suddenly bursting through her door and delivering yet another shock tonight.

But telling her would only make it worse. There was no explanation he could give her that would make up for what she'd suffered already, for him allowing her to think that he was dead for more than a year.

The right thing to do was to stay the hell away from her. Leave town to protect her.

Except dammit, now that he'd seen her again and potentially endangered her, he couldn't find the will to do it.

Marley was his weakness. Had been from the day he'd met her. She made the rest of the world fall away, made him forget everything but her. One touch from her and his resolve to keep his distance would turn to ash.

He clenched his jaw, remembering the utter shock on her face when he'd walked through that door earlier. The raw pain that continued to claw at his insides.

It was hell being so close to her and not being able to be with her. But then hell was what he deserved.

Ripping his attention from her house, he slipped through the trees and past her fence to survey the darkened, quiet street once more. The shooter wasn't coming back. But his gut said there was still danger out there somewhere.

A threat to him and anyone who got close to him. He couldn't let that be Marley.

A wave of loathing washed over him. He never should have come here. He'd known that from the start. Known he should have stayed the hell away. But now he had to stay, watching over her from afar, protecting her without her knowing until he was certain she was safe.

Once he was sure of that, he would leave for good. And hopefully take whatever danger was looming with him.

FOUR

"Granddad, look!"

Roland paused in the midst of packing his luggage and smiled as his four-year-old granddaughter raced through the bedroom door clutching something in her hands. He was a granddad three times over and while he loved them all dearly, he and Nelly had a special bond. "What've you got there, darling?"

"A unicorn!" She thrust it toward him so he could see the cuddly toy with its sparkly rainbow horn, then hugged it to her chest. "Isn't she beautiful?"

"She certainly is, but I'll tell you a secret." He lowered his voice to a whisper. "She's not as beautiful as you."

Nelly giggled and hugged her new toy harder. "Did you pick her out for me?"

"I might have. What do you think?"

"You *did*! I knew it." Beaming, she clambered up on the end of the bed and made herself comfortable to watch him, still hugging her toy. "Where are you going?"

"To a place called San Francisco."

"Is it far away?"

"Very far. On the other side of the world."

"Where though?"

He loved her curious mind. "I'll show you. Come on." He took her by the hand, helped her hop down and led her down the hall to his study where the antique globe sat on a table in the corner. One of his greatest pleasures in life was having his children and grandchildren over for dinners on the weekend. "Do you remember where England is?"

"That's where we live," she said, pointing to it.

"That's right. We're just south of London on the River Thames. Can you see where it is?"

"Here." She picked out the tiny, faint line immediately because they'd done this several times before.

"Clever girl." He ruffled her curls. She was a quick little thing and had firmly wrapped him around her little finger mere hours after being born. "I'm catching a plane in the morning and flying waaaay over here across the Atlantic Ocean…" He traced a fingertip across the route the plane would take. "And waaaay over here to this country called the United States, to the city I'm going to on the far West Coast. Right here." He tapped the city.

She studied it for a moment, taking it all in. "That's a long way."

"It's a very long way."

She looked up at him with big brown eyes that were identical to her mother's. "When are you coming back?"

The way this child tugged at his heart. "Soon. Maybe a week or two, that's all." It all depended on what the situation was like when he finished his initial meetings.

"Will you be lonely? You can take my unicorn with you if you want."

"I think your unicorn would be much happier staying with

you. And I won't be lonely as long as you and your mum send me messages and videos."

"And Rainbow, too."

He raised his eyebrows. "Is that her name?" He nodded at the unicorn.

She grinned. "Yes." She looped one arm around his leg, hugged him. "I love her. Thank you!" she cried and skipped out the door.

The indulgent smile on his face slowly faded along with the patter of her little feet as she raced downstairs to join the rest of the family relaxing in the living room. Foreboding crept in, the cold reality of his current predicament hitting him.

It was impossible to keep smiling with Warwick James still in the wind.

After the operation in Durham in which Isaac Grey had been killed, James had suddenly disappeared. For two whole weeks, Roland hadn't been able to find out where he was, until he'd suddenly popped up on a flight from Heathrow to the US. The person tasked with following him had tracked him as far as Portland, Oregon, several days ago. There'd been nothing else since.

No online activity. No credit card activity to tell where he was or what he was up to. James had simply gone to ground somewhere on the West Coast.

Saying it alarmed him would be an understatement. It made him more suspicious than ever that trouble was brewing, and he was too busy currently to delve further into this personally at the moment, but something more had to be done.

He'd first become suspicious of James just prior to the Lake District op last summer. He was increasingly concerned that James had seen or heard or deduced things he shouldn't about the Grey case prior to being wounded. Things that incriminated Roland directly and would spell the end of his career, reputation, and land him in jail if they ever came to light.

The only silver lining was that James had suffered a severe concussion and short-term memory loss in the explosion. Roland had watched him carefully during his recovery. James hadn't appeared to talk to anyone else involved in the parts that Roland intended to ensure stayed buried. Hadn't revealed anything worrisome or suspicious during questioning. He hadn't been nosing around asking questions since. So it was possible he either didn't know, or didn't remember.

But if he *had* known and then forgotten due to his injuries, it was also possible that he could regain his memory at some point.

Roland had kept tabs on James throughout the past year because he simply couldn't be sure whether James knew too much…or nothing at all. Either way he was too dangerous to be left unmonitored. James suddenly disappearing like this after the Durham op raised too many red flags. He had to be brought in for a thorough debriefing to ascertain whether he was a threat or not.

There was no telling whether he'd remembered something, who he was in contact with, or who he'd been talking to. James was highly skilled and experienced as both a soldier and a covert operative. If he didn't want to be found it would take someone equally as skilled to track him down.

Roland needed answers so he could decide what measures to take next. He'd already risked so much during the Grey case. He couldn't afford to take another one this soon. So while it would be convenient to have James done away with somewhere out of view in another country, Roland wasn't prepared to make that call unless he knew James posed a credible threat.

Which he might. And that was the hell of it.

He strode back down the hall to the master bedroom and

straight into the en suite. On his side of the sink, he opened the mirror and took out the bottle of prescription medication he'd been taking daily since the gastric ulcer had first been diagnosed a year ago this past June. He'd never had stomach problems in his life—or any other serious health issues for that matter—until the op in the Lake District.

He swallowed the tablet with a sip of water, wiped the few drops he'd spilled on the marble vanity with a clean face towel before going back into the bedroom to finish packing. His family had no idea what was going on. What he was involved in. Or how much he stood to lose if it all came to light.

After spending a lifetime working in British intelligence and making his way up the chain to where he was now at MI6, he wasn't about to let that happen.

"Need a hand, darling?" his wife said from behind him.

He put on a smile to hide that something was wrong and looked at her. He never told her about work, had always tried to protect her from the stresses and darkness of his job. "No, I'm nearly done."

"You sure?"

"Yes. Be down in a few minutes."

"All right." Her quiet footsteps tracked back through the bedroom and out into the hall.

Roland clenched his jaw, hand tightening around the tie in his fist. The situation with James was untenable and taking a serious toll on his health, both mental and physical. Something had to be done, and he wasn't willing to risk getting more personally embroiled with this than he already was.

He also hadn't reached this level of stature in his career without good reason. A stature that just happened to come with a wide net of contacts to help in situations just such as this.

He strode to the walk-in closet. From the safe behind the custom-built shoe rack, he took out a burner phone and used it to access a secret database he used sporadically whenever a situation became too sticky.

A message was waiting from the American private investigator he'd hired to track James from Portland.

James verified in Crimson Point. A picture was attached. James, his facial scars unmistakable, getting out of a vehicle with the sea in the background.

He searched the name of the place. A small town on the Oregon Coast.

What the hell was James doing there? Talking to someone in the FBI or CIA? His stomach clenched tight at the thought. If James had remembered overhearing something he shouldn't have and was now talking about it…

Roland accessed an encrypted program. A list of qualified contractors popped up to choose from.

Within minutes he found someone already in the area, and sent out an activation message to the contact number listed beside the contractor's name.

He was just zipping up his suitcase on the bed minutes later when the response came back.

Tied up on a job at the moment.

How long until you're available? he replied.

A day or two. Maybe less.

He paused, considering his options. Decided that given the quality and profile of this particular contractor, waiting another twenty-four to forty-eight hours was worth it. Ordering a hit on James at this point was premature, and while Roland had his faults, James *had* been fundamental in hunting down Grey. That had to be taken into consideration here.

At the end of the day, he wasn't ready to order the execution of such a loyal asset without hard evidence against him. Better to be conservative for now.

That's fine, he answered. *Need the package brought in as soon as possible. By any means necessary. Contact me only when you have it.*

Got it.

He tucked the mobile away into his trouser pocket, already feeling better. One way or another, he intended to get the answers he needed.

And if those answers confirmed his fears, then James would have to be eliminated.

A THICK GRAY fog blanketed the shore as Warwick ran along the damp, packed sand at the edge of the waves. It was late afternoon now. In another hour it would be dark. He was exhausted but couldn't sleep.

He'd stayed outside Marley's place again last night—the second night in a row— until the sky had turned light this morning, hoping she might stop by before heading to work. When she hadn't, he'd gone to the care home and waited. Again. She hadn't shown there either.

So he'd finally gone back to his rental to crash. After an hour of fitful sleep, he'd been ready to come out of his skin, so he'd driven back toward town and wound up stopping at a deserted public access lot off the highway, feeling like he was being torn apart inside. Compelled to release all the pent-up energy and chaotic emotions he was struggling to lock down, he'd left his vehicle, wandered down to this deserted stretch of beach and started running.

He was the only soul out here except for the seabirds skimming through the fog. Large waves rolled into the cove in a powerful rush driven by the wind farther out to sea, drowning out the sound of his pulse in his ears and the soft thud of his treads. His bare feet were soaked and numb from the cold, his jeans wet up to his knees.

He ignored the discomfort and kept running, trying to clear his head. Except it wasn't working. Even with his heart pounding, even when he gasped for breath and his legs and chest screamed for mercy, he couldn't outrun the thoughts tumbling through his mind.

Marley. Grey. The op in Durham. The explosion. Waking up in hospital. The painful recovery. That nagging sense that he'd forgotten something critical. Something dangerous, though he didn't have a clue what it might be.

Marley again. Seeing her face-to-face two nights ago.

Where was she? Was she okay? He wanted to see her again. Talk to her.

No. You need to leave her the fuck alone, mate.

A large wave came in, soaking him to mid-thigh. He slowed to a stop. Bent over and braced his hands on his knees and sucked in air until he got his breath back. A gust of cold wind raked over him and his sweat-soaked shirt, making him shiver.

Straightening, he checked his watch. Was surprised when he realized he'd been out here for nearly an hour.

He turned around and headed back the way he'd come, at a quick walk this time. Throughout the entire trek back to the parking lot, he battled with himself. He owed her answers, but there was a very real chance that he might put her in danger if he gave them.

Yet the thought of leaving her behind now that she knew he was alive was like having his heart carved up by a dull knife.

He kept going, distracted and deep in thought, barely aware of the scenery anymore. Of the bleached driftwood logs lining the high-water mark on the curving beach. The dark drifts of seaweed and long bull kelp washed ashore by the crashing surf.

Then, out of the blanket of fog, he saw something else up

ahead lying on the sand. A body sprawled out facedown at the edge of the surf.

He broke into a run. Partway there he saw the soaked long black hair plastered to the wet sand, and the slender build of the dark form.

A woman in a wet suit. She appeared unconscious. Didn't move as he pounded over and dropped to one knee beside her.

He felt for her carotid pulse beneath the angle of her jaw. It was faint, but there. And she was breathing, albeit shallowly. She was ghostly pale except for the blue tinge around her lips and eyes. A surfer maybe? There was no one else in sight.

"Can you hear me?" he said close to her head. She didn't respond. Not so much as a flicker of her lashes. Definitely hypothermic.

Quickly checking her for injuries, he saw some cuts and bruises on her hands and face and a large laceration along the right side of her rib cage. He rolled her onto her other side and placed her in the recovery position, started to whip out his phone, then stopped. There was no service here and this woman didn't have time to wait for an ambulance anyway. He needed to get her dry, warm and to hospital as quickly as possible.

Bending low, he levered her across his shoulders and stood, his tired legs screaming in protest. He started back up the beach at a lope, the shifting sand making it twice as hard.

The woman was still unconscious when he made it back to the parking lot and put her in the backseat of his rental. He quickly stripped her wet suit and the shirt she had on underneath, leaving her in just her underwear. The wound on her side was deep and bleeding freely. Definitely a knife wound.

The chances of someone being stabbed while out surfing were pretty damn small. So what the hell had happened to her?

He wadded up a spare shirt from his suitcase in the trunk, pressed it to the wound and tied it there around her ribs using the arms of a sweatshirt. Wrapping her up in a blanket, he pulled the seatbelt across her limp form and buckled her in place before hopping behind the wheel and turning the heat on full blast as soon as he started the engine.

He checked his phone. Minimal reception but he dialed 911 anyway, told the operator what was going on and to alert the hospital that he was bringing the woman in.

Speeding out of the lot, he headed north on the highway back toward town. Whoever the woman in the back was, she was running out of time.

FIVE

Marley stifled another yawn, eyes watering, and struggled to focus on her computer screen. The promotion to assistant manager meant more money and less physical labor on the job, but some days she missed the close contact she'd had with the residents as a care aide.

"Another late night last night with someone?" said a rough voice behind her. "Or are they working you too hard as usual?"

She swiveled her chair around and smiled at Henry. He usually stopped by around this time every day to visit for a few minutes.

As assistant manager she technically shouldn't have favorites amongst the residents here, but Henry was absolutely her favorite—and one of a kind. A former Marine in his late eighties, he was a little rough around the edges with a wry sense of humor that was an acquired taste for many, and he had an adorably soft spot for her. They'd hit it off right away on her first week here when she'd first been hired.

"Long night," she said. After tossing and turning in Everleigh and Grady's guest-room bed for another night, then dealing with the police and insurance company again before work this morning, her concentration had been shit all day and she was fading fast.

On the bright side, she only had another hour to go and then she could head home. Not to bed where she belonged, because her brother was due to arrive around dinnertime.

She was really looking forward to his company, the sense of safety and stability he'd always given their broken little family. "What mischief are you getting up to today?"

His white, spiky eyebrows lifted. "Mischief? Me?"

"Now I'm even more concerned." She rested her forearms on her desk and gave him a playfully stern look. "What have you done?"

He blinked. "Nothin'."

"I'm not convinced."

He waved it away. "Don't try to deflect this at me. Is it a guy? It's a guy, isn't it." He sounded convinced.

"Henry. You know I can't talk about—"

"What'd he do?" he growled, a menacing look in his eye.

She sighed and held his gaze for a long moment, debating on how much to tell him. She made it a point not to share things about her personal life with residents, but she and Henry had grown close over the year she'd worked here. He knew more about her, her background and family than anyone else in Crimson Point besides Everleigh.

"He let me believe he's been dead for over a year, but it turns out that's not the case." She left out the shooting bit because he would worry about her too much. He was eighty-seven and had heart issues.

His watery blue eyes bulged. "Shit, are you serious?"

"Yes." She'd been tormenting herself about it ever since Warwick had walked through her door two nights ago.

"What the hell," he muttered, face darkening.

"Yeah. So it's been…kind of a long week so far." She was

still struggling to process everything. Wasn't sure it was even possible to process what had happened.

Henry shuffled his walker forward and leaned in to brace his forearms on the counter, eying her with fire burning in his faded eyes. "You give me his name and location, and I'll fuck him up."

A laugh burst out of her. She never knew what was going to come out of Henry's mouth. "You know what, Henry? I believe you would."

His chin came up. "You're damn right I would. Asshole. So where's he at?"

"I wish I knew." For all she knew he'd taken off again and left town. Might be on his way back to the UK or somewhere else overseas at that very moment.

Henry set his jaw. "Well, whoever he is, the bastard doesn't deserve you. You can do way better."

She smiled faintly. "Thanks." Her track record with romantic relationships wasn't exactly stellar. Her family relationships had been a bit rocky too, especially with Decker.

Then Warwick had blindsided her and she'd fallen head over heels, had honestly thought he was different. That what they'd had was something real and lasting she could build a future on.

Wrong again. The man had let her think he was dead all this time rather than tell her the truth. *Why?*

Sick of driving herself insane about it, she put her fingers back on the keyboard and cleared her throat. "Anyway, I'll be okay." She was strong. She'd been through painful shit before. She'd get through this too. Somehow.

"Yeah?" Henry didn't sound convinced.

"My brother's coming into town to stay with me for a few weeks."

"One of the twins?"

"The eldest. He's got an interview with a company here. If all goes well, he might be moving here permanently."

"Glad to hear it. Your family should appreciate you more."

"Henry?"

They both looked over at the young care aide who'd called his name from the hallway.

"It's time for your shave." She waved a bottle of shaving cream in her hand and smiled.

Henry scowled. "This new recruit is a pain in my ass," he muttered to Marley. "She's always fussing over me. I don't like being fussed over. I'm a goddamn Marine. Told her that, but it didn't make a damn bit of difference."

He was so adorably gruff. How could she not have a soft spot for him? "Your toughness is just one reason why I love you so much." She lowered her voice to a whisper. "And don't you dare tell anyone I said that."

His expression shifted. For a moment he looked almost embarrassed, then the tips of his ears turned pink and the side of his mouth tugged upward. "They couldn't torture it out of me."

"I don't doubt that."

"Good." He slapped his hands on the countertop and straightened. Slowly, his stiff joints hampering him. "Give me a SITREP on your situation if there's an update. And if you need anything, anything at all, I'm here for you." He paused to look her dead in the eye. "I know it probably doesn't seem like much because I'm an old fart with a walker, but I mean it. I still know how to use a weapon and hide a body."

The backs of her eyes began to sting. Shit, was he trying to make her cry right here in front of everybody? "I know. And same goes for me."

"But you're not an old fart."

She laughed again. "Not yet. Getting there though." Especially on the inside. She felt ancient right now.

His grin flashed in the midst of his white stubble.

"Henry? Come on." The new aide waved him over from the hallway. "Visiting time's over."

He rolled his eyes, a scowl falling into place as he shuffled his walker around and headed her way. "Damn fussy woman," he muttered under her breath.

The visit with Henry had actually made Marley feel a lot better. She was able to focus on the rest of the work she needed to get done, and the text from Decker confirming he'd arrived in Portland further lifted her mood.

On the drive home, she held on to the excitement at seeing her brother. Any nerves or awkwardness were obliterated in the face of everything else. Besides, she had zero control over the situation with Warwick. She didn't know where he was, didn't have a way of contacting him, and wasn't going to hire someone at Crimson Point Security to track him down.

She needed to accept that he was alive, didn't want her, and move on.

Resolved, she pushed aside her fatigue and got busy in the kitchen, losing herself in the familiar rhythm of cooking a meal. It only took twenty minutes to throw together Decker's favorite meal and pop it in the oven, and the time in the kitchen helped give her something else to focus on.

She heard a vehicle pull up out front. The window was still boarded up so she went over and looked through the peephole in the door.

Sheer joy filled her when she saw Decker's tall frame step out of the SUV. She threw open the door, stood there grinning like a lunatic as he wheeled his suitcase up the walkway.

"Hi." She wrapped her arms around his neck and hugged him hard. He was taller than her, almost six-four, with chocolate-brown hair and hazel eyes. "God it's good to see you."

He gave her a slightly awkward one-armed hug in return,

and her heart squeezed. Technically they were half-siblings but she'd only ever thought of him fully as her brother.

The one she'd secretly hero-worshipped her entire life. The one whose approval she'd always tried to earn. Only three years separated them, but she'd always seen him as a kind of father figure. Probably because he'd been forced to take on the role of provider and head of the family at eighteen.

"You too." The second she released him, he nodded at the window, face grim. Still imposing. Still frustratingly aloof. "You find out what happened yet?"

"No, but I'm fine. Come in and get settled. You must be starving."

He walked in, took off his shoes and inhaled appreciatively, shooting her a look. "No. Is that…"

"Homemade chicken pot pie? Why yes, it is." She used frozen puff pastry for the top and a rotisserie chicken and chopped frozen veggies in the filling, making it super simple to whip together. Bit of butter and flour and broth to make a nice roux, add in some broth, and cream, and voilà. Heaven in a casserole dish.

He groaned. "If I'd known you were making this, I'd have driven faster."

She lifted an eyebrow and snorted. "And I'm not reason enough to risk a speeding ticket for?"

His teasing expression turned serious. "That's not what I meant."

Apparently he wasn't in the mood for teasing. "I know. Come on." She directed him to the guestroom, let him put his stuff away and was plating them both pot pie when he walked into the kitchen several minutes later. "Beer?"

"Yeah, that'd be great." He joined her at the table, gave her a smile that tugged at the corners of his mouth and made his eyes twinkle. "It's good to see you, Mar."

She smiled back, chest tightening. "Happy to have you. It's been too long." She raised her own beer. "Cheers, Deck."

They tapped bottles, took a sip, and then dug into their dinner. "So tell me more about the job you're applying for at Crimson Point Security." Getting him to talk about financial or work-related stuff was always a sure way to keep the conversation going.

"There are two possible openings I'm interested in. One's for a specialized personal protection slot, and the other's for recruitment." He took another bite of the pastry and filling before continuing. "I've built up a good network and a lot of contacts over the years. Figured I could put them to good use. Guys—and women," he added hastily, "are looking for good options outside the military. The company's got a really good rep."

"I know. They're growing like crazy, too. Nadia said they're interviewing people all the time for different positions."

"Who?"

"Oh. Callum's wife." He was basically Ryder Locke's right-hand-man and helped run the company. "They both live in town and I'm in a book club with her."

He nodded, went back to eating. She loved seeing people she cared about eating and enjoying her cooking. Something about providing nourishment satisfied her on a deep level.

"The boys might be interested in applying too, once they're out."

He meant the twins. "Yeah? They've only got what, another six months left on their contracts?"

"Give or take. I told them I'd report back after my interview."

"It's next week, right?"

"Yeah."

"Great. That gives me the whole weekend to show you

around." And a much-needed distraction from her own heartache.

He didn't comment, just kept eating. When he finished, she took his plate and got him seconds. All three of her brothers were massive eaters. He picked up his fork, pinned her with a hard look. "So what's going on with the insurance company and whatever?"

She lowered her gaze and focused on her own dinner, not wanting to get into the details. "They're going to send out someone to do a report and give a quote in the next day or two."

"And the cops haven't said anything yet?"

"No, but I'm pretty sure the shooter meant to target next door instead."

He didn't look any happier about that, jaw tight as he eyed her. "And?"

"And...?"

"You're hiding something. I know it."

She shrugged. He was too damn perceptive with her. "No, it's nothing. Just a guy thing, but that's done now. He's gone." For the second time, again without a word. But goddammit, she was still furious with him for ripping her wounds open all over again. If he hadn't planned on sticking around, why bother coming here in the first place?

Her phone rang in her pocket. She fished it out. "It's work. I better take this." Decker grunted and kept eating, so she answered. "Hi."

"It's Bev."

"Hey. Everything okay?"

"Well...no, actually."

She straightened. "Why, what's wrong?"

"It's Henry."

No. "What happened?"

"We think he had a massive heart attack. The ambulance is rushing him to the hospital right now."

Oh, God, not Henry. "Was he conscious?"

"No. I'm sorry, Marley. Thought you'd want to know."

"Yes, thank you. I'm on my way." She shoved her chair back as she ended the call and stood, swallowing past the lump in her throat to face her brother.

"What's wrong?" Decker asked, frowning in concern.

She could handle a lot. She prided herself on it, on not getting flighty under stress. But too damn much had happened in the past forty-eight hours and she didn't think she was steady enough to drive herself. "I need to go to the hospital. Can you take me?"

"Yeah, of course," he said, jumping up and heading to the door with her.

An hour later, she walked out of Emergency into a cold rain, drained, sad…and angry. Henry was still holding on, but it didn't look good. The doctor had told her it was unlikely that Henry would make it.

It wasn't fair. He would hate lingering this way. If it was his time, she wanted it to be quick and painless. Not lying in an ICU bed strapped to a bunch of machines, waiting to die.

The only thing that had remotely helped was that Grady had been on shift. He'd let her in to see Henry briefly, had explained what was going on, then sat with her while she held Henry's gnarled, age-spotted hand for a few minutes.

The grizzled old Marine she'd come to love had no family left. No one to be with him. She'd wanted him to know he wasn't alone.

Rain pattered on her jacket as she stepped down off the curb and started toward the parking lot. Decker was parked somewhere on the other side waiting.

Partway there, she saw another man making his way across

the lot in front of her. He heard her footsteps and glanced back. Froze.

She stopped too, riveted to the spot.

Apparently the universe wasn't done throwing jabs at her yet, because for the second time in forty-eight hours, Warwick James was once again standing in front of her.

SIX

Quickly recovering from his surprise, Warwick took a step toward her, protective instincts on overdrive. It was dark out but the streetlamps around the parking lot gave enough light for him to see her face. And he could tell she'd been crying.

Raw protectiveness streaked through him. "What happened? Are you alright?" Jesus Christ, had someone targeted her again since he'd seen her last? Had she been in an accident?

She wrapped her arms around herself and raised her chin while the rain pattered the pavement softly. "No." He could feel her anger pulsing at him from where he stood.

Before he could open his mouth to say anything else, she turned her back on him and began to walk away. He started after her. "Wait—"

He stopped abruptly when she suddenly whirled to face him.

Squaring her shoulders, she marched right at him, the rain making her hair glisten. "What are you doing here?" she demanded, eyes narrowed.

"Are you okay?" he repeated firmly, refusing to budge until she told him she was truly okay.

"I'm not hurt if that's what you're asking—not that it's any of your damn business. Now answer me."

She was right, of course. Except it did feel very much like his business. She'd just walked out of the hospital, crying. Something was seriously wrong. It tore him up that she no longer felt safe turning to him. That he had lost the right to comfort her.

"I came across an unconscious woman on the beach south of town," he said, battling the urge to reach for her. "She was lyin' half in the water with a stab wound on her side."

Her brows contracted. "Stab wound?"

"She was hypothermic and unresponsive. They're treatin' her now. I just finished giving a statement to the sheriff. Now you."

"Now me what?"

"Why are you here? You've been cryin'."

For a long moment she stared at him with clear resentment burning in her eyes, her jaw clenched. So long that he was convinced she wouldn't answer. But just when he thought she was going to dismiss him and walk away again, she answered. "One of our residents had a major heart attack and was rushed here by ambulance. He's in the ICU."

That she'd answered him at all felt like a gift. But death at a nursing home was a common enough occurrence, and he doubted she got this emotional over them all. Clearly this particular resident meant something more to her. "Are you close to him?"

Unguarded emotion flitted across her face for an instant, then she firmed her lips together and glanced away. "Yes, his name's Henry. He's a grumpy former Marine and I love him. They don't think he's going to make it."

"I'm sorry to hear it. Are you alone?"

"No. Decker's waiting for me over there." She nodded across the lot.

Her brother was here? She'd told him their relationship was distant and a bit strained at times. Maybe they had reconciled since last summer. There was so much he didn't know about her life now, and he hated it.

He'd have given anything to pull her into his arms right now. Dammit, it was killing him to be this close to her again and have such a huge wall between them. A wall that existed purely because of him. "I can drive you home."

She snorted. "No," she said, and turned to leave again.

"Wait." He lunged after her, caught her arm to stop her. "Can we talk? Just talk. Please."

The muscles in her arm were as rigid as the rest of her, her normally warm brown eyes accusing. "About what? Why you faked your death to get away from me?"

He stared at her, aghast. That's what she thought? "I didn't—" He bit the rest back, knowing it would be useless at this point. "Let me explain. Not out here. In my vehicle."

"My brother's waiting," she said curtly.

"So tell him to leave. I'll drive you back after."

She threw him a look that said where he could shove his offer. "Like hell."

"Look, you have every right to be angry—"

"You're damn right I do," she shot back.

"But there are things I want to tell you. Things I need to explain. I know you must want answers." She deserved them as much as he owed them to her. He hadn't been able to tell her before. Now that she knew he was alive, he wanted her to at least know some things so she wouldn't always wonder or think the worst.

"I want the truth. No lies," she added with a hard look.

He dipped his chin in acknowledgment. "I'll tell you what I can."

"What you *can*? That's not good en—"

"Marley, please," he said impatiently. "Just hear me out. But not here." They were standing in the middle of a lit public parking lot. A busy one, in the rain, no less. They were too exposed. He didn't think anyone had tailed him, but he couldn't be sure about her after the other night, and there had to be security cameras around the place.

Scowling at him, she jerked her arm free of his grip and pulled her phone out of the bag looped over her shoulder. She shot off a quick text. "I'll give you *one* chance to explain. Then I'm leaving."

He was smart enough not to argue with her about that for the moment. Any opportunity for time with her, he was taking. So he nodded. "This way."

He stayed vigilant on the way to his rental car. Paused to look around once before opening the passenger door for her. After shutting it, he rushed around to the driver's side, started the engine.

"What are you doing?"

"Moving us."

She eyed him in annoyance.

"I just want to move us to a more secure spot," he said. "I'll explain after that."

She crossed her arms and snapped her head around to face forward, staring through the rain-streaked windshield while the silent tension thickened between them.

He drove them several blocks away to make as sure as he could that they hadn't been followed, then pulled onto a quiet, dark street lined with trees and parked across from an empty driveway. He turned off the ignition, plunging them into a brittle silence broken only by the rain on the roof.

"Okay, start talking," she said.

Where to begin? He'd thought of what he'd say so many times, had rehearsed it often enough, yet now he felt rattled and overwhelmed. One wrong word and this would be over almost before it began. "I didn't fake my death."

"No? Then how the hell do you explain the call I got from the cops saying you were dead? And the call I never received from you, telling me you *weren't*."

"It was a misunderstanding on their part. I *almost* died. Well, technically I guess I did briefly a couple of times initially, before the medical team resuscitated me."

Her eyes tracked over the scar on his face, down the side of his neck. And now he could see concern there in place of the anger and resentment.

"There was a clerical error. In the chaos a report was issued sayin' I was dead. The agency I worked for didn't correct it initially because they didn't expect me to pull through. I didn't find out about it until I came out of the coma three weeks later." The agency had corrected the mistake once they'd discovered it.

And then he'd had to make the hardest call of his life in deciding not to inform Marley that he was alive.

"And so why the hell didn't you call me then? You knew I must have been out of my mind with grief. You knew how and where to reach me if you'd wanted me there. One call and I would've been on a plane over there to see you."

"Aye. I know."

She studied him, wary and angry. "Are you a criminal or something?"

"What? No, course not." He rubbed a hand over his face, realized he needed to go further back. "I told you I worked for the UK government."

She didn't answer, just stared at him in stony silence.

"And that I was former military."

"Yeah. So?"

"It was more than that." So much more. "I served in the SAS. And when I met you, I was working for MI6."

She stilled, a frown tugging her perfectly arched eyebrows together, and watched him closely. "Seriously?"

"Yes. I'm out now. Obviously."

"MI6. As in the equivalent of our CIA."

"Aye." It felt risky to tell her even this much. But God, he'd wanted to tell her for so long. Needed her to understand at least this much, to make her believe him. "And the reason I couldn't tell you before was—"

"I know how security clearance protocol works," she said shortly, her expression still skeptical.

Aye. Of course she would, having served in the military herself. And he didn't blame her for doubting him now. "I couldn't tell you any of it before. Not about my military service, and not about my job. There are things I still can't tell you because they're classified." And others he wouldn't tell her because he didn't want to put her in any more danger.

"So what the hell happened after you got that call at the resort? Where did you go when you left me?"

"I was called away on a mission to capture a domestic terrorist. We tracked him to the Lake District, where the PM has a vacation home. But things went sideways and when we moved in to take him, there was an explosion. And this…" He gestured to the scars on the side of his face. There were plenty of others on his body as well, some from shrapnel or burns, and others from surgeries. "Was the result."

She stared at him for a long moment. "And after you woke up you decided to just let me keep believing you were dead."

He watched her, trapped in a hell of his own making. Marley was strong. Possibly the strongest woman he'd ever known. The last thing he wanted was to cause her more pain.

But he owed her this at least. "I felt it was better for you that way."

"Better for me?" She gave a humorless laugh. "That is such selfish *bull*shit—"

"You didn't know what was really goin' on. And I didn't want to involve you in any of it or make you a possible target—"

"What do you mean?" she asked, narrowing her eyes. "How would I be a possible target?"

He let out a long breath. "The terrorist's name was Isaac Grey."

Her gaze sharpened. "The dual British-American citizen who was killed a few weeks ago in the UK."

He nodded. "In Durham."

"You were there?"

"Aye. With Walker and Ivy. Do you know them? He works for a local security firm here in town."

"I know of Walker. Heard about him and Ivy from his daughter at book club." She paused, dragged a hand through her rain-dampened hair. Faced him again. "I thought you said you got out after you were wounded."

"I was medically discharged after the 'incident,' as they call it. Received my pension, such as it is. I thought I was done with it all. But then they called me back on a contract basis for the Grey job. I couldn't say no, not after what happened. I wanted to end that bastard."

She was still frowning. "If he's dead, why would you be a possible target now, let alone me?"

"Because there are…holes in my memory around the day of the explosion. Things I can't quite remember except I know that they're bad. Dangerous." It drove him crazy that he couldn't put the pieces together. Was it about someone connected to Grey? Home Front, the terrorist organization he'd been connected to?

Marley kept eyeing him, a hint of pity in her gaze. "Grey's gone, and you suffered a brain injury. Maybe it's paranoia."

He shook his head, tamping down the rising frustration. "No. It's not. I *feel* it, and it's been worse since Durham." He'd thought he'd seen two men following him there. Had brushed it off as heightened paranoia after an intense mission that had nearly gotten him and his team killed. But maybe they *had* been following him. Planning some kind of revenge for Grey's death.

"Somethin's off," he continued. "Somethin' happened either before or during the Lake District op that I can't explain, and I can't let it go. *That's* why I wanted to stay away from you. I couldn't be sure I wouldn't put you in danger." And he might already have.

"Yet you magically turn up in Crimson Point anyway. For what, a holiday? And I just happen to be living here? Come on."

"I saw a video with you in it on Walker's mobile in Durham." He'd sworn the world had stopped turning for a moment. "You were at the book club with his daughter, and I… wanted to come see you for myself. One last time, to see how you were doin' and make sure you were okay." She had no idea that she'd been his secret obsession the entire time they'd been apart. Still was.

"So you found out where I live."

There was no point denying it. "Aye. I parked down the street waiting for you to come home. I didn't mean for you to know I was there, but then the shooter hit your place and…" It all seemed so amateurish. The more he thought about it, the more he questioned whether they could have been trying to kill him the other night. Unless they'd chosen to shoot in Marley's direction right in front of him to send him a message?

"And then you burst back into my life for all of ten minutes before taking off again without any explanation or word since," she finished in a hard tone.

He had to admit, it looked selfish as fuck. "There's a chance the shooter could have fired those shots while I was there to make a point. And a few times since I arrived in Portland, I've felt like someone was trackin' me."

"Who? And why would they want to track you here?"

"I made a lot of enemies on the job. Enemies who would love to see me dead, and all it would take is for one of them to find out my identity in order to come after me." Anyone connected to Grey, for starters. "And I did come back later that first night, and again last night, but you were gone. I went by your work a few times as well, but you weren't there."

"I was there. I borrowed Everleigh's car instead of using mine and parked under the building instead of the outside lot, just in case." She gave him a hard look. "So you've been stalking me, is what you're saying. And if that shooter hadn't hit my window the other night, you would have left town without me ever knowing the truth."

Basically. Hell, how did he make her understand the kind of danger that might have followed him? "I was trying to protect you—"

"Yeah, you already said. But I'm done now." She reached for the door handle.

He shot out a hand to stop her, grabbed her wrist.

She whipped her head around to glare at him. "Don't touch me." Her voice was cold, sharp as a whip.

He withdrew his hand, the need to touch her a physical ache so painful it felt like his chest was being crushed. He wanted to pull her to him and lock his arms around her. Hold her as he'd wanted to for over a fucking year—the longest, darkest and loneliest of his life. Somehow make her understand he'd done all of this to keep her safe.

"Alright," he said instead, even though everything in him screamed not to let her walk away. Forcing her to stay would only make her hate him more. "I'll drive you home."

"No." She pulled out her mobile. "I'll get a ride."

He clamped his jaw shut with difficulty. He didn't like the idea of her getting a ride from a total stranger, but he also didn't want to risk her jumping out and storming off alone in the dark either. "At least stay in here until the driver shows up." He wanted to make sure the license plate matched what was on her mobile.

"Fine." She finished ordering a ride and put it on her lap, folded her arms and sat there stiffly, refusing to look at him.

It felt like a lead weight was stuck at the bottom of his stomach. Nothing he'd said had made any difference. Not that he blamed her. But Christ, he'd have given anything for things to be different.

"I'm sorry, Marley," he murmured into the brittle silence. "More sorry than you'll ever know. For everythin'."

For the things he'd hidden from her before. For letting her believe he was dead. For coming here and possibly putting her in danger, and hurting her all over again in the process.

"Did I ever mean anything to you at all?" she asked in a strained voice.

He stared at her, stricken that she could even ask that. My God. From the moment he'd met her, she'd been the beating heart in his chest. "Aye," he said in an agonized voice, reaching out to touch her face while choking back all the rest of the words flooding onto his tongue. Feelings for her that she wasn't ready to hear.

Marley recoiled as if he'd been about to strike her.

He reluctantly lowered his hand. Clenched it into a fist on his thigh, wanting to scream from the anguish tearing him apart. "Whatever else has happened, you must know I loved you. You must." Did even now. And always would. Even if it felt like he was dying from it right now.

She gave him an incredulous look. "You don't know what that word even means. Because if you did, there's no way you would've done what you did."

He set his jaw, feeling like he was about to come apart. "That decision was the worst and hardest thing I've ever had to do in my entire life." Worse than his miserable childhood. Worse than killing people throughout his career. Far worse than the physical agony he'd endured after the bombing.

Marley remained silent, unmoved by his words.

The frustration bubbled back to the surface, the anguish twisting inside him unbearable. "Do you think I wanted this? That I wouldn't have moved heaven and earth to be with you if I'd thought there was any way to make it work?"

"Stop talking," she snapped, folding her arms across her chest as she huddled against the door. Desperate to get away from him.

A myriad of desperate explanations tumbled through his mind as he tried to think of something else to say, anything that would make this better. He didn't deserve her forgiveness, but he couldn't live with her thinking he hadn't loved her with everything in him. That the decision he'd made wasn't a knife in his heart every waking hour—and plenty of sleeping ones also.

"I never meant to hurt you, I swear to God. And everything I felt for you then was real." *I still feel it now*, he almost said aloud. "Whatever else you think of me, please believe that at least."

She didn't answer. And there was nothing more he could say.

It felt like he was bleeding inside. Dying slowly in front of her.

So he shut his gob. An uncomfortable, endless fifteen minutes passed while they sat there without a single word more between them before the driver finally turned up. The license plate matched. He relaxed only slightly, didn't let his guard down.

Marley immediately opened her door. "Don't you dare follow me. And one more favor?"

"Anything."

"Just leave me the hell alone," she said without looking at him as she got out, then slammed the door shut.

Warwick shoved out a hard breath, hand clenching around the steering wheel as her tall, sleek silhouette walked away, torn between respecting her wishes and running after her. Holding her. Somehow break through the icy wall standing between them.

Show her he still loved her, had never stopped. Plunge his hand into her hair and kiss her with all the pent-up longing in his soul. Make her his again.

But that was all just an impossible dream now.

He stayed where he was, resolve hardening inside him. He still didn't know what kind of danger he faced, but until he could be sure she was safe, he was staying.

So once again he would have to break her trust. Because they both knew he was going to follow her home.

SEVEN

Warwick woke from a light doze at the sound of a vehicle pulling up out front of the rental he was staying in. He sat up, tensing. He'd only slept for maybe an hour total, awake all night thinking of Marley and everything that had happened. The way she'd stormed off had felt so damn final. Like she was shutting him out for good.

What the hell, mate? That's what you wanted. You know it's for the best. You have to let her go.

Except his heart refused to allow him to do that anymore. And he didn't know what the hell he was supposed to do with that.

He got up, glanced at his watch before yanking on the jeans and shirt he'd left on the foot of his bed. It was only seven.

A vehicle door closed. Then another. Moments later he heard faint footsteps approaching the house.

He went to stand next to the window, his back to the wall. Moving the edge of the blind aside a fraction of an inch, he saw the two people coming to his front door.

Walker and Ivy.

He relaxed, muscles easing even as unease spread through

his gut. He'd been extra vigilant about ensuring he hadn't been followed whenever he'd gone out anywhere. Ivy and Walker were no threat to him, but how had they found him?

He went down the hall to let them in. He'd find out soon enough what he wanted to know. "To what do I owe the pleasure of this early and unexpected mornin' visit?"

"Let us in and we'll tell you," Ivy said with a pointed smile. Walker was silent, not unusual for him.

Warwick stepped back and gestured for them to enter. "How'd you find me?" He'd even switched rental vehicles after the drive-by at Marley's and rented this place under an alias without using a personal credit card.

Ivy arched an eyebrow at him, hazel eyes laughing. "How do you think?"

Her. With her master-level hacking skills. He didn't know the specific details of her background, but he'd seen enough in Durham to convince him she'd been a highly trained operative of some sort. MI6 would kill to have someone like her on its payroll.

"No, I mean specifically." There were only a couple of ways she could have tracked him here. While she was in an elite class all her own, if she'd found him so quickly, anyone else following him might be closer than he realized.

Not a comforting thought.

"Tagged your phone while you were at the Sea Hag with us. Just to make sure I could find you if you needed us. You seemed a little…on edge, that's all."

He stared at her, a slight measure of relief hitting him that the only reason she'd found him was because she'd been so close to him before. He'd had his phone sitting face down on the table the entire time. "How could—right. Never mind." Obviously she'd done it with her own phone while sitting at the table and he hadn't realized it. Damn, he was glad she wasn't his enemy.

She waved a hand dismissively. "I'll let it slide this once." She seated herself on the sofa in the lounge and leaned back, making herself comfortable while Walker sat next to her. "Nice place. Plan on staying long?"

"No."

"Didn't think so. Not going down the coast to Cali after all?"

It's what he'd told them at dinner his first night in town. No point lying now. "No."

She nodded, narrowed her eyes as though he was a puzzle she was keen on figuring out. "Then why are you still here, laying low?"

"Bit of unfinished business."

"Something to do with Marley and the shooting at her place a few nights ago maybe? Or maybe the woman you pulled out of the ocean? You've been busy."

Given what he knew about Ivy's skills and capabilities, her knowing about that wasn't exactly a surprise. Though Crimson Point was a small town, so it could have been as simple as gossip. "Aye."

"I spoke to the sheriff yesterday about the incident at Marley's," Walker said in his calm, reserved way. His deep Mississippi drawl only added to the effect. So different from the slight twang in Marley's Kentucky accent. "He's certain it was a case of mistaken identity, and that Marley wasn't the intended target. They think it was drug related."

"Maybe." But there was enough doubt for him that he couldn't be sure. And he wasn't going to just leave without knowing she was safe.

Maybe he wouldn't be leaving at all.

"What else would it have been?" Ivy asked. When he didn't

respond, she huffed out a sigh. "Look. We'd both love to help you out with whatever's happening, but you need to come clean with us first because this is our home and if anything's going on, we want to know."

"*Is* there something else going on?" Walker asked him.

"I'm not sure," he said.

Ivy's gaze sharpened. "Okay, then what's your hunch?"

He trusted them. He did. There was absolutely no reason for him to keep the truth from them. They weren't the enemy, weren't a threat, and were just trying to look out for him. Yet he still hesitated to say anything more. He may have already put Marley in harm's way. Didn't want to put them there too.

And there was also something else that held him back. Something Marley had said last night. About how he'd suffered a brain injury from the concussion.

He'd been thinking about that more. About what the doctors had told him. There was a chance it had resulted in a certain degree of paranoia. That could explain the intermittent feeling that he was being followed. That telltale prickle along the back of his neck. Unless he was losing his mind.

But he wasn't willing to risk Marley's safety on any of that.

His mobile rang, giving him a reprieve as he dug it out of his jeans pocket. It was the police. "James," he answered.

"Warwick, it's Noah Buchanan."

"Areet, Sheriff?" Ivy and Walker were both watching him.

There was a slight pause. "Pardon?"

Sometimes his Geordie was tough for people to understand. "What can I do for you?"

"Nothing, I called to let you know that the woman you rescued has regained consciousness and all things considered, physically she's doing well. Well enough that she'll likely be released within the next day or two."

"Glad to hear it." He thought of the stab wound and the way

she'd been left to wash up on shore like that. "Did you find out anythin' about who injured her?" It had definitely been from a knife.

"Nothing yet. As for the shooting at Ms. Abrams'—"

"Walker just updated me."

"Oh. Any questions or further concerns then?"

Not that he was willing to share at the moment. "No."

"Okay. Well, if anything comes up, just give me a shout. And thanks again for what you did. You saved that woman's life."

"It was nothin'." He quickly ended the call.

Watching him, Ivy lifted her eyebrows. "So? What's going on?"

"I don't have anythin' concrete." No proof, and he didn't want to be a statistic. Or a cliché. Another washed-up soldier-turned-spy injured in the line of duty who wandered aimlessly through the rest of his life with a constant itch between the shoulder blades, becoming more and more suspicious every day and seeing things that weren't there.

Walked gazed at him steadily. "But you've got a gut feeling something's not right."

He clenched his jaw. Nodded. And finally just said it. "I think someone might be after me."

Ivy sat up straight, tension in every line of her body. "Who?"

"Dunno. Someone connected to Grey maybe. I first felt it in Durham the day after the op. Once or twice on the way to London. Then since I landed in Portland. The night of the shooting I noticed a car here in town that I initially thought might be tryin' to follow me when I left the restaurant."

She frowned. "And was it?"

"I decided it wasn't. But then another car similar to it appeared on Marley's street later and raced down it. The shooter hit Marley's front window, and there's a good chance that was a warning to me." Unless they were two different vehicles. He wasn't sure.

"You need to tell the sheriff," Walker said. "He's a stand-up guy. Thorough and trustworthy and good at his job."

"No. I'm not involving the police." Not yet, anyway. "Not until I know more."

"And what about Marley?" Ivy asked, then her expression changed. "Ah, got it. You're staying to watch out for her, just in case."

He didn't bother denying it. But more guilt slid through him.

He should leave. Once he did, there was a good chance he would take any hint of danger with him.

Except he wouldn't. Couldn't, and not only because he wanted to protect her.

Even after the way he'd hurt her, even though she clearly hated his guts now, he couldn't make himself walk away from the only woman he'd ever loved.

And that was the hell of it. He'd thought time and space between them would make everything fade.

Instead, it had only made the unbearable need for her worse.

ROLAND DIDN'T BOTHER with subtlety as he checked his watch and glanced past the CIA official to the huge plate-glass window framing the San Francisco skyline and the leaden gray bay beyond it, impatient to wrap up the meeting. It should have ended over an hour ago but several of the people involved had wanted to get all chatty and waste more time.

"Got somewhere to be, Roland?" the CIA representative asked with a grin.

"Yes, actually." Their business was done. Now they were just dragging this out unnecessarily.

The man sobered, cleared his throat and glanced around the room. "Better finish up the agenda then."

"I'd appreciate it."

It still took another twenty minutes to adjourn. He immediately excused himself and exited the high-security room into the hallway. The moment he did, the glass wall behind him turned from opaque frosted to clear in an instant, signaling someone in the room must have hit the button. He contacted his driver on his mobile. "I'm on my way down. Meet me out front."

He rode the elevator down to the lobby alone, hands clasped at his waist. He could see his reflection in the shiny metal of the doors, his tailored navy suit and crisp white shirt. The striped tie his wife had picked out for him from their closet.

He missed his family. Always did when he traveled. But right now all he could think about was the situation with James.

There had been no word from the recent asset he'd activated. He should have heard something by the time he'd woken up this morning.

He strode through the gleaming marble lobby and out through the secure doors to where his driver was waiting at the curb in the SUV with the tinted windows. He got straight in the back without a word, sent another message to the number he'd used before while his driver started for the hotel across town.

Now he needed to hedge his bets, just in case.

He dialed the number for Crimson Point Security, watching out the window. My God, San Francisco had become a shithole since the last time he was here.

Everywhere he looked he found evidence of crime, filth and homelessness. He hated to think it, but given the sorry state of the economy and no impending improvement anytime in the near future, major cities might start to look like this at home soon.

"Crimson Point Security," a pleasant female voice answered.

"It's Roland Yates." If she didn't know who he was, she would at least recognize his name from previous contact.

"Yes, Mr. Yates. How can I help you?"

"I'm in San Fran right now and have a day or two before I'm scheduled to fly back to the UK. I was thinking of heading up there first. Any chance of a meeting with Mr. Walker? And Ms. Johnson as well, if feasible. I want to thank them personally for their assistance with the recent operation and could be up there for tomorrow if that suits." He could easily have gotten Walker's mobile number and contacted him personally but didn't want to risk coming off as suspicious. Besides, going through his office made it seem more official.

"I'll check his schedule, sir. One moment." He heard the click of a keyboard in the background. "Would seven-thirty Monday morning work for you?"

He'd make it work. "That would be perfect, thank you."

"You're welcome. Can I help you with anything else? Will you need a ride from the airport, perhaps?"

"Lovely of you to offer, but no, I've got my own transportation. Thank you, I'll see them Monday."

As soon as he ended the call, he contacted the pilot of the jet he'd chartered for this trip. "Slight change in the itinerary," he said to his driver while he typed out the message. A former Royal Marine who'd been his pseudo-bodyguard for two years now. "We're flying to Oregon tonight."

"Yes, sir."

Roland settled back for the duration of the drive, deep in thought. Up in his hotel room, he ordered room service for an early dinner and called his wife quickly to check in. She was a nighthawk and would still be up. Sitting there in the quiet afterward, he checked for messages. There had been no further update from the PI. And still no response from the asset he'd hired prior to leaving the UK.

Which meant the operative was likely dead.

In any case, he couldn't afford to wait any longer for an update. He pulled up a name from his contact list. A man he knew personally who was now working as a contractor. One who wasn't afraid to get his hands dirty when necessary.

And he also had a personal score to settle with James.

Where are you now? he typed after the man had responded to the initial contact.

Chicago.

That would work out well. *There's a job for you on the Oregon Coast. Crimson Point area. How soon can you get here?*

The response came back moments later. *Who's the target?*

Telling him would practically guarantee he took the job, so he did. Because this man knew exactly who James was. And hated him enough to kill, should that order become necessary.

James, he sent.

I'm in.

Good. How soon can you be here?

Give me twelve hours.

You've got nine, he answered, and turned off the phone.

He unscrewed the cap from his medication bottle and swallowed the tablet, a faint burn already starting up in his chest. He needed the James situation dealt with, one way or another.

Hopefully in another day or two, this would all be over.

EIGHT

I'll be damned, Warwick James.

Merely seeing or hearing that name instantly triggered all kinds of memories and emotions for Simon. None of them good. Every last one of them enough to make his previous decision to take this job a no-brainer.

And a pleasure.

He finished his last set of push-ups, jumped to his feet and rolled his shoulders, letting the quiet surround him. The cabin he'd rented was on the outskirts of Crimson Point, high up in the hills away from any neighborhoods. All he could hear was the sound of the rain drumming on the roof.

A sense of peace rolled over him. A sense of rightness. As if psychologically he'd been waiting for this day to come. And now it was here.

He finally had the chance to get even.

This thing had fallen in his lap and moved fast. Much faster than his other jobs had. Roland had been in a rush to get him here, so much so that he was paying him double his usual fee. That alone would have made this worth it, but the chance to nail James?

Fucking bring it. That arrogant bastard had had this coming to him for *years*. Now he finally had a legitimate reason to go after him.

He took a quick shower, letting his mind clear as he stood under the hot spray. He'd done initial recon after arriving in town yesterday afternoon. Looking around, getting the lay of the land as it were, and then carefully asking around at places James was likely to visit. Starting with the bar at the waterfront, the Sea Hag, which locals had said was the place where everyone went.

His American accent was fairly decent. He'd kept it casual, careful not to arouse suspicion when he'd asked the bartender whether he'd seen someone matching Warwick's description. Made up a bullshit story about them being old friends who'd met while serving overseas a few years ago.

Simon's lip curled at the thought. Friends? Sod that. They had served together overseas, in the same unit. In the same troop. Right from the start, he and James had rubbed each other wrong. And it had gone downhill from there.

The bartender confirmed a Brit had been in just three nights before, and mentioned the scars on Warwick's face. He'd been eating with a local named Walker—who James had recently teamed up with to go after Isaac Grey in Durham—and a woman. But he hadn't seen James since.

Simon killed the shower, dried and dressed before checking the current mobile he was using for this job. He couldn't confirm that James was still in the area, but there was no way the wanker had flown all the way here from the UK just to meet up with someone he'd only met a few weeks ago and barely knew.

No way. There was another reason. Something important enough to make James come halfway across the world. Once Simon found out what it was, he would have him.

But he needed help to make that happen. Tech stuff and hacking weren't his strengths. His skillset was all about grabbing or taking out a target.

There was a new message. Presumably from Roland.

James spotted in Crimson Point as of 19:00h last night. Contact there listed this address as possible location. Go check it out.

Whatever local contact Roland was using must be low-level, or he would have had the person deal with James already. Simon entered the address into the GPS program. A pin popped up six miles away to the northwest, saying it was a twelve-minute drive from his current location.

On it, he replied, and gathered his gear into his bag before heading out to the rental he'd parked by the front steps. Supplies to bring James in with after he found him. Weapons in case James decided to make things interesting.

He memorized the directions and started down the road bordered by towering evergreens on either side. The rain was steady, traffic light as he wound his way up to the highway and started north.

His official instructions were to bring James in alive and hand him over for questioning. But Roland hadn't specified in what condition. If things wound up getting messy after Simon found James…he would consider that a bonus.

The target address was located in a small subdivision full of vacant lots and building sites. It was busy. Construction crews working at several sites. He slowed down the street from the small bungalow, staring at it through the rain while his wipers swished back and forth.

There were too many people around for him to risk exploring the house up close, and there was no vehicle parked in the driveway or carport. There were only a few cars parked along this block that weren't grouped with the construction crew.

He sent the plate number of each one to a contact Roland had given him, a trained tech expert he used frequently, and asked him to run them. Then doubled back to a spot down and across from the house and studied the house again.

Every window was covered by curtains or blinds, preventing him from seeing in. That and the empty driveway were things someone like him or James would do as basic precautions.

His contact sent back details on the vehicles minutes later. One caught his attention. It was a rental, had been picked up two days ago near Crimson Point. The name on the agreement wasn't James, but he would never use his real name on something like that if he was trying to stay off the radar. Combined with the possible sighting here last night, the rental car's position around the corner from the house merely added to the theory that this was the right place.

He found a spot just up the street between a row of vehicles parked along the curb at one of the building sites, allowing him a better view of the front of the house. Stakeouts were boring as shite and he'd always hated them, but having James as his target galvanized him.

Over three hours later, his patience paid off.

He sat up straighter, attention riveted to the red sports car as it slowed in front of the bungalow, reversed, then pulled into the driveway next to the rental. Making sure no one nearby was watching him, he took out the small pair of binos to get a better look.

A tall redhead emerged from the car. She tossed her hair back, slammed the door shut and marched for the front of the house.

Whoever the woman was, she was hot. And on a mission.

Simon made a note of her and her license plate. Watched her knock on the door and stand there waiting with hands on hips.

The door opened a few inches. Not enough for him to see inside. But the woman shoved a hand against it and swept inside. Giving Simon a fleeting glimpse of a tall, dark-haired man before it quickly shut behind her.

He stared at the closed door, his intuition buzzing while his pulse accelerated. That definitely could have been James. Had he come here for the woman?

His gut said yes. And if he was right, this was something he could use to his advantage.

He sent the woman's plate to his contact, then looked back at the house as a little smile curved his lips.

Almost time to settle this personal score once and for all.

THE ENTIRE DRIVE over here from the hospital after she'd stopped to visit Henry, Marley had been bracing herself for the moment she came face-to-face with Warwick again. But the moment he cracked the door open, it felt like the world stopped.

Quickly recovering, she pushed the door open and stepped inside. They were not having this conversation out in the open.

Staring at her in surprise, he shut the door behind her. "What are you doin' here?" he asked, sounding confused.

"I called Shae and asked if her dad might know where you were. Ivy was there and gave me your address herself."

"Did she?" The hint of a rueful grin tugged at the side of his mouth and her stupid heart swooned.

"Yep." She tore her gaze off him and looked around the place instead. It was smaller than her cottage even, but he wouldn't need more space since he probably wasn't planning on staying long.

Her eyes stopped on a packed suitcase standing in the corner, her insides grabbing. She faced him again, battling another ridiculous wave of hurt. By now she should have been immune to hurt where he was concerned. "So that's it, huh? You're leaving town." Though to be fair, last night she *had* told him to leave her the hell alone.

He stood there unmoving while some undecipherable emotion moved in his eyes. "I thought that's what you wanted."

"It is," she said. Lying through her teeth and hoping he couldn't see how much this was killing her.

God, what was wrong with her? Even after everything that had happened, everything he'd done—the lies, the manipulation, the cruelty of him allowing her to grieve all this time—shutting him out of her heart now that she knew he was alive wasn't so easy.

The sight of him took her breath away and made her go weak.

God help her, she still wanted him. Wanted him so much that just standing this close to him had her entire body aching with need.

She wanted to slap his scarred, handsome face. Scream at him. Grab him. Shake him. Shove him against the wall behind him and capture his lips with hers, kiss him until she broke through his infuriating remoteness and let pure need consume them both.

"Why have you come, Mar?" he asked in a low voice. That dark gaze was so intense. Not just watching her. Seeing into her. Maybe even right through her.

She swallowed, her heart thudding way too hard and fast against her ribs. "I don't know." All she knew was, after another exhausting night spent rehashing everything he'd said, she'd woken from a fitful sleep with the burning need to find him and speak her mind in a desperate bid for some kind of closure.

Her plan had been to show up and blast him, unleash the anger burning a hole in her chest. Tell him *exactly* what he'd done to her and what she thought of him before she stormed out and tried to start the process of mending her broken heart all over again.

Except that had all changed the moment he'd opened the door. One look at him and she forgot herself. Now she didn't know what the hell to do or say. Or even what she wanted anymore.

He studied her for another moment while the tension inside her pulled ever tighter, ready to snap. "Do you want to sit down?" He gestured to the couch in the adjoining living room. "I can make you some coffee."

"I don't want coffee." She wanted *him*, goddammit, and couldn't have him.

It cut knife deep. Sliced right through all the pent-up emotion trapped inside her. Made her want to scream and cry and rage against whatever cruel fate had torn them apart.

She'd thought the razor-sharp edge of grief after being told he was dead was unbearable. But this? Standing here looking at the man she'd once given her heart to, so alive and vital and gorgeous while he watched her with those deep, dark brown eyes she could drown in? Eyes that had once warmed for her, creasing at the corners when he'd smiled or laughed.

Eyes that had delved straight into her soul while he made love to her, making her feel things she'd never known existed before him.

Marley drew in a steadying breath, struggling to rally her weakening anger. It would be so much easier if she could hate him. But her heart and body refused to cooperate. They didn't give a shit that he'd devastated her so completely before. Didn't care that he was unavailable. They only cared that he was right here in front of her, whole and alive.

No! Too much had happened. Maybe if he told her exactly what was going on, made her understand why he believed he was protecting her by staying away, maybe then she could make peace with it and move on.

Maybe. But she also deserved to speak her truth too.

"Losing you gutted me," she finally said in a hoarse voice.

He shook his head, pain stealing into his expression. "Marley, I swear to you I never meant—"

"To hurt me. Well, you did. Unbearably. And I can never forgive you for that, no matter what your reasons. Or for showing up now and blowing up the life I've struggled to rebuild." Shit, now her voice was shaking. *She* was shaking—a former Marine.

Fuck him for doing this to her. For opening this up all over again. "The least you could do is spell it all out for me. Tell me exactly what kind of danger you think you're protecting me from. Who's involved, and why. Maybe then I might have a chance at understanding what you did, and hopefully make peace with it someday."

"Marley, I *can't*." He stepped toward her, shoulders taut, expression urgent.

"Then there's nothing left to say. But at least this time one of us should have the balls to actually end this like adults—"

"I wish I could undo it all. All of it." The sincerity on his face tore at her.

She closed her eyes, shook her head as anguish twisted through her. Because she wished that too. More than anything. "Stop." She opened her eyes. Found him coming closer.

Panic streaked through her, the sincerity in his tone, in his face, making her crack inside. "*Don't*," she warned, throwing up a hand and stepping back. Afraid she would shatter if he touched her. That she might splinter into a thousand jagged pieces that could never be put back together again.

But he didn't stop.

He caught her wrist, his long fingers locking around it in a strong yet terrifyingly tender grip that made her lower belly somersault, reminding her exactly of how that same touch translated to the way he was in bed.

She sucked in a sharp breath, tugged hard even as she opened her mouth to tell him to go to hell but found herself enveloped by his arms instead, her cheek pressed to the solid muscle of his chest.

Her entire body snapped taut, a quiver rippling through her as he buried his mouth in the hair at her temple, his hold at once possessive and desperate. "I need to let you go, but I can't," he said in a ragged whisper, one hand planted between her shoulder blades and the other buried in the back of her hair. "I fuckin' can't let you go again now, Marley, I can't. I *won't*."

The taut, impassioned words had barely penetrated the rushing sound in her ears before he angled her face toward his and his mouth found hers.

A high-pitched, wounded sound tore from her throat. Shock. Pain. Denial. But as his lips slanted across hers, his arms locking her to the big, powerful body she'd dreamed about for over a year, a tidal wave of need slammed into her.

It sucked her under. Pulled her so deep that there was no way to escape. There was only this. Only Warwick crushing her to him, his mouth on hers, tongue demanding entrance.

No, no, no…

She shoved at his chest and stumbled back, breathing unsteadily. Terrified by the unquenchable need between them, and how close she'd just come to allowing him in again.

Warwick stared back at her, his breathing just as unsteady as hers, dark eyes molten with the same unfulfilled hunger she felt. Along with something raw and possessive that sent another shot of alarm through her.

Letting him in again would be reckless. She couldn't take the risk of him up and leaving her again. Just couldn't. And he'd proven that not only would he not open up to her about what was really going on, he also couldn't be trusted to stay.

To save herself, she had to leave. Now.

She drew herself upright, holding his gaze. "If you won't tell me everything, then there's nothing more to say. And if you still care about me at all, if you ever really loved me, you'll let me go now. *Please*," she choked out, unable to take this a second longer. Slowly being ripped apart with each second she lingered.

"Marley," he whispered, face twisting as he reached for her again.

"*No*," she cried, spinning for the door. Not daring to look back, she burst out into the cold October rain and ran for her car, the sound of him calling her name making her chest hitch and her eyes flood with scalding tears.

She had barely backed out of the driveway before the first tears fell. God, she was an idiot. And a glutton for punishment.

She'd come here for answers to help her get closure. But she was leaving with the exact opposite.

NINE

Decker stopped reading through the checklist he'd downloaded on his phone in preparation for his upcoming interview when he reached point number nine.

Be yourself.

His derisive snort was loud in Marley's empty living room. Yeah, being himself for any extended period of time wasn't going to do him any favors, least of all at Crimson Point Security. The military might have trained him to work with and as part of a team, but he was a loner at heart. Hadn't always been that way, but that's how it was now, and it wasn't going to change anytime soon.

He shook his head, skimmed the rest of the list and decided to ditch the remainder, unsure why he was so wound up about this. It wasn't his first interview rodeo, he already knew how this all worked. It was just as much about impression during the interview as what was on his resume.

He'd already done research on the company before applying for an interview. He'd also done some homework on the main players there, Ryder Locke, Callum Falconer, and the guy simply known as Walker. So no matter who wound up interviewing him at the office, he at least knew the basics about them and wouldn't feel like he was at a total disadvantage.

He looked up when he heard footsteps on the front walkway. The lock mechanism whirred a moment later, then Marley stepped inside. Her face was blotchy, eyes puffy.

He shot from his chair, alarm popping inside him. "What's going on?" He could count on one hand how many times he'd seen Marley in tears, even with all the awful shit they'd been through as kids. "Is it Henry?"

"No. Well, I guess partly." She dumped her oversized purse onto the upholstered bench in the entry, along with her keys. "He was awake when I went in to see him, but really weak. He recognized me though. Squeezed my hand. I told him I loved him. He doesn't have anyone else. I wanted him to know someone cared, just in case he doesn't pull through." She wiped under her eyes.

"Then what else?" he asked, confused.

"After I left I…" She winced, rubbed a hand over her face and walked over to collapse on the couch with a groan. "I went to see someone."

He narrowed his eyes. "Someone?" A guy. Some asshole who must have done something really fucking bad to upset her this much.

She finally met his gaze. Nodded, looking utterly miserable and…lost.

That part concerned him most. Marley was tough. Way tougher than she looked, and not just courtesy of the Marine Corps. She'd had to be strong with everything life had thrown at her. And he wasn't proud to admit that he hadn't been there enough for her to lighten the burden the way he should have.

Part of his decision to apply for a job here was to hopefully change that.

"The guy who broke my heart last year," she finally said, her voice barely carrying.

His eyebrows snapped together. "What guy?" She hadn't said anything to him about a guy. The twins hadn't told him anything either, and she talked to them about a lot more than she did him.

"I fell for someone last year. And not long after that I was told he died."

Oh, shit. For real? "I'm sorry, Mar. I didn't know." How had he not known something that major? Damn, he really had drifted from everyone.

She gave him a sad smile that tugged at the hidden soft spot he'd always had for her. "No one did. Anyway, really long story short, it turns out he's still very much alive."

He frowned at her, not liking the sudden plot twist happening here. "Are you sure?"

"Yeah, because he barged through my front door about five seconds after those shots went through the window the other night."

He stared at her in stunned silence for a moment. "What the *fuck*?" he finally got out. The guy reappearing just after her house had been shot up meant the two things had to be connected.

She eyed him, looking tired and dispirited. The opposite of his bright, energetic sister. "You'd better sit down."

"No." He folded his arms across his chest. An imposing posture that had intimidated many of the Marines he'd dealt with as an MP. Whoever this asshole was, he sounded like bad news, and Decker didn't want him within fifty miles of his sister. "Start talking."

After a long pause, she did. Haltingly at first. Then she got going and the words seemed to pour out of her.

With each one, the anger in him grew hotter. Increasing

from a simmer to a rolling boil, blending with a gut-deep fear. By the time she finished explaining how she'd gotten the prick's address this morning, his jaw was so tight he was surprised he didn't crack a molar. "And he's still here?"

She looked up at him, expression wary. "Yeah, but just forget it. It's over."

Forget it? Like it never happened? Like she wasn't in possible danger now because of the guy? Nope. "Like hell it is," he growled, and stalked past her.

She jumped up, face filled with alarm. "What are you doing?"

He ignored her, marching for the door. After feeling numb and purposeless for so long, the anger felt good. He was going to go over there and get to the bottom of this, make sure Marley was safe from this guy.

"What are you— Deck, no," she blurted when he grabbed her keys and phone and walked out the door.

He unlocked the phone using the code she'd always used, and sure enough, there was the address in her text messages.

"Just leave it alone," she called from the doorway. "Deck!"

Nope.

God knew he hadn't been there for her enough over the years. Hadn't had a clue about what she'd gone through last spring, and he couldn't change any of it.

But he was damn well going to be here for her now. And *no* one. *No fucking one* threatened or put his sister in danger. Not happening.

"Deck, stop!" she called frantically. "You can't just drive over there and confront him—"

"Watch me."

He slammed the driver's-side door shut and started the engine. Ignored her when she came running down the walkway toward him. And whaddya know, there was the address still sitting in her car's GPS system.

Ignoring her frantic pleas to stay put, he drove away, the rage inside him shifting. Turning icy. Laser focused.

Whatever it took, he was going to make damn good and sure his sister was safe from Warwick James and whatever threat he'd brought here with him.

"GOD DAMMIT," Warwick snarled into the empty yet deafening silence, gripping the back of his hair in his fists. It had been fifteen minutes since Marley had driven away and he still felt like he was being split apart with a sodding crowbar. The impulse to chase after her was so damn strong his muscles twitched.

The fear of pushing her away forever if he did was the only thing that stopped him.

He slammed the end of his fist into the kitchen doorframe, a cry of frustration and anguish tearing from him. He could still feel her. The imprint of her long, lithe body against his. Could still taste her. Smell her.

He was ready to come unglued from the need pulsing through him.

He'd meant what he'd said to her at the end. He couldn't let her go now. It was too late for that. But charging after her, no matter how badly he wanted to, would only cause another confrontation and make her retreat harder.

Much as he hated it, he had to give her time and space. All he could do for now was try to protect her from whatever unseen threat was out there. And hopefully win her back when the danger was gone.

Whirling, he turned and stalked to the short hallway, heading for the bedroom to get his phone.

A sound from the back door made him pause. A quiet snick.

As if someone was trying to pick the lock.

The air around him crackled with static electricity as he turned, nape tingling, his focus narrowed on the source of that sound. No one could see into the house. He'd pulled all the blinds down over the windows as soon as he'd arrived. Was this a simple break-in attempt?

Or something more.

He walked silently through the small kitchen to the door beyond it, pulling a knife from the butcher block on the counter on the way. He flicked it in his hand and clenched the handle in his fist, blade pointed down, staring at the doorknob.

It didn't move. There was no further sound, no telltale snick or scraping, but he knew what he'd heard. And that whoever was on the other side of this door was no friend to him.

He waited, back pressed to the wall behind the door in case whoever it was tried to fire a shot through it. A minute passed. Two. Then he thought he heard the faintest whisper of movement beyond the door.

The intruder was on the move again.

With silent treads he quickly retraced his steps and went into the bedroom to ease the corner of the blind aside to look out front. There was nothing but the gray gloom of the rain as he pulled on his boots, carefully eased the blind aside and slid the window open.

Inch by inch, careful not to make any sound while watching for the intruder the whole time, until it was wide enough for him to slip through.

He hopped down into the flowerbed beneath the window and crouched slightly, still clenching the knife in his fist, watching the far corner of the house. He started creeping along the side of it, pulse slowing now that he was on the move. Becoming the hunter instead of prey.

At the end of the front exterior wall he paused, glancing behind him quickly before focusing on what was happening around the corner. A cedar-plank fence wrapped around the backyard, hiding it from his view. But through the rain he heard hushed footsteps on the grass.

Then he caught a glimpse of someone jumping the fence and disappearing from view.

Whether the intruder was leaving or planning to circle back and try again, Warwick wasn't waiting to find out.

Nah, mate. You're mine.

He burst away from the house and charged into the band of forest bordering the side of the yard, heading in the direction he'd seen the person moving. There was no time for stealth. He had to stop whoever it was before they got away.

His boots thudded on the carpet of cedar needles as he ran. He ducked and dodged branches, leapt over protruding roots and logs.

Something whipped past him and buried itself into a tree trunk, a telltale crackle sending an electrical charge through the Taser wires. A solid weight hit him in the ribs a split second later.

The impact knocked him off his feet. They hit the ground side by side with a thud. Warwick immediately twisted toward the attacker. Raised the knife as he turned. A fist clamped around his wrist. Drove the blade toward the ground as a blow to the side of the face made him see stars.

With a throttled growl, he wrenched to the side, heaving the man off him. He had only a vague impression of his size in the shadowy forest, the dark balaclava covering the face as he jumped to his feet.

A boot came hurtling up at his knife hand. He ducked,

twisted to the side just in time, grunted as the kick made contact with his shoulder instead, knocking him sideways.

He stumbled, threw out his arms to catch himself. The edge of the blade snagged on a cedar trunk. Tore out of his hand and spun away into the underbrush beyond.

Catching himself on the rough bark, Warwick regained his balance and struck out behind him with a back kick.

The sole of his boot made solid contact, a grunted *oof* reaching him. Warwick whirled, snapping his other leg around in a roundhouse kick aimed at head height. This time he caught the bastard in the back.

His attacker lost his balance and staggered to the side. Warwick seized his chance and dove at him.

They crashed into the ground, Warwick on the bottom. But the bastard was strong, and from the moment he'd first taken Warwick down, he'd known.

This wasn't a mere street thug or drug dealer bent on breaking in and stealing shit. This big bastard was trained and knew what he was doing.

A fist shot out, connecting with Warwick's face. The pain dazed him but he lashed out with an elbow. The man's head snapped to the side with the impact, the sudden shift in momentum throwing him off Warwick.

They both staggered to their feet, less than ten feet apart.

Warwick lunged. Caught the bastard's arm as a fist came at his face again and wrenched it backward, immediately spinning around behind him to put him in an arm lock.

The man snarled and twisted hard. Something popped.

A throttled scream filled the air a heartbeat before an elbow rammed him in the solar plexus. Warwick stumbled back at the unexpected force of the blow, doubled over as he fought to suck in air, preparing for another attack.

But the man suddenly turned to run in the opposite direction. Warwick darted forward and swept his leg out, tripping him.

Another scream as the bloke hit the ground. Warwick moved in to grab him. Deflected a kick to the head that caught him in the ribs instead, punching the little remaining air out of him.

He dropped to a knee, biting back a curse as pain lit up his side. Lurched upward as the bastard suddenly shot to his feet and took off, racing like a deer through the trees.

Warwick tore after him, still fighting for breath. But the forest grew denser. Darker. The tangle of underbrush thicker.

Within a minute he'd lost sight of his quarry.

He stopped. Debated his options for a moment and ran back toward the house to get another weapon in case the bastard wanted to come at him again.

Just as he neared the fence line, he skidded to a halt when he saw another large figure coming toward the front door.

The guy's head snapped toward him. He stopped. Stared at Warwick. Then his brows lowered in a menacing scowl and he stormed right at him.

Warwick cursed under his breath, winced as he put a hand to his ribs. He didn't think they were cracked but he'd have one hell of a bruise come morning, and he could feel blood trickling from his nose. "Decker." He recognized him from pictures Marley had shown him.

Decker slowed in surprise, the black scowl turning into a dark frown as he ran his gaze over him. "What the hell happened to you?"

"Where's Marley?" he demanded, fear curling in the pit of his stomach. There was no time to explain, but whoever had just come after him was a pro and might try to target Marley next.

Decker's eyebrows snapped back together. "None of your fucking business."

He didn't have time for this shit. He glanced at Marley's car parked at the end of the driveway. She wasn't in it. "You didn't leave her alone, did you?" When Decker blinked at him in clear surprise and opened his mouth to respond, Warwick talked right over top of him. "Go," he commanded. "Get back there now and don't leave her for a second."

"Why, what's going on?" He looked concerned now, edging back toward Marley's car.

"Just go, mate!" he snapped, jumping back through the bedroom window to grab his phone. When he came back out, Decker was gone.

He dialed 911 as he ran for his rental car, then drove like hell for Marley's place.

TEN

"Oh, thank God," Marley breathed, looking through the peephole in the front door when she heard her car arrive out front.

The whole time Decker had been gone, she'd been worried about what would happen when he saw Warwick, but there'd barely been enough time for him to get there and back, so maybe Warwick hadn't been there.

She flung the door open and ran outside in her socks, ready to interrogate him. Only to stop dead halfway to the curb when another car sped up and Warwick climbed out.

He was bleeding, blood dripping from his face onto his shirt.

She shot Decker an accusing look as he came toward her. "Oh my God, what the hell did you do?" She couldn't believe her brother had attacked him.

"Nothing," he said, rushing toward her.

She backed up a step at the set look on his face, alarm curling inside her. "What—"

"Inside, now," he said, grabbing her arm and practically running her back into the house.

"What's going on? Why's he bleeding?"

"He was fighting someone." He gave her a little push toward her bedroom. "Go pack a bag. We're leaving."

She whipped around to face him. "What? Why?"

"Just do it, Mar." He went to the kitchen to look into the backyard.

Warwick came in before she could ask anything else, quickly scanning the outside one last time before shutting the door and looking at her. He was bleeding from his nose and lower lip. If Decker hadn't hit him, who had?

"You need to leave. It's not safe here," he told her.

"Go, Mar," Decker ordered, still looking into the backyard.

"Somebody better tell me what the hell is going on right now," she snapped. "And why are you bleeding?" she said to Warwick.

His expression was set. "You've got five minutes, pet."

Decker nailed him with a hard stare. "You stay out of this. I'll handle it."

"No. It's too late for that now," Warwick told him.

Marley opened her mouth to blast him for not telling them what was going on, but the look on his and her brother's faces made ice slide down her spine. Something really bad was going down.

Relenting, she grabbed a bag from her closet and started pulling out clothes. "How long will I be gone? And where am I going?"

"Not sure yet," Warwick said behind her from the doorway.

Decker shouldered past him, giving him a look that was downright scary. "You're not in charge here. I'll find us a place," he added to her.

"She's comin' with me, mate." Warwick's voice was steely.

"Like hell she is," Decker said, squaring off with him, almost seeming to grow in size. "You're the reason she's in this position. I'm her brother, so you can fuck off. You really think I'd let you take her anywhere after what—"

"Deck, no. I'm going with him," she said, stepping in before this escalated into something ugly. Whatever happened, Warwick was deadly serious, and she didn't want to see him and Decker beat the hell out of each other.

Her brother whipped his head around to stare at her, incredulous. "You can't be serious. Neither one of us knows what the hell's happening here, but you were shot at a few nights ago, now someone just attacked him at his place and he's saying you're not safe here anymore. Because of *him*." He stabbed a finger at Warwick, who hadn't budged from the doorway.

"I know, and I hate it too. But if I'm in danger I'm not dragging you into this with me. And besides, you've got your interview coming up."

"Fuck the interview," he growled. "And fuck this. We're family. And I don't give a shit what it says on his resume, I can protect you better than he can." He shot Warwick a venomous glare. "And after what he did to you, there's no way you can trust him."

She exhaled. "I'm not saying I forgive him. But I'm not risking endangering you, so end of discussion. And whatever else he's done—I *do* at least trust him to protect me."

She looked away from her stunned brother to Warwick, and the proud, almost grateful expression on his face clogged her chest with a confusing mass of emotions.

"I don't fucking believe this," Decker muttered, raking a hand through his hair in agitation. "You can't go with him." He sounded outraged that she'd even consider it.

"Well, I am. So stop arguing." She stuffed a few sweaters and an extra pair of jeans into the bag along with a fistful of underthings, then went into her bathroom to grab toiletries, mind spinning.

Decker followed her in. He caught her by the upper arm. "Mar, please don't do this."

She pulled free and kept packing her things. "My mind's made up, Deck. Drop it now."

He stood there staring at her for several tense seconds before turning around and walking out. Her stomach sank. The last thing she wanted was more tension with her brother.

Her gut said she'd made the right decision. Whatever else he'd done in the past, Warwick would do everything in his power to keep her safe. She knew that on a bone-deep level, and she didn't want Decker in harm's way because of any of this.

When she emerged from her room a minute later, both men were waiting by the front door, arms folded across their chests as they faced one another, having a staring contest.

She suppressed a sigh. What a hell of an introduction to her brother. "Do you want me to call someone to find you somewhere to stay?" she asked Decker.

"No." His expression was all kinds of pissed off, but he would just have to deal. This was happening. "I'll deal with it."

"I'm sorry you're mad," she told him, for whatever that was worth.

"He won't tell me a fucking thing," he said, his stare locked with Warwick's.

She hoped he told her everything once they left. Otherwise she was going to explode. "I'll keep you updated when I can. Hopefully this will all blow over soon, but…" She looked at Warwick, so many questions spinning through her mind. If she went with her brother, she might never get the answers she needed. It had to be this way.

"Hey." Decker curled a hand around her arm, turned her toward him. His jaw flexed, the tormented, almost guilty look in his eyes tugging at her. "I'm here for you if you need me. For anything. You know that, right?" He seemed concerned that she didn't feel she could count on him.

Her throat tightened as she forced a smile. This was a shift in their relationship. A turning point heading them back in the right direction. "Course I know. Love you." She wrapped her arms around him, closed her eyes when he hugged her back. Not an awkward God-I-hate-hugs-and-showing-affection hug. A hard one, as if he was afraid to let her go, his arms tight around her.

She'd needed this hug for so damn long. Craved it her whole life, and even under these shitty circumstances, she could feel it healing something deep inside her.

He sighed. "Switch cars with me at least. I'll pick up a new one."

If someone had tracked Warwick's vehicle, then Decker might be in danger just driving it to the rental company. "But—"

"No." He gave her one last squeeze and released her, then aimed one last warning look at Warwick. "You better take care of her like she's your reason for breathing. Or whatever's happening won't be the only thing you need to watch your back for."

"I will." He looked straight at her as he said it. "Because she is," he added, knocking the breath from her as he bent to pick up her bag. "Ready?"

Honestly? No. And his response just now had her reeling, completely off-balance in a moment when it seemed like her entire life was spinning out of control. So she nodded woodenly and followed him outside. The rain had eased slightly, gusts of cool wind tugging at her hair and jacket. This was surreal. And too damn unsettling.

She was still so angry at him. Angry at what he'd done, and angry that she still wanted him so badly it made her ache. And now they were going to be forced to stay together, alone, until whatever danger they faced was taken care of.

Warwick stayed in front of her, watching their surroundings in a way that had her gut tightening. He put her in Decker's car, went around to the driver's side and set her bag on the backseat before getting in and heading up the street.

"Where are we going?" she asked.

"Not sure yet." He put his phone on his lap, hit a button. "Ring Walker," he said to it.

"Warwick, hey," Walker answered moments later.

"I need a favor, mate."

"Sure, what's up?"

"I've got Marley with me now. Someone tried to break into my place about thirty minutes ago. I fought him in the woods. He was trained. Marley was at my place just before that. It's possible he saw her. We need a place to lie low for a few days until I figure out what the hell's going on."

"Where are you now?" Walker's voice was calm but had an edge to it.

"Still in Crimson Point. Just left Marley's place in her brother's rental. He's returning mine now."

"Let me make a call. You armed?"

"Just a blade."

"I'm armed," Marley said, earning a startled look from Warwick. She nodded her chin at the bag in the backseat. "Got my Glock from my gun safe." Given the circumstances, there was no way she was going unarmed.

"I'll get you set up," Walker said. "Hang tight." He ended the call.

"When's the last time you shot it?" Warwick asked her.

She glanced in the side mirror. Didn't see anyone following them. "Couple weeks ago. I go at least once a month. Who was this guy?" She gestured to his face.

"Don't know. He was wearing a balaclava. But he was good."

"How good?"

"As good as me."

Oh, shit. That was scary.

His phone rang and he answered immediately. "Walker. Good news?"

"Yeah, Beckett Hollister is former SF and owns a local construction business. He says they just bought a place up in the hills south of town you guys can stay in. It needs work but it's still furnished and in a private spot."

"That's perfect."

"I'll let him know and text you the address. You guys need anything else?"

"We'll need supplies. About a week's worth."

"Got it. Ivy and I'll grab everything and meet you over there asap."

"Thanks, mate."

"No worries. And if you have any leads you want us to help follow up on, we can talk when we get there."

"Sounds good. See you soon." He ended the call.

"You really think it'll be a week?" Marley asked, typing out a text to Everleigh to let her know the gist of what was going on and that she'd contact her when it was safer.

"I don't know. I don't know what's goin' on yet, but I promise you I'm going to get to the bottom of it." He looked over at her, dark eyes intense. "And I promise you I'll keep you safe."

"I'm not helpless," she said in a hard voice, then softened her tone. Her stupid heart was still fluttering from the protective way he'd said it. Neither of them had any idea what they were facing or why, and that made the situation even more dangerous. "But I believe you." She turned away to look out her window, unable to bear the sight of his beautiful, bleeding face right now.

She might not trust him with her heart anymore. But the rest of her was another matter.

SIMON'S VISION went hazy again as he steered up the street to the place he'd rented. He sucked in a breath, clenched his jaw against the pain shooting through his left arm. It hung limply at his side, his hand and forearm in his lap. His fingers were pale and numb.

He'd dislocated his shoulder before, the first time on a training course with Warwick of all people back when they'd been SAS. The doc on base had put it back in joint, but it had been a few weeks of rest and rehab before he'd been able to use it much, and it had popped out twice more since because of the ligament damage.

He parked in the alley behind the small rancher-style house in a quiet neighborhood north of Crimson Point and stumbled through the back door, holding his useless arm. Every single muscle in it was locked in spasm, pain streaking up his neck and right down to his wrist.

There was no way James could have recognized him with the balaclava on. He hadn't said anything, so James wouldn't have picked up on his accent. Wait, had he said anything when his shoulder had popped out? He couldn't remember, just that he'd screamed.

It was that fucking useless Taser. If he'd been able to use a real weapon instead of a non-lethal one, James would have bled out on the ground in that forest.

He made his way into the bedroom. Paused to grasp the doorframe and catch his breath, closing his eyes. He couldn't function like this and going to a hospital or even urgent care was out of the question. So he'd have to deal with this himself.

From his open bag sitting on the dresser he took out a leather belt, did it up on the loosest notch and then stretched out on his back on the floor. The room spun for a moment and he grimaced, then gritted his teeth as he wrapped one end of the belt around his left wrist.

Staring up at the ceiling, he slid the sole of his boot in the other end of the loop. Remembered when James had taken exception to how he had conducted himself on a particular mission in Afghanistan. How James had called him out in front of the rest of the troop, grabbed him by the throat and slammed him into the wall, threatening to cut off his balls.

The others had pulled them apart after they'd bloodied each other, but by then it had been too late. The damage was done even before James had reported him to their commanding officer. Simon had hated him ever since, and working on the same detail together later at MI6 had been nearly unbearable.

Until the bombing had landed James in a coma. Simon wished he'd died then and there.

He closed his eyes. Focused on the memory of James's bleeding face as he clenched his jaw and pulled the belt with his boot as hard as he could.

Pain seared his shoulder and arm, his throttled scream lost under the roar of blood in his ears.

Pop.

He stopped, panting. Shaking all over as he opened his eyes.

The room spun for a moment. He gagged. Withdrew his boot from the belt and sat up, gingerly moving his left arm. The joint was back in place.

Sensation returned to his fingers in a rush of hot pins and needles. He flexed them, curled them into a fist and used his other hand to push to his feet.

From his bag he dug out two pain tablets, downing them with a gulp of bottled water before folding a T-shirt into a sling and casing his left forearm into it. There was ice in the freezer. He made his way into the kitchen, dumped some ice into a Ziploc bag and wrapped it in a damp tea towel before tucking it over his shoulder under the strap of the sling.

Having done all he could for himself, he went back to the bedroom and stretched out on the sheets before messaging Roland.

Located James but he escaped. A lie, but it had the same result. *He'll be on the move.*

Did he recognize you?

No. And there's a woman involved, he added. If he found out who she was and where to find her, he could use her to flush James out of hiding.

Does she matter to him? came the reply.

Yes. He didn't know for sure, but his gut said she did. And he was sure that if she was under threat, James would come for her.

Do what you have to do.

All right then. He laid the phone aside, closed his eyes and willed the pain meds to kick in and take the throb in his shoulder down to a tolerable level.

Another message pinged just as he was dozing off. From the hacker.

Marley Abrams. Thirty-one. Assistant manager at a care home in Crimson Point. Former Marine.

That last bit was interesting but didn't concern him. He plugged her address into his mobile, gauged the distance and it wasn't far.

There was his starting point. Once he found her, James was his.

ELEVEN

Warwick remained on alert as they reached the address Walker had sent them. A small house perched up on the hill surrounded by forest that looked like it had been built at the beginning of the last century. No one had followed them. He was certain of it.

A pickup was parked on one side of the two-car driveway. The driver stepped out. Big dark-haired bloke with a scar through one eyebrow. He wore a holstered pistol on his hip.

"Stay here," he said to Marley, and got out to talk to him.

"You must be Warwick. I'm Beckett." The man stepped forward to offer his hand.

Warwick shook it. "Thanks for this. We really appreciate it."

"Nah, it's no problem." He glanced past him to Marley in the car. "You both wanna come in and I'll show you around? The guest bath shower isn't working, but the en suite in the master is still good."

"That's fine." He waved Marley in. Watched all around as she got out and came toward them, waited until she was past him before falling in behind her while Beckett introduced himself.

"Like I told Walker, this place needs a lot of work," Becket said to her. "We're not scheduled to start demo for another six weeks, but it should do for you guys for now."

"I'm sure it'll be great," Marley said diplomatically, stepping inside after him.

The dead-end street was empty as Warwick took one last look around outside before following them in and locking the door behind them.

"It's not that big a place, so you won't have to worry about getting lost." Beckett led the way and gave a quick tour.

When they got to the guest bedroom, Warwick saw a problem. It was empty.

"There's a queen-size in the master," Beckett said. "I brought you towels and sheets and I've got an air mattress in my truck if—"

"That's okay," Marley said. "We can share the queen if we need to."

Warwick glanced at her, surprised. He'd thought the last thing she would want was to be that close to him. And he honestly didn't know if he could take lying next to her with this tension between them. Not when he wanted her more than he wanted his next breath.

"I'll leave the other bed here in case you change your mind," Beckett said, then turned to him. "If you come down to the crawlspace with me, I'll show you where the furnace and boiler are. They're both kinda finicky."

He left Marley to get settled in the master bedroom and went out back with Beckett to a wooden hatch near the rear wall of the house. Beckett pulled a small torch from his pocket, put it in his mouth and lifted the hatch. The crawlspace under the house was just that. They both had to get on their hands and knees and crawl through the thick layer of dust on the concrete floor to get around.

The furnace looked ancient. "It's old, but it still works," Beckett said, firing it up. Then he went to the boiler. "Pilot light's a bit temperamental on this." He used a lighter to ignite the tiny flame with a soft whoosh. "You might want to check it in the morning just to be sure it's still on. Water heater's directly above it in a service closet, along with the electrical panel. Which we'll also be tearing out when we gut the place."

"It's all good," he said, and crawled back out.

Beckett came through after him, closed the hatch behind him and stood, brushing off his clothes as he eyed him. "I don't know the situation, but if you need backup, gimme a call. The boys and I can be here in twenty minutes."

Warwick didn't know who "the boys" were, but he appreciated the offer, and that Beckett wasn't pressing him for details. Especially since Warwick didn't have any answers for him at the moment. "Cheers." They shook hands again.

Beckett went around front to collect the air mattress, put it in the entryway, and left.

Warwick was about to close the front door when he saw Walker's vehicle coming down the street. It parked where Beckett's truck had just been, then he and Ivy stepped out and started pulling bags from the back.

Warwick hurried out to help. "Hiya."

"Hi. We didn't know what kind of stuff to get you guys, so we asked Shae, since she knows Marley a bit," Ivy explained, shoving bags into his arms. "And there was a small British section so I grabbed a bunch of stuff for you. Just to make sure you don't get homesick."

"That was nice of you."

"It wasn't completely altruistic. I got myself some Jammie Dodgers too." She grabbed a few other bags while Walker stacked two cases of bottled water and carried them to the door. "And just wait until you see what else we brought you."

"I'm in a fair agony of suspense." He was sure that whatever Ivy had brought, it would be interesting.

They carried everything into the kitchen. Marley walked in, smiled at them, and even though it wasn't meant for him it hit Warwick in the heart anyway. "We meet in person at last. I'm just sorry it's under these circumstances."

"Don't be sorry." Ivy smiled back, tossing her hair over her shoulder. "Shae says hi. She told me you make killer biscuits and gravy so we got all the ingredients for you. Well, Walker did, your fellow Southerner. He does most of the cooking at our place, and I've never made biscuits and gravy in my life."

"Oh, that's so sweet of you. I can't believe she remembered me saying that."

"It was no trouble. And I know you've already got your own weapon, but we brought these for you guys just in case." She opened a duffel on the floor, revealing two more pistols and a rifle. "There's plenty of ammo in there too. Hopefully you won't need it, but you never know."

Looking past Marley at the tall sidelights flanking the front door, Warwick tensed when he saw another vehicle come into view at the end of the driveway.

"What?" Marley asked.

Seeing who it was, he relaxed. "It's the sheriff. I texted him earlier." He went to meet him at the door, and moments later, Sheriff Noah Buchanan strode into the kitchen in full uniform.

"Hey," he said to the others. "I need to talk to Warwick in private for a few minutes."

"We can talk in the guestroom," Warwick said, meeting Marley's gaze briefly on the way by. She was a people person. She'd be fine talking with Walker and Ivy alone for a bit. And he'd bet she was more than a little curious about Ivy after what she'd heard anyway.

Buchanan followed him down the hall and closed the guestroom door behind them, blue gaze steady. "I heard what happened at your rental, but I need you to run me through it from the top."

Warwick did while Buchanan took notes, explaining how at first the intruder had been thinking about breaking in, then changed his mind for some reason and the resulting chase and altercation in the woods.

"He didn't have a gun on him or anything?"

"A Taser. The probes just missed me and it got dumped into the brush early on. That's the weird part. He obviously wasn't there to kill me."

"What then?"

"I dunno. Capture me and take me somewhere, I'm guessing." Torture. Interrogation. Both. Then execution. Eventually.

Buchanan assessed him in silence for a moment. "Have you been a hundred percent honest with me about why you're here and everything that's happened up till now?"

"No," he answered, not seeing the point in denying it. "But I can tell you that whoever that bloke was, he had serious training. His CQB skills were just as good as mine." That was disturbing too.

"And you have no idea what he wanted with you."

He shook his head, unwilling to voice any of his theories out loud. They were all guesses at this point.

"Do you know of anyone who might be targeting you?"

"There are people out there who might want to come after me," was all he said.

"Because of Isaac Grey and the op in Durham? Yeah, I heard," he said when Warwick didn't answer right away. "Small town. Word gets around my inner circle about things like that when it involves one of our own."

By one of our own, he meant Walker, of course. Warwick inclined his head. "Aye. It could be related to Grey." That was his best guess, though given the number of jobs under his belt, it could be something else.

"Someone connected to Home Front?"

"Aye, exactly."

"But no one specific?"

"Not that I can think of."

"And you're sure that whoever it was wanted you alive," Buchanan answered.

"Aye. Bloke could easily have shot me down the moment I hopped the fence otherwise." That was the rub. What was he missing? Did someone want to use him as a hostage to force someone's hand? No point in that. He wasn't worth much anymore as far as the UK government was concerned.

Buchanan made some more notes before continuing. "I've got some deputies at your rental right now looking at everything. Forensics will look for the taser, see if they can get any prints."

"There won't be any. He was a pro, and wearin' gloves and a balaclava besides."

"Well, we'll check it all out and see if we can get anything to help ID him anyway. Is there anything else you want to add to your statement?"

"No." It wasn't that he didn't trust Buchanan not to betray them. It was because of exactly what the sheriff had just said. Word got around in small towns. Anyone spreading intel or their location could get him and Marley killed.

"All right. Does anyone else other than Ivy, Walker and Beckett know you're here?"

"How do you know Beckett?"

"We grew up together. And now he's married to my sister. So, anyone else know?"

"No." Even Marley's brother didn't know their location.

"Okay, good. I'll do everything I can to find a lead on my end." He held Warwick's gaze. "And if you have anything else you want to share in the meantime, you know how to reach me."

"Aye. I appreciate it."

He saw the sheriff out and returned to the kitchen. Walker straightened from leaning against the countertop. "Ivy and I have to get going. You guys need anything else?"

"No, I think we're set for now," Marley said. "Thank you for all this, we really appreciate it."

"We already told her we're not taking any money from either of you, so don't bother arguing," Ivy said as she walked toward him, then lowered her voice to a murmur when she got close. "I like her. You take good care of her."

"I will." Anyone trying to get to her would have to go through him and his dead body first. And he wasn't easy to kill.

She stopped, hazel eyes intense. "But if anything feels off and you want backup, call and we'll be here. No questions asked."

He nodded, knowing she not only meant it, but that she could back up that claim both technically and tactically.

"Yeah," Walker added. "If you need anything, just holler."

"Will do." He wouldn't call them unless it was necessary, but if it was, he wouldn't hesitate to have them watch his and Marley's backs. That's how much he trusted them. "Cheers for this."

"No problem." Ivy shot him a wink and clapped him on the shoulder on the way to the door.

Warwick locked up behind them, waited until they drove off before pulling the curtains and blinds shut on every window that had them. Marley followed suit, beginning in the kitchen. "That Ivy is something else. Is she really as badass as I think she is?"

It was a relief that she was making conversation. "Aye, and then some."

"Amazing. I'll have to have her over for drinks and find out more once this is all over."

More guilt hit him. Her life was on hold because of him. He'd dreamed so many times of sharing a roof with her again. But never because of a situation like this. "I really am sorry, Mar."

She stopped and looked back at him over her shoulder, long auburn hair spilling down her back. So damn beautiful she made him ache. "I believe you. But it doesn't change anything if you still won't tell me what's really going on." Then she turned to face him, pulled a wet wipe from a package on the counter and crossed the kitchen toward him.

She stopped less than two feet away, close enough that her familiar, intoxicating scent hit him. Close enough that he could see the warm flecks of amber in her big brown eyes as she reached up to gently dab at the blood under his nose.

He didn't dare move. Barely even dared to breathe while she carefully cleaned his face, her touch so tender it simultaneously eased the tight knot in his chest and made him want to crush her to him and never let go. Claim that soft, sexy mouth again. Kiss her until she was clinging and begging for more.

And he would give her all of him. Nothing held back this time.

When she was done, she lowered her hand and searched his eyes for a long moment. Then her gaze dipped to his mouth and a rush of pure need ripped through him. Made his fingers clench to stop himself from reaching for her. Knowing that if he touched her intimately again, there would be no going back. For either of them.

She cleared her throat and stepped back, breaking the spell. Leaving him strung taut as a wire. And if they had to share a bed later it would be even harder. "Why don't you go shower and get cleaned up. I'll fix us something to eat." She turned away before he could answer.

He made himself walk down the hall to the master bedroom and into the en suite. Finally got a good look at himself in the mirror. He was a damn mess.

He stripped, wincing as the sore spot on his side pulled with the motion, and caught sight of the bruise forming on the left side of his rib cage where the attacker's boot had slammed into him. It could've been a hell of a lot worse.

The old pipes groaned and rattled when he started the shower. As soon as it was warm enough, he got under the spray and began soaping himself. He thought of Marley just down the hall and instantly got hard.

He ignored his poorly-timed erection, finished cleaning up, then toweled off and dressed. In the bedroom he checked his phone for messages, and opened the email account he rarely used anymore. A string of emails popped up. Including one sent less than an hour ago.

Come in now or she's fair game.

There was a picture of Marley beneath it, showing her walking to his front door this morning.

He'd been right. "Fuck me," he muttered, opening the file in a full-screen format. Who the hell had sent this? He didn't recognize the sender's address. There was nothing to figure out who had sent it or where the email had originated.

But he knew someone who probably could.

He rang Ivy.

"Need us to turn around?" she asked the instant she picked up.

"No, but I need your help tracin' an email. I need to find out where it was sent from, and if possible, who sent it." Though he was guessing the second part wasn't going to happen. But if anyone could do it, it was Ivy.

She didn't hesitate. "Send it to me and I'll get on it right away."

TWELVE

"Tris, it's me. Call me when you get five. Thanks." Sitting in his rental vehicle parked out in front of a hotel near the waterfront, Decker ended the call and dialed his other brother.

"Wow, to what do I owe this honor?" Gavin answered, giving a little dig about how long it had been since they'd last talked.

An uncomfortable weight settled in his chest. When was that, anyway? Had to be over a month by now. Gavin had left him a message but he'd never gotten around to calling back. He'd been so wrapped up in getting his life sorted out after receiving his honorable discharge, everything else had been shoved to the background.

Including his siblings, the only family he had.

He winced inside, vowing to do better going forward. Circumstances at home while they were growing up and the five-year age gap between him and the twins had permanently altered their relationship, and not necessarily in a good way. Their sibling dynamic had shifted—unnaturally forced, to be honest—into something else long ago and they'd never moved past it. "You got a minute?"

Gav must have picked up on the tension in his voice because he dropped the mocking tone. "Yeah, I've got ten. What's up? Where are you?"

"In Crimson Point. And there's something going down with Marley."

"Is she okay?" A note of alarm tinged his voice.

"Not really, no. There's an unknown threat against her and she just went into hiding—with a guy she used to date who she thought was dead up until a few days ago when he barged into her house unannounced."

"Say *what*?"

"Yeah. Did you or Tris know about her and this guy named Warwick? They were apparently together last year for a while."

"No, never heard of him. Are you sure?"

"I'm sure." He sighed. Set his jaw as he gathered his thoughts. It was his fault Marley hadn't told him any of it before. He'd been fulfilling the role of head of the family for so long, acting the part of father until he didn't even know how to be a brother anymore. "He's a Brit. She was really into him for a while, then he went back to the UK for a job, and she was notified not long after that he'd been killed. This whole time she thought he was dead, and then he shows up at her place out of the blue the other night—right after someone shot at her place, and it's all linked to him."

"What the hell?" Gav blurted, sounding shocked.

He quickly explained the rest in a condensed version. "Someone jumped him outside his rental this morning and now he's taken her somewhere to supposedly protect her."

"And you just let her go with him?" The accusation in his voice was unmistakable.

"She didn't give me a choice. You know that look she gives where you know anything else you say or do is a complete lost cause?"

"Yeah."

"That, but on steroids." Marley had a million amazing qualities, but she was also as stubborn as hell. Maybe it was genetic, because that was one of his faults too. "Her mind was made up and there was no budging her. So she's with him right now and I don't know what the fuck's going on or how to help her." Just...fuck.

"Okay, damn. I wasn't expecting to hear anything like this when I saw your number come up."

"For real. I just wanted to tell you what's going on. I tried Tris but he didn't pick up." Okay, he'd needed to talk to someone he trusted. No matter what issues he and his siblings had, they were still family and he trusted them all completely. "She said she'd get in touch when she could." Hardly comforting under the circumstances.

"Who is this guy?"

"Former British military. Not sure what branch, but from what I've seen, he can handle himself." Maybe even SOF. Didn't matter, he hated entrusting Marley's safety to someone he didn't know or trust.

"Well, for her sake, I hope you're right." Disapproval dripped from every word.

Another stab of guilt hit him. Christ, he shouldn't have let her go without a fight, but she'd seemed so determined and he'd been so torn about pushing it. He might not like Warwick, might want to deck him for everything that had happened, but he at least believed the guy would keep her safe. The way he'd looked at Marley had convinced Decker that he cared deeply about her.

An incoming call came through. "Tris is calling. I'll keep you posted, okay?"

"You better."

He answered the other call, filled Tristan in and then headed inside to the lobby with his bag while they talked, fielding a barrage of questions from his brother while he checked in at the front counter.

Afterward he took the stairs to the fourth floor, paused outside his room to fish the plastic key card out of his pocket. "Look, I don't know anything more right now, okay? I've told you everything I can, and I can't do anything more until she contacts me." Even if it rubbed him raw inside.

"I can't believe you just let her go with him."

Yeah, that was the consensus. "Like I told Gav, she didn't give me a—" He stopped when the door to the next room opened and an Asian woman stepped out. She was pretty, with long black hair.

And then he saw the other side of her face as she turned toward him.

She froze when she saw him, looked ready to bolt.

He zeroed in on the bruising on her skin, noted the way she was hunched over slightly, one hand pressed to her side as if she was in pain.

Something flared to life inside him, hot and quick like a match strike. A blend of outrage and protectiveness.

She stared back at him for a moment, body tense, expression almost wary, then quickly disappeared back into her room and shut the door.

"Deck? You still there?"

"Yeah." He let himself into his room, bothered by what he'd just seen, and thinking of Marley. And how sick he'd feel if someone ever hurt her like that.

. . .

TEAGAN STOOD AT the closed door for a few seconds, listening as the man's voice trailed away into his room and the door shut behind him. Her heart was racing.

She didn't know the man in the next room. Hadn't recognized him. But he was big. Something about his size, about the hard look on his face, had triggered the instinct to flee.

She closed her eyes, rested her forehead against the cool wooden surface. This sucked. Everything was so damn confusing. She knew her first name but not her last, couldn't remember her birthday or anything else significant.

She'd had no ID on her when that stranger had pulled her from the water. Had no recollection of where she was from, what she was doing here, or how she'd ended up on that beach with a knife wound in her side. Someone had freaking stabbed her, and she couldn't remember a damn thing.

All she knew was, she was afraid.

The doctors had told her amnesia wasn't uncommon after suffering from shock and hypothermia, and the knot on the side of her head might explain it too. They'd said her memory could return in a rush, maybe in pieces, or maybe not at all, and ordered her to rest while she recuperated.

Real hard to rest when someone had apparently tried to kill her, and she didn't even know who the hell she was.

She straightened, winced as the stitches across her ribs pulled and the throbbing in her head suddenly intensified, and went back to the bed. Gingerly stretching out on her other side, she gazed out the large window at the ocean. The waves rolled in one after the other, crashing on the beach in rhythmic thuds that should have been soothing.

Except she was beyond soothing.

From the moment she'd woken up in that hospital bed she'd been struggling to fill the holes in her memory. There were flashes of things from her childhood. Her parents' faces. A sparkling Christmas tree surrounded by brightly wrapped presents. Birthday cakes. Her first car. Wearing a cap and gown to her graduation.

And then there were recent, murky memories of being on a boat. It was dark out. The deck rocking. She remembered turning around suddenly. A blaze of pain across her side, followed by a flash of terror as she plunged over the railing. Then the moment she'd hit the surface of the icy water.

Nothing else. Not what she'd been doing on the boat in the first place. Or who had stabbed her or why.

She didn't remember getting to shore. Lying on the beach. Had no recollection of her rescuer finding her, carrying her to his car and taking her to the hospital.

Warwick James, the sheriff had told her. That was the name of the man who had saved her.

Someone knocked on the door.

She jackknifed up, one hand going to her hip, reaching for something that wasn't there. Then she sucked in a breath as pain raked across her ribs at the sudden movement, pressed a hand to her side and sat there, heart pounding.

They've found me.

"Teagan? It's Sheriff Buchanan."

The sudden spike in fear receded, but that last thought was disturbing. Who were *they*? What was her subconscious trying to warn her about? "Coming." She got up, checked through the peephole before letting the sheriff in.

He stepped into the room, gave her a polite smile as his gaze scanned her in a clinical way. "How are you feeling?"

"Fine." She wasn't sure why she'd just lied to him, because she definitely wasn't fine, mentally or physically.

"I came to bring you this." He pulled a phone from a pocket

inside his uniform jacket. "It was tucked inside your wet suit. The bag it was in was punctured, so it was damaged by the seawater." He handed it to her. "Unfortunately, your prints aren't in any state or federal databases, so it's unlikely you have a passport or anything."

She pressed the power button. When the screen remained black she turned it over in her fingers, hoping it would spark some kind of memory. But her mind remained as frustratingly empty as the screen.

"There's a tech place in the next town north, about fifteen minutes from here. Or you could take it in to Crimson Point Security here, just a few blocks away. They've got a good tech department, and someone there might be able to at least recover the data on it. I can call them if you want, let them know to expect you. Maybe tomorrow morning?"

"Yes, that'd be fine. Thank you." Even her voice sounded foreign to her ears. She didn't have much of the cash left that had been tucked into another hidden, waterproof pocket inside her wetsuit. She was only in this hotel room because the man who'd pulled her out of the water had left a donation for her. She couldn't believe he'd done that on top of everything else.

"You're welcome." Buchanan watched her for another moment. "We're continuing our investigation into your assault, and we've sent your picture and prints to the FBI. Is there anyone you can think of who I can call who might be able to help you?"

"No. The doctors said I just need to give it time."

He smiled. "Yeah, I'm sure everything will come back to you soon."

"I hope so."

She thanked him and let him out, took the phone back to her bed and gazed back at the ocean, trying to suppress the bubble of rising panic as she watched the waves. Something about the water made unease curl in the pit of her stomach. Was it because she'd nearly drowned? Or was it something else?

She was starting to fear she'd never know. And with her past a blank slate and no known family, she was all on her own.

THIRTEEN

"Are you sure I can't do anything?" Everleigh asked.

Phone to her ear, Marley sat propped up against the headboard in the master bedroom of the old rental house. She'd just poured out the entire story to her bestie and felt better for it. "I'm sure. But I love you for asking. Please thank Grady for the update on Henry." Obviously she couldn't go visit him at the hospital in person right now, but Grady was on shift and had passed on a message for her.

Somehow, Henry was still hanging tough. Not improving, still incredibly weak, but holding on. Marley wanted him to recover and return to the care home, but if that wasn't going to happen, she wanted him to just go now, quickly, and not have the end dragged out. She didn't want him to suffer, and he wouldn't want that either.

"I will." Everleigh paused. "So how's it…going there? With the two of you. Is it hideously awkward?"

Her plan was to avoid him as much as possible. Things were too messy otherwise and this entire situation was hard enough already. "You could say that, yeah. I'm still mad as hell at him." It wasn't that simple anymore, however. "But the longer I'm with him, the harder it is to hold onto that. I get that he thought he was trying to protect me. Whatever this is, it's dangerous. He's apologized a few times and he's trying to do the right thing now by guarding me himself."

As well as making it clear that he still wanted her more than ever. That was the toughest part, and something she was trying not to think about. Because the pull he exerted on her was too strong. Heightened because of nearly having lost him and the time they'd spent apart, rather than diminished by everything.

"But? I can hear a but in there."

Everleigh knew her so well. "But I know I can't trust him not to leave again."

Ev made a sympathetic sound. "Sweetie, I'm so sorry. That's so hard."

"Yeah." She lowered her voice. Warwick was down the other end of the hall in the living room working on something, so it's not like he could hear her, but still. "What makes it even harder is the chemistry's still there. No, chemistry's the wrong word for it. Too bland."

"Fireworks?"

"No." She contemplated it for a moment. "Just fire," she said. That's what it was. A white-hot fire between them, and if she wasn't careful, she was going to get incinerated. "I've never felt anything so intense with anyone else."

"I totally get it. It's like that for me with Grady."

She made an understanding sound, glad her friend had found that kind of connection with someone. "And then today he…"

"He what?" Ev pressed.

"He told me there's been no one else since me."

"Oh, wow. Oh, Mar…"

"I know." That comment had really hit her hard. Made her heart hurt to know he'd been holding onto the memory of her all this time while keeping his distance because he had been wanting to protect her from something he didn't even understand himself. "I can't say the same, of course." About six months after being told Warwick was dead, she'd forced herself to start dating again. Not that it had ever gone anywhere.

"You don't feel guilty about that, do you? You thought he was gone forever. You had to move on."

"No, I know." Nothing had ever lasted more than a week at most anyway. "Even though I had fun sometimes, I always ended up feeling more alone after. Empty. And now that he's back and made it clear he still cares about me, I…"

"Can't stop wanting him."

"Yup." She blew out a breath. "So yeah, that's how it's going, and we're stuck here together for God knows how long. Oh, and there's also someone out there trying to target both of us. It's good times," she added sarcastically.

Everleigh chuckled. "I'm sorry, I know it's not supposed to be funny, but your wit is so cute."

She couldn't help but smile a little. "Thanks. I guess bridesmaid gown shopping is out for the next while, huh?"

"Don't even worry about that! We'll find you something awesome when this is all over. Hopefully soon."

"Yeah, hopefully." The wedding was in a little over a month. Surely this would all be behind her by then.

"We're so going out to do something fun as soon as you're home."

"Hell yes, we are. And by fun, I hope you don't mean another quilting class or book club night. No offense."

Everleigh laughed. "No. Something a little more lively than that. I was thinking a girls' date. Winery tour and dinner. Hell, I'll even go dancing with you at a club after."

"I'm in." She smiled again, feeling a tiny bit lighter inside. Venting to Everleigh had helped more than she'd expected. "I love you, you know. I'm so thankful you moved in down the hall from me that day." They'd hit it off immediately. Just clicked, both of them somehow recognizing the other as a kindred spirit who had gone through their own version of hell and were trying to put their lives back together again.

"Me too, and you know I love you back."

A dinging sound came from the kitchen. The ancient oven timer still worked. "Oh, my biscuits are done. Gotta go."

Time to gird her loins and face Warwick again.

"Okay, but call me if you need anything. And stay safe. Promise?"

"Promise." She opened the bedroom door and hurried into the kitchen, steeling herself.

Warwick was already there turning off the timer. He glanced over his shoulder at her, and her stomach did a little flip. Even scarred up and bruised, he was a gorgeous man, all masculine grace and controlled power. The ridges of muscle outlined by his shirt had her itching to run her hands all over him.

"I think they're done, but you're the expert," he said, his deep, accented voice surrounding her.

He moved aside slightly for her while she stepped closer to open the oven door and take a peek. The oven temperature was hotter than what the gauge read, because the biscuits were dark brown on the bottom. "They're a little overdone, but not bad," she said, pulling on an oven mitt to slide the pan out and set it on the counter.

He inhaled appreciatively. "They look amazin'."

Marley froze, the oven mitt still holding the edge of the pan. He was so close she could smell the soap he'd used in the shower earlier. So close that if she turned around, they would be face-to-face and only inches apart.

So close that if she turned around, she might forget all the reasons she needed to keep her walls up and give in to the crushing need swirling inside her.

"I'll get the plates," he said, stepping away to the cupboard and allowing her to breathe again. He took down two, got them each some silverware while she stirred the sausage gravy she'd left to simmer in the pan on the stove.

"Okay, it's ready," she announced, and began plating their meals. Focusing on the task at hand so she wouldn't have to focus on him. Two biscuits for him, one for her, with a generous ladle of creamy sausage gravy over the top for both.

Warwick took the plates for her and carried them to the small round table in the tiny breakfast nook in front of the covered window. "I've dreamed about these," he told her with a little grin as he picked up his knife and fork. "Ever since you made them for me that first time."

She hadn't made them since, because they reminded her of him, and it had been way too painful. "I'm out of practice, but hopefully it'll taste okay."

He cut a bite of biscuit. Scooped up more gravy with it. Popped it in his mouth. The low sound of pleasure he made, part groan, part hum, went right to her core. Utterly sensual and decadent, just like the man himself.

Marley forced her concentration to her own plate. As soon as they both started eating, a strained silence crept in. Thickening with each passing second.

It felt unbearably intimate, the two of them eating alone in here together. Not only that, but in spite of her resolve her gaze kept straying to him.

Watching his mouth. Remembering it on hers. The feel of it on her naked body while he learned all the things that drove her wild. The way he'd savored her, pushing her to the point of desperation and then devotedly lingering on the exact spots that gave her maximum pleasure.

Shit.

She tore her eyes off him and concentrated on her meal, barely tasting anything. The gravy was decent, but the biscuits were definitely overdone and a bit dry. But that wasn't the only reason she struggled to get hers down her throat every time she swallowed.

The air around them had become charged with an electric current. She could feel it tingling along her skin, her body acutely aware of his. And that he was more than willing to satisfy the unbearable craving he'd lit inside her.

She couldn't help but think about their kiss this morning. The terrifying hunger it had unleashed, the way he'd threatened to break her control simply by standing in front of her.

No, she told herself firmly. *That's all over.*

It had to be if she was going to survive this unscathed.

"What were you working on?" she asked him to get out of her head.

"Tryin' to piece things together. Starting with the Lake District op."

She finally looked up at him, lowered her fork. Hoping he was finally going to open up about all this. There was no point in keeping it from her now. They were in the shit together. "What do you remember?"

"The lead up to it. My team. I remember being kitted up and waiting outside the house for the order to breach." He paused, a faraway look in his dark eyes. "I remember the teammate behind me squeezin' me shoulder to signal he was ready. I broke in the door." He frowned. "I…can't remember exactly what happened after that. Just a vague sense of thinkin' 'oh, shite,' and seeing a tripwire. Then a quick flash. And flyin' backward."

Her heartbeat accelerated. God, that sounded terrifying. She had training but had never been deployed or seen combat.

Knowing how close he'd come to dying had every muscle in her body clenching in denial.

"I don't remember being hit. Or the impact when I hit the wall. The first responders or being in the ambulance afterward. Naught at all until I woke up in my hospital room and seeing a nurse and my commander there."

Her gaze traveled over the length of the scar on the side of his face. She wanted to trace her fingers over it. Kiss it. Kiss every single mark on his body to try and take away the suffering he must have endured during his recovery. "You were lucky." Her voice was rough, all her emotions rising to the surface.

His eyes focused on her. Deep and dark and full of yearning. For her. "Aye."

That painful ache started up behind her sternum again, the gulf of time and loss and pain standing between them. She couldn't let him in again. Just couldn't. "You think whatever's going on now is connected to that somehow?" she asked to keep him talking.

"It has to be." He shook his head, frustration bleeding into his expression. "There's something more to it. My gut's tellin' me there is. That there's a critical piece I'm missin', something that happened before that op, and I can't remember what the hell it is. Somethin' I saw? Or heard?" He shook his head again. "I just know it has somethin' to do with Grey."

Since Grey had been involved in a terror network that now operated on both sides of the Atlantic, that could mean any number of things. "Have you talked with anyone else involved with it? Someone you think might be able to fill in the blanks?"

"No. All three other men on that breaching team either died in the blast or of their injuries shortly after. My commander was reassigned before I came out of the coma. We had brief contact right after the Durham op. I've thought about reachin' out to him now, though I'm not sure what he could do to help at this point. I need to remember the bits I'm missing, and so far, there's naught."

His frustration was palpable, and she didn't know how to help him.

He looked down at his plate, cut another bite of biscuit smothered in gravy. "Anyway, enough of that for now. Did you speak to Everleigh?"

"Yes." She didn't dare look up at him again. Afraid that if she looked into those deep dark eyes right now, she'd never be able to pull free again. "Henry's still fighting."

"That's good news."

She nodded, cut another bite of biscuit. She wasn't hungry. Too on edge to even attempt to enjoy what she'd made, the worry about the threat hanging over them and the strained tension between them pulling her stomach into a knot.

But somehow this silence was worse. So she broke it. "I still have a lot of questions."

He stilled, looked up at her. "Aye, I figured," he said softly, and she could see his guard drop. "What do you want to know?"

Everything. "Are you really from Newcastle?" She had no idea if anything he'd told her about himself last year had been true at all.

"Aye."

"You told me you don't have any family left."

"I don't. Me mum died about seven years back. Now there's no one."

"Were you close?"

"No." He sighed, put the forkful in his mouth—lucky biscuit—and chewed thoughtfully. "She was a single mum. Did the best she could, I suppose, but it was hard for her. She didn't want to be a mum. At least, not on her own. She didn't bother hidin' it."

"In what way?" She so badly wanted to know him better. Understand him.

He shrugged. "I was a burden to her and I knew it. An obligation. She fed me and kept a roof over my head and clothes on my back, but that was about the extent of it. As soon as she felt I was old enough to take care of myself, she was done with me and let me know it was time for me to go."

Oh, God, how awful. "How old were you?"

"Sixteen. Old enough."

"What did you do?" She was afraid he'd wound up on the streets.

"Lived with friends here and there, but never for long. Wound up at a shelter for teenage boys until I finished school and then went into the military. Turned out to be the making of me."

Her chest tightened as her own past flooded back. She and Warwick had more in common than she'd realized. "For me, too. Well, us," she added when he looked up at her.

"Us?"

"My brothers and I."

He held her gaze, completely focused on her and what she was saying. "Aye, you told me you lost both your parents when you were young."

She nodded. She'd told him some of it one night after dinner while they'd been walking along the beach at the resort. "My dad died of a heart attack when I was nine. Decker was twelve, and the twins were only seven. Our mom basically worked and drank herself to death afterward, but honestly, she was gone long before she died."

Warwick remained silent, watching her. Waiting for her to go on.

So she did. "Even before she died, she couldn't take care of us properly, so Deck and I took over. He was the provider, out working part-time jobs after school and on weekends to make sure we could eat and stay in the house together."

He made a quiet sound. "And you?"

"I raised the twins. Took care of them and the house. Made sure they were fed and got to school and got their homework done." It had been so completely overwhelming at first, she'd thought she would drown under the weight of it all, struggling to balance all of that with her own schoolwork.

And then, over time, it had somehow become normal. "Mom died right before Decker graduated. He went straight into the Marine Corps, sent home all the money he could to us. I held down the fort while he was gone, waited until the twins graduated before enlisting."

"What about your degree?"

"I used the GI bill to get my degree in business management. Decker and I both sent the twins money every month to help them get by until they enlisted and were making enough to take care of themselves." Well, she and Decker still pitched in financially for the twins from time to time, like at Christmas or on their birthday, to help build them a little nest egg to tuck away. Neither of them wanted the twins to have to struggle as much as they had.

His eyes shone with admiration. "It's incredible how you took care of all that on your own."

"We're family." And she hated that Warwick had never experienced that kind of love and support. Even Decker with his frustratingly distant edge, she knew he loved her and the twins. Through everything, all the hard times they'd endured, at least they'd all known what unconditional love was, and that they had each other's backs.

No matter how bad things had gotten, they'd had each other. While Warwick hadn't had anyone.

"But our background is also why all of us are careful with our money. I still clip coupons and look for sales when I grocery shop, and I have to have my freezer and pantry stocked at all times. I've only started spending money on extras recently, and I sometimes feel guilty after I do."

"Makes sense. You learned early on to put yourself last."

She stilled, his words resonating deep inside.

He was right. She had done that. And she'd be lying if she didn't admit that it had cost her in her life.

Her living situation, for example. She was still renting rather than looking for a place to buy because she hadn't been able to save much until the past few years and was still socking away whatever money she had left at the end of each month. Waiting until she had enough to pay for at least half a home to minimize the stress of a big mortgage.

"I guess I did," she said quietly, a little shaken by how clearly and deeply he saw her. It only made her feel more drawn to him.

She looked back down at her plate. Quickly finished off the last bite and stood abruptly. "There's plenty more, so help yourself. I'm just gonna go take a quick nap."

Liar. You're running away.

Yup. She hurried to the sink to deal with her plate, relieved to have her back to him.

She needed space from him. Now, before she gave into all the feelings and the tide of need he created inside her.

With every step she took down the hall to the bedroom, she could feel the weight of that dark gaze following her until the moment she shut the door behind her.

FOURTEEN

Warwick stopped reading to rub his tired, burning eyes for a moment before sitting back against the old, tattered couch cushion and staring at the glowing screen of his laptop.

He'd spent the past few hours going over everything he could remember that might be linked to the threat against him, then made a list of everything and everyone he thought might be involved in the current threat facing him and Marley. Had racked his brain for every detail and recorded it all, even things that seemed insignificant or unlikely.

He still couldn't put the pieces together. Was still no closer to finding out what the hell was going on and who was after him. There was no obvious thread to tug on. No common links that might explain what had happened.

The only thing that made any sense was at the top of his list. Home Front was still active in the area despite recent FBI and other law enforcement efforts to break the organization and shut down local cells. It was still his best guess as to who might be after him. But why target him specifically? How would they know he was here?

He thought of the men he'd seen following him in Durham. It was possible that someone linked to Home Front in the UK had tracked him there initially after Grey was killed, and had someone pick up his trail from Portland. And he still wasn't certain whether the drive-by car was the same one he'd seen at the waterfront previously. It was possible there were more people involved in this than he'd first imagined.

It didn't seem likely he'd been followed without picking up on it, but if it was true, it meant he'd been inexcusably careless at some critical point. And now Marley was paying for it along with him.

He shut the laptop, plunging the room into instant darkness. It was just after midnight but there was no way he could sleep.

Glancing down the hall, he saw there was no strip of light coming from beneath the master bedroom door. Marley must have turned it off in the past hour or so while he'd been preoccupied. She'd done her best to avoid him all night and was probably asleep. Or at least pretending to be.

Standing, he made his way down the hall with silent treads. Paused within reach of the master door.

All around him, the house was silent. He could hear the wind outside, sighing in the trees surrounding the property. A steady barrage of raindrops drummed on the roof.

They were alone. Safe. That should have been enough for the moment.

But all he could think about was Marley lying in the bed on the other side of this door.

All he could think about was climbing into it with her. And what a selfish bastard he would be if he did.

There was a zero percent chance that he could lie next to her and not touch her. Not draw her to him, wake her with kisses, slide his hands beneath covers and clothing to find her smooth, bare skin.

And not stop until he was buried as deep as he could get inside her. Until they were joined as intimately and completely as humanly possible and she was crying out in the throes of orgasm. More than once before the night was through.

He was starving for her. Had been starving for her for almost a year and a half. Their kiss this morning told him she still wanted him too.

His body tensed, knowing she was right here, right on the other side of this door…

With a mental curse, he turned around and forced himself to walk back down the hall for the air mattress Beckett had left inside the front door. Partway there, he paused. The guestroom was right beside Marley's. Inflating that thing now would surely wake her, no matter how quiet he tried to be.

So the sofa it was.

Back in the living room, he winced as he folded up his tall frame on the worn cushions. His side throbbed where he'd taken the impact of that boot. But that was nothing compared to the current ache he felt inside.

The rain continued to patter on the roof as he lay there, the wind gusting through the trees and around the eaves with a low moan. Tired as he was, he couldn't sleep. Too amped up, too uncomfortable, too caught up in his head about Marley and how the hell he was supposed to get them out of this.

He desperately wanted to break through the wall she'd put up between them. To bring it crashing down so they could recapture the way things had been between them before. So he could have another chance to make things right. Build a future with her once this was done.

That was like wishing for the damn moon.

He tossed and turned for hours on his lumpy, uncomfortable bed while the wind turned from a moan to a low howl along the eaves. Finally, toward dawn, he drifted off at last. Only to jolt awake when his mobile buzzed on the low table beside him. He reached for it automatically, winced as his bruised side protested, and squinted at the screen.

Ivy was calling and it wasn't yet seven. "Areet, Ivy?" He kept his voice low. The house was still quiet, Marley still in her room. Either asleep or determined to keep avoiding him as long as possible.

"Hi. Did I wake you?"

"No, it's alright."

"How's Marley?"

Something about her tone told him she was fishing for intel about the two of them. He put a stop to any speculation now. "Still asleep in her room."

"Oh." If he wasn't mistaken, she sounded a little disappointed. "Cracked your email mystery overnight. The sender wasn't that sophisticated about trying to hide their location. Whoever it was bounced the email off a different server inland, but it wasn't hard to trace it back and then triangulate to find the origin."

"Which was?"

"Crimson Point. Right on the northern edge of town from a house up on the hill. I looked up the address and it's listed as a rental. I hacked into the host company's site and got the credit card number used for the booking, but if this guy's really a pro like you think he is, then it won't go anywhere. Name on the account is Chris Stringer."

She was a bit scary with what she could do on her own without being caught, but in a cracking way, and this sort of thing was child's play for her. "Don't know anyone by that name." Probably a stolen card or an alias anyway, but he would find out who's staying at the property.

"I'll keep digging. Or I'll get Amber on it, because Walker and I have meetings at CPS starting first thing this morning."

"Marley's brother has an interview there this morning too. Not sure what time."

"I'll keep an eye out for him while we're there. You guys need anything else?"

Short of finding the bloke who'd attacked him, no. "No, everythin' you've already done is more than enough. Thank you."

"It's my pleasure. Has the sheriff's department uncovered anything yet?"

"No."

"Not surprising. They're a small unit with limited resources. I'll look more into this later when I get back and update you if I find anything else."

"Cheers." He ended the call, sat up and opened his laptop, thinking hard. Ivy or Amber may yet uncover something that would give him a solid lead to follow. But as of right now, he'd exhausted all the resources currently available to him and was no further ahead.

Restless and needing something to do, he got up and checked the perimeter of the property for any sign that someone had been here overnight. The rain had left the ground soft, but there were no footprints or vehicle tracks near the house.

Satisfied that all was as it should be, he went back inside. Marley's door was still shut. At this rate she might be planning to stay in there until she was on the verge of starving to avoid him. It was making him mental.

The kitchen hadn't been touched since he'd tidied it after eating with Marley yesterday. He put on coffee for her and filled the kettle to make himself a cuppa of the strong Yorkshire tea Ivy had bought him. After downing two cups and updating and reviewing all the notes he'd compiled so far, almost two hours had passed since Ivy's call.

An online search on Chris Stringer didn't turn up anything

helpful. The next step was to do recon on the actual rental to see if he could get a look at the person staying there, but he wasn't leaving Marley here alone and didn't want to put her at further risk by bringing her. He would need Ivy and Walker's help to uncover more.

The cursor blinked at the end of his notes, waiting for him to add more. But with the holes in his memory blocking his efforts to put them together, everything he'd thought of was a dead end.

There was nothing more he could do to crack this on his own. No other threads for him to pull on. It was time to reach out and ask for help from further afield.

He found the number he needed in his contact list and dialed it. "Commander," he said when the man answered. "It's Warwick James." He was one of the few people who had been there for him while he was in hospital.

"Warwick? God, it's been a long time. How are you?"

He could hear indistinct voices in the background. "I've been better, to be honest."

"Why, what's going on?"

"I need your help."

"Yes, of course, anything you need. Where are you, anyway?"

"It's a bit of a long story." Taking a deep breath, Warwick told him the gist of what was happening. He left out Marley's name but explained everything else, including the attacker, the email and where it had been sent from. "Cardholder is listed as Chris Stringer. That name mean aught to you?"

A pause. "No, I'm afraid it doesn't. How certain are you that this has something to do with the Grey case?" More voices in the background, muffled. As if his former commander had stepped into another room for privacy. Warwick pictured him standing at his office window overlooking the London traffic moving across the Thames.

"I'm sure." Nothing else seemed plausible.

"Ah. Well. That's good enough for me, then. Where are you, exactly?"

"Somewhere safe." He wouldn't disclose the location directly, even to him.

"Good, good. Listen, I have a meeting right now, but I'm going to look into this as soon as I'm done and get back to you. All right?"

"Aye. Thank you." Any help at all would be appreciated.

"No need to thank me. We'll get to the bottom of this together, okay?"

"Okay," he said, a measure of relief sliding through him. With his former commander and Ivy helping them, things were bound to start moving soon.

ROLAND SHOT off a quick text and tucked his phone away when he entered the meeting room on the top floor of Crimson Point Security, put on a smile for Walker and Ivy in spite of the renewed sense of alarm coursing through him as they both stood from their seats at the conference table. "I'm sorry to keep you waiting. I had to take an important call."

And send an even more important message.

"Not at all," Walker said.

"Thank you for meeting with me. It's nice to see you both in person."

"Likewise," said Walker as they shook hands.

He turned to Ivy, shook with her too. She was decidedly cooler, her expression unreadable.

Releasing her hand, he pulled out a chair for himself, unable to shake the feeling that she was assessing him. It didn't help that her background was a complete blank for him, even after his enquiries. Whoever she really was, the Americans had gone to a lot of trouble to hide her true identity. "Well. I've heard a lot of good things about this company recently." He glanced around the room, past Ivy and Walker to the view of the sea beyond the large windows lining the west side of the building. "Not a bad spot for headquarters, if a bit unconventional and off the beaten track."

"We like it," Walker said, his posture relaxed. Deceptively so. From what Roland knew about him and the events in Durham, Walker was not only a skilled interrogator, he wasn't someone you would want as an enemy. "So, what brings you to Crimson Point?"

"I'm on my way to Seattle from San Fran for more meetings and thought I'd stop in to see you both in person to thank you again for everything you did to assist with the Grey case. It's been a few weeks since we've spoken but security services in the UK are still working hard on identifying people linked to him and Home Front. We've made several key arrests as well."

"Yes, we're aware," Ivy said, reminding him not so subtly that she was able to stay apprised of sensitive intel all on her own without official permission or any kind of security clearance. A bit disconcerting, but at least they were on the same side.

"How are the cleanup efforts going in Durham?" Walker asked.

He and Ivy had a good cop-bad cop dynamic going. Roland couldn't help but feel like he was in a kind of subtle interrogation. "Slowly coming along. Engineers are reinforcing the last section of the tunnel right before the crypt. They're still unsure whether there's enough structural integrity in the vault itself to allow it to be saved. But we're hopeful that it can. After all the press since the Grey op, there's been massive public interest in the city. Reopening the tunnel and crypt would be a great tourist draw for the region."

"Yeah, well, I won't be going back in there anytime soon," Ivy said.

"Understandable. You all had a close call down there."

"Several close calls, actually."

"Yes. And then there's James, who was nearly killed by another of Grey's devices last year. Have either of you heard from him since you got back, by the way? I reached out to him but he never responded."

"No, we haven't heard anything," Walker said. "But if we do, we'll let him know to get in touch with you."

"I'd appreciate it. Maybe he's on a well-deserved holiday somewhere then, eh?" Roland smiled, trying to figure out if they were lying to him. Both were impossible to read, even for him. Neither gave away a single clue with their body language or eye movement. But the chances that James would travel all the way here to this small coastal town where they lived and *not* make contact?

Zero as far as Roland was concerned. He knew James was digging for intel about what was happening. Were they protecting him?

A subtle buzz in his pocket signaled he had a new message. He was anxious to see if it was what he'd been waiting for but would check it in private. "Well," he said, straightening in his chair. "I won't keep you. I need to be in Seattle by lunchtime."

"Thanks for making the trip to stop in and see us," Walker said as he and Ivy both stood in a movement that was almost synchronized.

He shook hands with them both and took his leave. On his way out he went through the reception area. His heart jolted when he saw the young Asian woman sitting on a bench at the side of the room. Long black hair. One side of her face marred by bruises.

She glanced his way for a mere instant then looked right past him, absently massaging the back of her neck.

His muscles unlocked. They'd never met in person, but it was definitely her.

He kept going, said goodbye to the executive receptionist who had arranged the meeting for him and continued to the elevator. Once downstairs and outside the secure building, he waited until he was in the backseat behind the privacy of the SUV's tinted windows before checking the message on his mobile.

The PI had sent him an address and a map. And it wasn't far from Crimson Point.

I've been following the cop, the accompanying message read. *Was able to put a tracker on his vehicle. Took me a while to get anything useful because he's alert and almost spotted me once. But there's this place he went yesterday in an isolated area. Really isolated, down a long dead-end road. I couldn't get close enough to verify everyone there without being seen, but after the cop left, I saw Walker drive past me coming from the same place. Might be worth having your guy check it out.*

The sheriff and Walker both stopping at an isolated property outside of town soon after Warwick had escaped from Simon yesterday? No way that was all coincidence.

Elation surged through him. He relayed the intel to Simon immediately. There was no time to lose.

Wherever James was, he knew something. Roland was sure of it. James now knew for certain he was being targeted. Law enforcement would be involved. The FBI might be brought in. The possibility that James knew something was too great a risk to take now.

Nerves prickled along his spine. The danger to him was

only increasing the longer this thing dragged on. He could almost feel the walls closing in.

This couldn't wait any longer. He had no choice now. There was only one way to protect himself.

James had to die.

He composed a message to Simon. Hesitated only a few seconds before pressing send. It had to be this way. There was too much at stake otherwise and he couldn't take the risk of being exposed.

His driver got into the vehicle, reversed and steered out of the parking lot. Roland stared out the window at the restless, churning waves as they drove along the waterfront, lost in thought.

He set aside the guilt burning in his stomach with a mental shove. Ridiculous to feel guilty or have second thoughts now. As difficult as the decision had been, it was necessary. His message had already set the wheels into motion. No going back now.

Just like the explosion that had nearly cost James his life and compromised his memory, he would never see this one coming either.

FIFTEEN

Simon stumbled into the adjoining bathroom at 06:30 hours, eyes half-closed against the morning light as he fumbled in his shaving kit with his free hand for the bottle of pain meds. His left arm was still bound up in the sling, and he'd barely slept all night because of it. Every single muscle around the joint was in spasm, the entire thing tender and inflamed.

He managed to uncap the bottle and shake out two tablets into his left palm. Downed them and then angled his head in the sink to take a sip of water from the tap.

This was worse than the previous dislocations. Maybe there was ligament or even bone damage, he wasn't sure, but he couldn't seek medical treatment at the moment anyway.

Didn't matter. He wasn't out of the game. Far from it. He wasn't stopping until he had James under his boot, trussed up and delivered to Roland for whatever came next.

A hot shower at least got him clean and made him feel more alert. He went into the kitchen to make coffee and checked his phone. Found a new message from Roland.

An address and a map with a red pin showing the location.

Along with a short message changing the mission from capture to a kill order.

He set the phone on the counter, excitement racing through his bloodstream in a heady rush. Using his right thumb and forefinger, he zoomed out on the map to see what he was looking at. Realized with a start that it was less than ten miles from him in a sparsely populated area.

His pulse kicked hard, triumph and determination coalescing in his gut. This was what he did best. The kind of mission he preferred.

Locate target. Set up the shot. Eliminate target. Leave.

He switched the map to satellite view to get a better look at the terrain surrounding the target house. The property was fairly isolated, up on the hillside surrounded by trees on three sides and located on what appeared to be a dead-end road that stopped against a ravine. The house itself appeared small.

If James was there, a long-range rifle shot would be easiest, but not necessarily practical. Faster to just sneak in and take James off guard up close. And if Marley was with him, she would meet the same fate to eliminate any loose ends. Maybe he'd kill her in front of James first to make him suffer more.

Smiling to himself, he strode to the bedroom to gather his gear, the lift in his mood making the pain in his arm recede even before the pain meds kicked in. He grabbed the rifle case as insurance, then tucked away his blade and pistol with its silencer into its holster. But he'd already made up his mind.

This kill was going to be up close. And as personal as they came.

"COME ON, YOU BLOODY BASTARD, *THINK*," Warwick growled under his breath into the empty room.

But no matter how hard he tried to remember, to join the dots, those gray, blurry spots teasing the edge of his subconscious remained infuriatingly out of reach.

He shoved to his feet and paced the length of the silent living room, ready to tear his hair out. After going through every memory around the Lake District op all over again, after reviewing all his notes in the hopes that it would trigger something in his brain, something at the back of his mind had finally stirred. A missing piece to this puzzle, something he'd either seen or heard that would explain everything that was happening now.

Yet right as it had begun to take shape, it faded away like mist just as quickly.

It was bloody maddening. He was sick to death of this. And he wasn't crazy.

All he knew was, he couldn't take much more, and sitting here doing nothing while the threat continued to hang over his and Marley's heads was enough to drive him insane. He owed it to her to end this. Quickly. So she could resume her life after being forced to put it on hold because of him.

The pacing didn't help. Nothing seemed to. He had to concentrate harder. Break through the brick wall blocking access to the bits of memory eluding him.

He crossed back to the couch. Sat down. Stared at his notes again. Then closed his eyes and rested his head in his hands, elbows braced on his knees.

Think, he commanded himself angrily. *Remember.*

He went back to the first clear memory he had prior to the explosion. Recalled standing with his teammates, dressed in his tactical uniform, breaching tool gripped in his hands as he waited next to the door they were about to break through in the target house.

The Prime Minister's vacation home perched high up on a

hill overlooking the lake. They were acting on a late tip, and all indications were that Grey was likely inside right now.

He remembered how surprisingly muggy the pre-dawn air had been. Could see his teammates' faces in the green glow of his night-optic device.

He knew their names and exactly where each one was positioned in the stack along the side of the house. Could feel the weight of the breaching tool in his gloved hands. The solid feel of his rifle slung across his chest. The sense of calm that always settled over him prior to an op.

The bit missing was before that.

He skipped back in time. Remembered bits of the mission brief. Piling into the van afterward to head out to the target.

No. Further back.

There was…something before that. Vague and nebulous. A jumble of bits and pieces. Disjointed. Like a satellite feed that was constantly interrupted.

He'd been walking out of the building with a teammate where the brief had been held. It was dark. They walked around the corner. Stopped when they heard low voices coming from the shadows.

The video in his head skipped forward again.

"James. Broughton," a man said when they rounded the corner. "Didn't see you there."

And there was another piece. Soon after that, they'd been hauled back into the briefing room. A last-minute tip had come in, placing Grey at another possible location several miles away where the PM sometimes stayed.

Warwick remembered his commander making the decision to call in a second team last minute. It was sent to the original location, and Warwick's team to the new one.

The screen in his mind went blank again. But all that was clear now, and it was vivid enough that he knew it must be important somehow. And the voice he'd heard before walking around that corner was so damn familiar. Who was it?

He kept his eyes squeezed shut, struggling to hold onto that moment. To stretch it out beyond the end of the video in his mind and put a face to that voice. Weave all the threads together until they made sense.

Dammit, he was so close. On the verge of remembering the critical pieces, he could feel it. And it was so goddamn maddening to sense it hovering *right there* at the edge of his consciousness and not be able to quite grasp it.

"You okay?"

His eyes snapped open to find Marley standing just inside the room. Freshly showered, long hair still slightly damp around her shoulders. She was dressed in dark jeans and a form-fitting lavender sweater that hugged her lean curves, the V-neckline dipping down to expose the top of the valley of her breasts.

His mind went instantly, completely blank, the memory he'd been holding onto disappearing in a puff of smoke. "Sleep well?" he made himself ask once he could unstick his tongue from the roof of his mouth.

"Okay." She was still wary of him. Keeping her distance. "You?"

"Not bad." Terrible, and not likely to get better anytime in the foreseeable future. Wanting her, his need for her, was a living thing inside him.

Her gaze ran over him, lingering on his scarred cheek. He probably looked rough, face battered and full of scruff, his hair mussed. "Have you eaten yet?"

"Tea and toast earlier. Coffee's ready for you if you want some."

She paused. "You made me coffee?"

"Aye." He wanted to take care of her in every way she'd let him.

"Thank you," she murmured, and walked to the kitchen.

He got up and followed her, unable to stay put. Heated the kettle up again on the stove just to have an excuse to be close to her.

She stood off to the side, pouring a mug of coffee and adding flavored creamer, her back stiff. The brittle tension between them grated on his already stretched nerves. He wanted to grab her. Spin her around and force her to look into his eyes before he crushed his lips to hers. Make her stop avoiding him.

They both turned toward the sink at the same time. She bumped into his side. He froze as pain shot through his ribs, sucked in a quick breath before he could stop himself.

"Sorry." She set her mug down, frowning at him in concern as she reached out a tentative hand and laid her palm against his ribs.

He stayed completely still. Barely dared to breathe as she grasped the hem of his T-shirt. "Let me see." She started pulling the material up.

"No, it's—"

She made a soft sound when she saw the bruise on his ribs. Dark blue, purple around the edges, in the perfect shape of a boot heel. "This looks bad," she murmured, gently laying her hand against his skin.

His breath hissed out. Her eyes darted up to meet his.

Pure, raw hunger tore through him. Dark and territorial, the feel of her touching his bare skin lighting up his whole body. He went rock hard in his jeans, every muscle contracting.

For a moment, neither of them moved. Then, slowly, she reached up with her other hand and traced her fingertips along the scar on his cheek. Her touch was light, following it down over the side of his throat to his collarbone, her right palm cool and soft against the bruised skin over his ribs.

"I thought I'd die too for a while, after I was told about you," she murmured. "Sometimes I thought I wanted to."

He grasped her wrist to stop her from going any lower. Coiled his fingers around it, already riding the edge of his control. Knowing how deeply she'd cared for him was like a dagger in his heart. "Don't say that."

Her eyes lifted to meet his. Held. Her fingertips remained poised on the scar. "Did you wish I was there? When you woke up. Honestly."

His heart was racing, the blood thundering in his ears. "Aye," he whispered, aching inside and out. "Every damn hour of every day." Throughout the constant pain and confusion. All the surgeries and grueling rehab that followed. "I would have given anythin' to have you there beside me."

"I wish I had been."

"Even though this wasn't how I wanted it to happen, I'm glad you're with me now."

Marley's gaze dipped to his mouth. Her thumb eased over his cheek to the edge of his lips. Feathered across them, her gaze intent.

The tension between them shot up sharply. Stretching out painfully like an elastic band ready to break, pulling tighter and tighter.

Her dark lashes lowered. She leaned in slightly. Her lips brushed the scar on his cheek, light as a butterfly's wings.

The skin there was numb, but he felt that faint contact all the way to the core of his being.

She nuzzled him. Warwick slid his fingers into the back of her hair, the other going to the side of her face as she pressed a trail of soft kisses down to the edge of his jaw. As if she was trying to kiss away the pain he'd gone through.

Possessiveness and hunger roared through him.

He tipped her face up to his, her height putting them almost at the exact same level. Their gazes locked. Her pupils expanded, the look in her eyes mirroring the same desperate yearning crashing over him.

His hands tightened as he brought his lips down on hers.

And the moment they made contact, he was utterly fucking lost.

Marley made a soft, plaintive sound that cut right through him, her hands going to his shoulders. Gripping tight, fingers digging into his muscles while she pressed the length of her tall, lithe body to him.

He backed her up against the wall behind her, needing to feel all of her. Groaned into her mouth when she opened for him, slid his tongue in to stroke hers. He couldn't get close enough. Couldn't touch enough of her, kissing her deep and hard.

She reached between them to grip the front of his shirt and started pulling upward. He released her only long enough to let her strip it off him, ignoring the pain in his ribs when he raised his arms over his head. She broke the kiss to nip at his jaw. Looked down at his torso.

Pain flickered across her face. Her hands cradled his rib cage between them, careful of the bruise, and she pressed soft kisses over every scar on his chest and side. Every inch of surgical scar. Each whorl of burn scar.

The hand he'd locked in her hair tightened, his heart pounding out of control as he pulled her back up to claim her mouth again. She wound her arms around his neck and sank into the kiss. Into him, rubbing that sinuous body against every hard, aching inch of his.

"I want you so fuckin' much," he rasped out. "Never stopped. Never will."

She nipped at his lower lip, then looked him dead in the eye. "Take me to bed, Warwick."

Oh, Christ yes.

He picked her up by the hips, locked his arms around her and carried her down the hall to her room, desperate to make her his again.

SIXTEEN

She couldn't believe this was really happening.

Marley wound her arms and legs around him and held on tight as he shoved the bedroom door open and kept going, her mouth busy on the side of his neck. She had thrown herself into the whirlwind, unable to hold back a moment longer. The fire between them, the constant longing, were too much, even for her.

Her feelings for Warwick hadn't diminished one bit. They were stronger than ever, and being trapped in here alone with him had pushed her past her breaking point.

If this was all they could have together, then so be it. She needed to get him out of her system. Had to be able to move past him somehow and get on with her life once this was over.

In the meantime, she was going to enjoy the hell out of him while she could.

Her back hit the mattress as he lowered her onto the bed. He came down on top of her, pressing her down with that long, powerful body, his hips settling between her open thighs.

She moaned into his mouth at the feel of him. It had been so long. So damn long, and for months she'd been left wondering if she'd only imagined how good it had been between them.

She hadn't. This was real. He was here in her arms, the hard ridge of his erection pressed against the throb between her legs, their tongues twining as she ran her hands down his naked back.

There were more scars here. Shrapnel and burns, from the feel of them. They made her ache with the thought of what he must have gone through during his recovery, alone. She wished again that she could have been there for him.

No. She wasn't going to waste a moment more being caught in the past. Or thinking about the future. There was only the here and now, the two of them tangled in this bed while the rain drummed on the roof above them, and the painful level of arousal only he could satisfy.

"I missed you every day," he rasped out, pushing up on his knees to grab the bottom of her sweater. "Every day, Mar. Dreamed of you. Of this. Us."

His words set off a bittersweet pain in her heart. She'd grieved for him. Ached for him. Dreamed of him. "Me too." She arched her back to help him peel it off, her hungry hands traveling over the powerful muscles on his scarred torso. The evidence of his strength and survival made him even more gorgeous to her.

Her bra came undone with a quick flick of his wrist. He swept it off her, tossed it aside and bent close, his mouth on the side of her neck while his big hands cupped the sensitive mounds of her breasts with firm pressure.

His dominant, possessive edge in bed turned her on as much as it turned her body liquid.

Yes, yes, yes…

She slid her hands into his thick, dark hair, let her eyes fall closed when his lips closed around one hard nipple. Instant pleasure punched through her, every flick of his tongue sending streamers of heat to the tight throb between her legs.

She'd never felt this way with anyone else. So damn hot for him that she couldn't even think, could only feel, and she'd never thought she would experience this with him ever again.

His long fingers found the button on her jeans. He undid it, worked the denim over her hips and down her legs, his lips and tongue now teasing her other nipple. She was so wet. So hot and wet she felt like she was about to vaporize, her heart thundering out of control.

He released her nipple and slid lower. Nipped at her belly as he cupped her mound through the scrap of lace barring his way. She made a hungry sound, lifting into his touch. The pressure and heat of his palm only made the ache worse, made the emptiness inside her more acute.

"Don't stop," she whispered, uncaring how desperate she sounded. She wanted to feel him everywhere at once.

He drew the lace down. Dipped his head as his big hands settled on the tops of her thighs and gripped tight. She felt the heat of his breath on her flushed, swollen folds. Gripped handfuls of his hair, just before…

"Oh, God, Warwick…" Liquid heat. The smooth stroke of his tongue right across her most sensitive flesh. She bucked her hips, squirmed, needing more.

His grip on her thighs tightened. "Nah, pet. Stay still," he said in a low voice. "I've dreamt about this for too long."

He flattened his tongue against her, unerringly found the exact spot on her swollen clit that made her see stars. His hands held her in place, refusing to allow her to move while he licked and caressed every sensitive millimeter until she was climbing toward the release she wanted more than she wanted air to breathe.

Still he refused to let her move. Refused to be rushed,

ignoring her gasping moans, the way her hands clenched impatiently in his hair. She was so close already, every nerve ending sizzling under the steady, decadent stroke of his tongue.

The pleasure turned molten, spreading outward even as her muscles tightened. Her vision started to haze over. She squeezed her eyes shut, a soft cry of need coming from her.

His tongue lifted a second too soon, leaving her hanging. He nipped at her abdomen. She opened her eyes in time to see him rising to his knees and shoving his jeans down his thighs. Hungrily reached down to wrap her fingers around his cock.

He hissed in a breath at her touch. Growled and grasped both her wrists, raising them up high to pin them to the bed on either side of her head in an implacable grip that turned her on even more.

Warwick paused to stare down at her for several heartbeats, that powerful, scarred body kneeling between her open thighs. She clenched them around his hips, trying to pull him to her, his dark brown eyes blazing with desire…

And a naked possessiveness that sent a secret shiver through her.

Holding her down, he eased his hips forward slightly. She stared back at him, held captive by them as much as his dominant hold while the head of his cock slid along her slick folds. She made a soft sound of need, lifting into him. He stroked it along the edge of her clit, making her hiss in a breath and arch, needing more, then finally nudged inside her a fraction.

She held her breath at the feeling of pressure, the anticipation building. Because she knew what was coming. Remembered how his thick length had stretched and stretched her. Remembered how the slow penetration had stolen her breath, filling her to the limit.

The look on his face told her he remembered it too. Watching her with a hungry expression, he eased more of his weight down on her. Pushing the head of his cock into her with a slow surge of his hips.

A thousand tiny nerve endings flared suddenly and painfully to life. She tensed, bit her lip and squirmed, the pleasure already spreading outward. Oh God, he was so thick. And hard.

Sensation streaked up her spine. He was barely inside her and she needed more, this instant. Needed it so badly—

He pushed deeper.

Oh, Jesus…

She squeezed her eyes shut and cried out at the sudden increase in pressure, the shocking fullness while her body stretched and quivered around him, the sensation balanced right on the knife edge of pleasure and pain.

There was no escaping it. Or him. He was so big, so hard and thick inside her, every inch of him stroking swollen, sensitive tissue, and the way he held her down made it impossible for her to move. He was clearly determined to make her insane.

He withdrew. Ignored her whimper as he paused a moment, then surged forward halfway.

"Warwiiiick," she cried, trembling all over. It had always been this way with him. So fucking intense.

"Shh, pet," he rasped out, making her wait. He brushed his lips across her eyelids. Her cheeks. Soothing her even as the feel of him half-buried inside her made her want to writhe. "God, the way you feel clenchin' around me. You were made to take me." His voice was rough, his breathing unsteady.

More. More…

She must have said it aloud because he pushed deeper, his hold on her wrists demanding her surrender. She made a sound of distress, pinned there, open and helpless while the rising pleasure took her apart. Not enough and yet too much all at the same time.

"Please," she managed to gasp out, half-delirious with pleasure as she tugged against his grip. She wanted to flip him over. Pin him down and ride him until release finally eased this unbearable, pleasurable ache inside her. "Please…"

The pressure around her wrists disappeared. He plunged one hand into her hair, the other sliding beneath her, pulling her lower body tight to his as he surged deep.

His low growl of pleasure was lost in the high-pitched wail that came from her throat. Her body clenched around him, inner muscles fluttering as the pleasure suddenly expanded.

She was lost. Helpless under him and reveling in it.

There was nothing but what he made her feel. The white-hot blaze of ecstasy as he began to fuck her with a firm, steady rhythm that slid his cock across the sweet spot inside her, his steely arm locked beneath her. Angling her hips so that each stroke of his cock rubbed her engorged clit against his pelvis.

Her hands flew to his back. She sank her fingers deep into the bunching muscles there while she squirmed beneath him, rubbing and grinding her way to the orgasm he was hurtling her toward.

She choked out his name as it hit. Unbearably sweet waves of ecstasy swept through her. Every thrust of his hips prolonged it, his heavy weight keeping her pinned to the bed. Anchored.

Safe. At least physically.

She barely had time to start coming back to her senses when he suddenly picked up his rhythm. Thrusting faster, faster, his expression as taut as his body. Seconds later he went rigid, burying his face in her neck as his deep, ragged cry of pleasure filled the room.

Marley lay sprawled out beneath him, gasping for breath. Their damp skin was glued together, her heart hammering in her ears. Her body turned boneless under the warm, heavy blanket he made, her muscles turning into melted wax.

He was like a dead weight atop her. Warm and solid and so damn perfect it made her throat close up.

I can't lose you again. How am I supposed to let you go again?

She ruthlessly shut down the voice in her head and wrapped her arms around him. Shoved her face into the curve of his neck while they clung together, determined to stay in the moment.

It had been perfect.

But perfection was an illusion. And it never lasted.

She couldn't get past the feeling that he was with her now only because of the circumstances and his need to protect her. But once the threat had passed, he would leave, whether because he thought it would protect her or for reasons only he knew.

Once he did, in her heart she knew she would never see him again after that.

Warwick groaned softly and stirred, his lips dragging lazy kisses along her shoulder and neck, along the underside of her jaw. "Mar," he whispered, finding her mouth with his. All slow and tender and sensual now that the intense storm had passed, his long fingers sliding through her hair.

I love you.

Her chest hitched, the bittersweet pain piercing her heart as she choked the words back. Oh God, she couldn't bear it.

But neither could she bear to end this, or let him go. Not yet. And never completely. He was part of her and always would be. No matter what happened going forward.

Holding on to the moment, she sank a hand into the back of his hair and returned the kiss. Pouring everything she felt for him into it even as the secret knowledge burned deep in her chest.

He lifted his head to look at her. Searched her eyes, his dark gaze intense. "Mar, I l—"

She put a hand over his mouth to stop him. Unable to bear hearing the words she saw mirrored in his eyes when she knew there was no chance of a future for them.

There would always be a reason for him to leave. Another unseen threat from his past hanging over him. She wasn't getting crushed like that again. She'd had enough heartache in her life.

"Don't," she whispered back. "Not now. Not when you—"

A ringtone went off from beside the bed, saving her from finishing that painful sentence.

"No, what?" he insisted, blocking her when she tried to rise.

She shook her head, started to roll toward her phone. "Never mind."

He pinned her flat on her back and trapped her beneath him again, his eyebrows drawn together in a frown that was equal parts confusion and annoyance. "Not when I what?"

"When we both know you'll be leaving as soon as this is over," she snapped, pushing his restraining hand off her and sitting up to grab her phone. It was her brother calling. And he couldn't have picked a better time.

"Hey," she answered, forcing a lightness she didn't feel into her voice as she grabbed her sweater from the floor and tugged it on. She felt too vulnerable being naked in front of Warwick now.

The sweater covered her to just below her ass, and it was better than nothing under the circumstances. "How did the interview go?" she asked Decker as she left the bedroom and closed the door behind her, avoiding looking at Warwick. Her heart hurt too much.

"Pretty well. They've asked me to come back for a second one next week."

"That's great!" she said with far more enthusiasm than she actually felt, her whole chest hurting and her throat tight with the threat of tears. "I'm sure you'll get the job. They'd be crazy not to hire you."

"Well, we'll see how it goes, but I'm just worried about you. Are you okay?"

"Me? I'm fine." Bleeding inside, but whatever. That was her own doing. "It'll be so great having you here in town."

Crimson Point was her home now. She had a job here that she loved. A best friend she loved even more. People who cared about her. And hopefully her brother would be moving here soon too.

Because once this was over and Warwick left, she was going to need all the support she could get in order to pick up the pieces yet again.

SEVENTEEN

"Teagan?"

She glanced up from the history magazine she'd been absently flipping through without reading anything and looked across the waiting area to find a woman with short, dark brown hair and dark-rimmed glasses smiling politely at her. Unlike everyone else who worked here at Crimson Point Security, she was dressed in jeans, knee-high boots and a pink cable knit sweater rather than business attire.

Teagan set down the magazine and stood. "Yes?"

"I've got your phone for you. I'm Ember by the way," she said as she closed the distance between them.

"Hi." She took the phone. It still didn't look familiar at all. Didn't trigger anything in her memory. Was it even hers? Or had someone planted it on her? "Thank you."

"You're welcome. Callum called and asked if I could come in to take a look at it. I was able to get it working again but it's password protected. If you enter it now, we can check to make sure everything's functional before you leave."

Teagan pressed the home button and stared at the password prompt, thinking hard. But she had no idea what it was. "I...

don't remember." The modicum of hope she'd been clinging to for the past two hours faded. She'd been counting on the phone jogging her memory and giving her vital information about her identity and life. But it was just another dead end.

"Oh. Well, maybe it will come to you later. I can take a crack at it myself if you want, or let someone in the tech department here try for you."

"No, it's okay. I'm sure it'll come to me." She didn't know where the refusal came from, but it was automatic. Some inner sense telling her to keep whatever was on the phone private.

"Sure. If you change your mind, just contact reception here and they'll be able to reach me." She smiled again. "Good luck."

Teagan returned the smile but her whole face felt stiff doing it. She was going to need all the help she could get. Her cash was running out fast and she was lucky to have been given a room at a local hotel rather than a shelter.

She took the stairs to the ground level rather than taking the elevator, the idea of being in the enclosed space making her uncomfortable. The phone was in her right hand as she exited the building, trying to figure out what the password might be. A sequence of numbers? A word?

She tried a few numbers that didn't work. Tried her name. That didn't work either.

"Hey—"

She whirled toward the source of a deep voice, glimpsed the big man looming close behind her and reacted without thinking, driving her fist at his throat.

He blocked it just in time with his forearm even as she winced at the pain along her ribs, snapping his head to the side and stepping back with his hands held up in a non-threatening manner. "Whoa," he said, staring at her like she was crazy.

And maybe she was.

They stood feet apart, staring at each other. She recognized him as the man staying in the hotel room next to hers. Tall. Short, medium-brown hair. Powerfully built with a commanding presence. She'd seen him upstairs earlier waiting for an appointment.

"I'm sorry," she said, shocked by what she'd just done. The complete overreaction and automatic nature of it. And that it had all felt completely natural. "I...sorry." She didn't know what the hell else to say.

"It's okay." He eyed her warily. "I didn't mean to scare you."

"You didn't scare me." Her answer was swift and instinctive. She didn't know where the defensive edge was coming from. Only that she refused to admit that he'd startled her.

Never show fear. Never show weakness.

She didn't know where that voice at the back of her mind came from. "Just caught me off guard." But that reaction. The way she'd instinctively planted her feet and aimed her fist directly at his throat... It felt familiar. Natural.

Something slid into place at the back of her mind. An easing that brought a measure of comfort, but no answers. Leaving her more confused.

The man's hazel eyes tracked over her face, making her conscious of the bruises and swelling there. "I was just heading back to the hotel and wanted to say you're welcome to ride with me if you're heading over there. I'm Decker, by the way."

She checked her gut. Felt no fear or foreboding. And with limited funds and not knowing who she was, making an acquaintance wasn't a bad idea. "Okay, yeah, that'd be great. And I'm Teagan."

He nodded once, the hint of a smile softening his hard features. "This way." He kept a respectful distance from her on the way to his car and opened the door for her.

She murmured her thanks and got in the passenger seat, not in the least bit uncomfortable with him for some reason.

He settled in the driver's seat and started the engine. "Are you a martial artist?"

"I don't think so." Unless…maybe?

He shot her a funny look. "You're not sure?"

"No." She didn't want to talk about this, but something about him made her feel safe in spite of her initial reaction. Which was crazy, since she'd literally just tried to throat punch him a minute ago. "I had an accident and hit my head pretty hard. My memory's not as sharp as it should be." It was pretty much blank right now.

He glanced at her in concern, then focused back on the road. "That has to be tough."

"Yeah."

"Were you at CPS for an interview?"

"No. Trying to get my phone fixed. It was damaged in the accident and the sheriff told me to bring it in there."

"Ah. Did they fix it?"

"I think so." But she wouldn't know for sure until she figured out what the hell her password was. "Were you there for an interview?"

He nodded. "Personal protection position."

"You former military?" He looked it, and he'd blocked her punch expertly. He definitely had training.

"Marines. Just got out. My sister moved here, so I figured I'd apply for the job and see how things went."

"Did you get it?"

"Not yet. Got a second interview next week though."

"That's good."

He made a sound of agreement and they lapsed into silence. She got the feeling that he didn't like small talk much either. And it was odd to know she didn't like small talk but couldn't remember her last name or what had happened to her.

At the hotel, he pulled into a parking spot behind the building and cut the engine. "Look," he said, swiveling slightly in his seat to face her. "Are you in trouble? If you are, I can help you."

She stared at him, taken aback by the offer. And also touched. Was she in trouble? Yeah, something told her she might be. A vague sense of foreboding she couldn't shake. But then she realized he probably thought she was a domestic violence victim. "I'm okay. Thanks though."

He nodded once, looking unconvinced. He had gorgeous eyes. Actually, he was pretty gorgeous all over with that square jaw and powerful body. And he'd been kind to her even though she'd tried to punch him earlier. "All right. But if you change your mind, I'm right next door. Probably for the next few days, anyway."

She gave him a polite smile. "Well. Thanks for the ride."

"Welcome. See you around."

"Yeah, see you." She got out and quickly hurried to the door before he could reach it, breathing a small sigh of relief when she made it up the stairs and to her room just as the stairwell door opened and he stepped through. She locked her door behind her, then sat on the bed facing the water and guessed at more passwords, none of which worked.

This was so damn frustrating. Who was she? What was she doing here in this little town? Who had attacked her? The sheriff was still trying to help identify her, and had contacted the FBI to assist with their databases.

The memory of being on that boat was sharp in her mind. She remembered standing on the deck, the feel of it rocking beneath her.

Destiny.

The word popped into her mind, clear as if she'd spoken it aloud. Not expecting it to actually work, she typed it into the password screen in lowercase letters.

The phone magically came to life. She sat up straighter, held her breath as she checked the apps on it. She found images of the boat in the photo section.

Her heart started beating faster when she saw the name painted across its stern. *Destiny*.

There were a dozen more, showing it moored at a dock at night. But nothing personal. No pictures of her or anyone else. No pets, no smiling faces that could have been friends or family. Had she known the owner of the boat?

She checked the text messages next. Shock rippled through her when she found a short chain of messages there. All from the same number. One of them included a picture.

She tapped on it.

A thirty-something man with dark brown hair and eyes appeared. Grim expression. Looked like either a military or government ID, though she wasn't sure how she knew that.

Below it was a name.

Warwick James.

She sucked in a breath, winced and pressed a hand to her stitches, staring at the man's image. She knew that name. He had rescued her from the beach.

Why did she have his picture on…

Her eyes stopped on the final message. She went cold all over as the truth hit her in a rush, along with a barrage of information that suddenly flooded back, filling the empty spaces in her mind.

And what it revealed wasn't comforting.

That saying careful what you wish for had never rung so true. She'd wanted to remember who she was and what she was doing here. Now she knew.

But Warwick James had saved her life and paid to put a roof over her head without even knowing who she was.

She owed him for that.

SIMON SKIRTED the edge of the park on the way back to where he'd left his car earlier. Marley's car was out front of her house but after checking the property thoroughly he was satisfied she wasn't home. He'd needed to verify that prior to heading to the other location.

He was betting James had taken her with him. If he had come all the way from the UK to see her, there was no way he would leave her behind now.

Simon had hoped to take her first. She was a much softer target than James, but the two of them being together might work in Simon's favor. She was James's weakness. He could exploit that.

He shot off a quick message to Roland first. *On way to suspect house.*

His mobile's GPS got him to the area within twenty minutes. But rather than heading down the dead-end street in broad daylight, he pulled to the side of a road two streets away alongside a stretch of heavily wooded land and got out to do his recon on foot.

The dense forest gave him the perfect camouflage as he moved close to the edge of the road toward his target. All the rain had made the ground soft, would leave prints in the earth so he had to be careful where he went so as not to leave a trail for anyone to find or follow.

Within minutes he was hidden just behind the tree line directly across from the house. Older, wood-sided thing in dire need of a paint job. Or a bulldozer.

There wasn't another soul around, no other properties on this stretch of road. The driveway was empty and all the windows facing the road were covered. There was no smoke or steam leaving from the chimney either.

He kept going, moving through the woods to skirt around the far end of the dead-end street, then up the hill to the edge of the property. The trees began to thin here, allowing him to see the chain-link fence enclosing a decent-sized back lawn. More forest sat behind it, enclosing the property on three sides.

A steady rain was falling now, the wind picking up as he crept all the way around the back of the property line, carefully using the trees as cover. The windows at the back and sides of the house were all covered as well. And the car sitting in a pullout behind the house, while a rental, wasn't the same one he'd seen in front of James's rental yesterday.

There was no cell service out here so he used a sat phone to message his contact, asking him to run this new plate.

Gimme a few minutes.

He kept scouting the property in the meantime, searching for a way to see inside without revealing himself or tripping any cameras or sensors James might have put up outside. And then a message came through.

Rental agreement names Decker Abrams, from Kentucky.

No way he wasn't related to Marley.

Simon smiled to himself as he tucked the phone away, staring at the darkened house. If Marley was inside, James would be with her.

Gotcha, you righteous bastard.

Much as he wanted to end James immediately, entering the house now would be reckless. So he kept going, tamping down the sudden spike in impatience and wound his way through the trees until he was well clear of the property before crossing the road and backtracking to his vehicle. While he carefully checked and readied his weapons, he considered his options.

It took less than a minute for him to formulate a plan and make his decision. He messaged Roland from the sat phone.

It's him. Moving into position.

The dead-end road gave him a major tactical advantage, as did the element of surprise. A direct assault was too risky. Now that he knew where James was, he had time. He could wait for James to leave, or he could flush him out. Both worked with his plan.

Either way, James was down to his last day on this earth.

EIGHTEEN

"That's great!" Marley said, her enthusiastic voice carrying down the hall. "What did you think of Ryder and Callum?"

Lying in the rumpled bed, Warwick listened to her speaking on her mobile to who he'd surmised had to be Decker. It sounded like his interview with Crimson Point Security must have gone well. Bully for him.

Things here had just taken a turn again. The abrupt way she'd left the bed earlier made it clear she was going to avoid him again.

It frustrated him, especially after what they'd just shared, but he wouldn't push for now. She was dealing with a lot, was no doubt gun shy about him. He would have to be patient and give her room to begin to trust him again. It would take time to prove to her that he wasn't leaving her.

He sat up, winced at his sore ribs, and went to the en suite to shower, hoping the hot water would help banish the fatigue and clear his head. He needed to try to get things moving again with his own investigation.

The shower/tub combination was small but the water pressure was good and the temperature hot. He tipped his head forward. Let it run over his hair and down his back, the heat soothing.

He tensed when the edge of the shower curtain pulled back. Marley stepped in with him a second later, utterly naked. The hungry look she raked over him made his cock go rock hard against his lower belly.

"This is all your fault," she said softly, stepping so close that their faces were only inches apart.

"I know—"

"I told myself to keep my distance because I knew damn well what would happen if I didn't. And now it's too late," she said, the raw edge in her voice slicing him. "I can't shut off my feelings for you, and I can't get enough of you. Even if I know you hold the power to break me again," she finished, grabbing hold of his head to plant her mouth on his.

Holding back a growl, Warwick coiled his arms around her and pulled her flush to him. The last thing he ever wanted was to break her. Not her heart or her incredible spirit. He was fucking thrilled that she'd sought him out again. That she wanted him so much she couldn't stay away.

The need to break down her defenses rode him hard. As much as he craved this intense, passionate connection they had, he wanted more than just her body. He wound one hand in the back of her long, wet hair. Their tongues twined as she rubbed her breasts against his chest, her body plastered to his.

"I've missed you," she breathed between kisses. "Missed this, the way you make me feel. The way you make the rest of the world disappear when we're together."

That's exactly what he wanted right now. To block out the whole fucking world and all the shite going on outside these walls and focus completely on her. There was nothing but this.

Nothing but Marley and what he felt for her in these stolen minutes together.

She'd never been a shy lover and she wasn't now, kissing him hard, the fingers of one hand digging into his scalp while she reached between them with the other to wrap around his rigid cock.

He growled into her mouth. Nipped at her lower lip before gliding his tongue across it to soothe the little sting, and used the hand in her hair to pull her head back.

She stared back at him, breathing hard. Her pupils were dilated, her eyes filled with a bottomless yearning that made his heart swell. She needed him. He could live off that feeling forever.

The water rushed down on his shoulders, flowing over them both. Cocooning them in sound and warmth. He ran the pad of his thumb across her lower lip. Tightened his jaw when she caught it between her teeth, staring boldly into his eyes while she flicked her tongue against it. Leaving no question as to what she wanted.

Right. He tightened his grip on her hair. Lowered his voice to just above a growl. "On your knees then, pet." He tugged to underscore the command.

Holding his gaze, Marley slowly, gracefully sank to her knees in front of him in a way that made him ache. She dropped her gaze to where she had her hand wrapped around the rigid length of his cock.

Anticipation tingled over his skin. He kept his grip tight on her hair, his whole body cording in anticipation. The thought of sliding between those soft pink lips again, watching her suck him off after fantasizing about it for so damn long, almost made him dizzy.

She set her free hand on the front of his thigh. Ran it up and down, her fingers trailing over the sensitive skin and sliding up and in to tease his balls at the exact same moment she ran her tongue around the flared, flushed head of his cock.

He sucked in a breath, heart pounding out of control as he watched her lick at him. Slow and sensual, like he was her favorite treat. Then she lifted those big brown eyes to his, lips parting again, her head dipping to take him into her mouth.

His fingers locked tight in her hair, a rough, raw sound of animal pleasure coming from the depths of his chest. Sweet, agonizing pleasure arrowed through him. Every flick of her tongue, every pull of that wicked mouth as she bobbed up and down, one hand working up and down the shaft while her other fingers played with his balls.

"Christ, Marley," he rasped out, breathing faster, muscles tightening.

Her hand tightened around the base of his cock and she lowered her head, taking him deep. Sucked. Swallowed.

He threw his head back, eyes slamming shut at the wild lash of pleasure flaying him alive. His balls drew up tight, his cock swelling. And the little witch knew how close he was to the edge of his control, her hum of satisfaction telling him how much she got off on pushing him to his limit.

A low growl vibrated in his chest. He seized her by the shoulders and hauled her up, his hands finding her hips. Gripping tight, he turned her and shoved her flat against the slick fiberglass wall, fusing his mouth with hers while he pulled her thighs apart and wedged his hips between them. Melding them together from chest to groin.

Marley made a mewling sound that acted like a whip on his raging libido and wrapped around him, rubbing her open folds against the length of his cock. He cupped a breast. Gently pinched and rolled the tight nipple the way she liked. Drinking in her soft cry while he stroked his hard length over her slick heat.

When she was good and wet, he reached down to position himself against her. Backed off just enough to watch her face as he pushed inside her. Her lips parted, head falling back as her eyes closed, an expression of pure ecstasy flitting across her face.

"All of me," he rasped out while pleasure streaked up his spine and pulled his balls taut. "You're gonna take all of me again, pet, and milk my cock while you explode."

She whimpered and clung to his shoulders, heels digging into his arse while he let gravity do the work and eased her down on him until he was buried to the hilt in her heat.

Her fingers bit into his shoulders. "Warwick," she moaned, struggling to move her hips.

"Aye," he answered, drinking in that lost, dreamy look on her face. Absorbing the feel of her clenching around him. "Come all the way undone for me."

He slipped a hand between them to find her clit with the edge of his thumb. Caught her soft cry with another deep, wet kiss while he began to thrust, pinning her to the shower wall as he took her. Within moments he could feel her tightening around him, inner muscles clenching, her breathing ragged.

She was so damn beautiful. The woman who had haunted his dreams and owned him body and soul.

I love you. I love you so fucking much.

A little more pressure and she climaxed, crying out and bucking in his hold. He gritted his teeth, fighting to hold on until she began to calm, then thrust quick and hard, allowing his own release to slam into him.

He barely remembered coming down from the high afterward. Was only aware of the thundering of his heart and a sense of rightness and belonging he'd never felt with anyone else.

He leaned into her, pinning her against the slick wall, and rested his face in the crook of her neck. Breathing her in.

Savoring the peace of the moment. How right it felt, every stroke of her fingers through his wet hair healing a place deep inside him.

Words crowded his throat, all but choking him. He wanted it all with her. Everything. A home, his wedding band on her finger, and maybe even a family one day.

He was utterly gone over her. More in love than ever but when he'd tried to tell her before in bed she'd cut him off, clearly not wanting—or not yet ready—to hear it. Now part of him was afraid to even hope for a future with her.

After a few minutes the water began to turn cold. She kissed the top of his head and gently disentangled herself from his embrace, breaking the spell. "We'd both better get ready in case we need to move again." She slipped through the shower curtain, disappearing from view.

He could all but feel her rebuilding the wall between them, gathering bricks as she went. Taking a deep breath, he curbed the impulse to rush after her, pin her flat to the bed and make her listen to everything he was holding in. Reminded himself that in spite of everything that had happened, she still wanted him. So much that she couldn't stay away even though she'd wanted to.

He could work with that. He *would* work with that, with every tool available to him.

Words wouldn't mean enough to her at this point. Not after what he'd done. He needed to give her time and show that she could count on him. Needed to prove that she could trust him. And prove that he wasn't going anywhere when this was over.

When he emerged from the bathroom into the bedroom a few minutes later, she was already gone. He finished toweling off and started getting dressed. Had just pulled his jeans on when his mobile rang on the bedside table.

Glancing at it, he saw his former commander's name.

"James," he answered, hoping for good news. Just one piece of good news or intel that would help him fill in the blanks so he could end this.

"I just wanted to let you know I've been looking into things a bit since we last spoke."

"Did you find anythin'?"

"Unfortunately, no."

His heart sank and he closed his eyes.

"There's no lead that I can see connected to the Grey case. Nothing logical, anyhow. I found no evidence of any chatter concerning you with the people we're watching here on the home front. No pun intended," he added wryly.

Damn. So much for that. "Thanks for tryin'. I appreciate the effort."

"I wish I had something for you. How are you holding up?"

"Fine." He just wanted this over with so he could move on with his life—and with Marley.

"I'll keep my eyes and ears open for anything and pass it on to you if I find something. For now, keep your head down."

"I will." He disconnected, mulling over the short conversation. Something about it tugged at the back of his mind. Insistent. Telling him to pay attention. Something that made his pulse pick up, his instincts humming.

Marley appeared in the doorway pulling a brush through her damp hair. "Who was that?"

"My former commander. He hasn't found aught to help us."

She leaned a hip against the doorframe. "Something else wrong? You look like something's bothering you."

He hesitated, then thought better of lying to her about this. She was trapped here with him. She deserved to know, and keeping her in the dark wouldn't protect her. "Just something he said that…" He replayed the commander's words again in his head. What was his subconscious trying to tell him?

"What?" she pressed.

...on the home front...

His mind flashed back to the night of the Lake District op. To the conversation he and his teammate had overheard before they'd walked around the corner of the building that night. His commander had said it to the man he'd been talking to. Who was it?

Marley was watching him expectantly.

"Home Front," he said. "This has everythin' to do with Home Front and Grey. I just don't know how it's all connected yet."

But his gut told him it was the answer to everything.

NINETEEN

As soon as Roland finished activating the trace on Simon's sat phone, he rang his wife. It was dinnertime in London. She would no doubt be cooking something while enjoying a glass of wine with one of the children who'd dropped by. It would be at least another day or two before he could go back to the UK, once this nightmare was behind him for good.

"Hello, darling. How are things on the home front?" he asked.

"Fair to middling. Are you in Seattle now?"

"Not yet. I made a stop on the Oregon Coast to meet with some Americans who assisted us on the Durham op. What are you up to?"

"Just making toad in the hole with onion gravy for Beth and I. She dropped over after work."

"Lovely." It had always been Beth's favorite meal. "Tell her hello from me."

"I will. Are you still due home tomorrow night? Reg and Jane have invited us out to the new Turkish restaurant."

"I might be a day or two longer. Just depends on how things go." And how quickly Simon got the job done.

They talked for another few minutes about the kids and grands. "I'll call again once I know my flight details, all right?"

"All right, darling. Be safe."

"Of course. Bye, love." Pocketing his mobile, he stared out the hotel room window. From up here he had an unobstructed view of the sea. But he wasn't looking at the view. He was planning his next steps.

Shrugging into his coat, he strode down the hall and knocked on his driver's door. Bill answered it, looking concerned. "Everything all right?"

"Fine, I just feel like exploring the area for a bit. Think I'll take a drive down the coast a ways."

Bill nodded and turned away. "I'll get my jacket—"

"No, I meant I want to go on my own. I'll be back in a few hours. Just came to get the keys."

Bill blinked at him, and for a moment looked as if he would argue. "What about Seattle?"

"I've rescheduled the meeting for tomorrow." There was no meeting. He'd invented it as an excuse to come here.

Looking confused, Bill went to retrieve the keys and reluctantly handed them over. "If you change your mind, come back and I'll drive you."

"I won't, but thanks. Just enjoy your downtime."

He found the SUV parked right outside the rear doors of the hotel, backed into its spot. A habit anyone in the trade did automatically. He connected his mobile to the hands-free device, got a lock on Simon's current location then steered out of the lot and drove south on Front Street.

The sky was a solid, leaden gray mirrored by the wind-whipped waves, the clouds heavy with the promise of more rain. Traffic was light, barely anyone else on the road as he turned east and drove toward the hills, heading for the coastal highway. He merged into the southbound lane, the tension inside him winding tighter with each mile he passed on the way to the target house.

Simon was in position. It was only a matter of time now.

When it happened, Roland would be there to verify it personally.

He'd taken a huge risk in coming here and didn't want to get any more involved, but too much had gone wrong already. There were still too many loose ends he needed to make sure were severed once and for all before they entangled him.

He would see to it that James took all his secrets to the grave.

WALKER POURED himself a cup of coffee and carried it into Ryder's office at the far end of the hall. The biggest office in the building, all exposed brick and plate-glass windows overlooking the bay.

Ryder sat behind his desk perusing the file in front of him. Callum sat in one of the armchairs across the desk. Both men looked up at him when he entered the room.

"Well? Find any great candidates in this batch of interviews?" he asked, taking the other armchair next to Callum.

"A few. One stands out in particular." Ryder turned the file around so Walker could see it. "Decker Abrams."

He nodded. "Marley's brother."

Ryder raised a black eyebrow. "You know him?"

"No. You both liked him?"

"He's a no BS guy. Takes his work seriously. He's got a lot of good experience as an MP in the Corps. Solid service record, has the skillset and temperament we're looking for in a bodyguard."

"His references were all awesome. Every single one I spoke

to gave a glowing report of his conduct and character," Callum added. "What's going on with his sister, by the way? I hear there's something going down with her and Warwick?"

Walker swallowed a sip of coffee and lowered his mug. "Yeah. You know how he was injured in an explosion on an op last summer? He says he's felt like he's been followed or watched off and on since, but especially after the Durham op. And when he got into town there was a shooting at her place. He witnessed it. The cops think it was a case of mistaken identity and drug or gang related, but Warwick's not too sure about that. He thinks it might be connected to him."

"Is she in danger too?" Ryder asked.

"Possibly. They were in a relationship last year before he was injured."

"And is it true he let her believe he was dead all this time?" Callum said.

He'd probably heard all this from Nadia. She and Ivy talked a lot, though Ivy wouldn't say anything she shouldn't. "Yeah. He had his reasons. They're laying low together now in a place Beckett set them up in, until Warwick can figure out what's going on. Ivy's helping where she can. There's something else though." Both men continued watching him. "Ivy and I were called into a meeting added to our schedule first thing this morning."

"The MI6 guy," Ryder said, leaning back in his leather chair.

"Roland Yates. We had contact with him briefly over the phone after the Durham op. He was in San Fran for meetings and is due in Seattle later today. He made an appointment to meet Ivy and me in person before he heads up north."

"You thought something was off about him?" Ryder asked.

"Not at first. I mean, springing the meeting on us like that last minute was weird, but that's not the bit that bothered me.

He asked specifically about Warwick. Whether we'd heard from him since Durham. We both said no. Gut instinct. But it felt like he was fishing."

Callum frowned. "You think he's keeping tabs on Warwick?"

"Maybe." He didn't like the feel of it. But before he could say anything else there was a knock at the door.

"Come in," Ryder said.

It opened and Ember stood there, looking at the three of them. "Hey. Sorry to interrupt."

"Didn't know you were still here," Callum said. "Any luck with Teagan's phone?"

"Yes." Her expression turned somber. "I gave it back to her, but she couldn't seem to remember the password. Things weren't adding up, so I went in and accessed the data I'd downloaded from it this morning just in case. And look what I found."

She turned the tablet she was holding, showing them the screen. A picture of Warwick with his name underneath.

An ominous weight formed in the pit of Walker's stomach. "He was the one who found her on the beach."

"I know. And there are also some other text messages that concerned me. The wording is vague, as if it's some kind of code. None of it makes any sense to me but it clearly means something to her and whoever she was communicating with. I tried to trace the other number involved but it's from a burner phone."

Walker, Ryder and Callum all looked at each other. "Something's not right here," Ryder said.

Yep, and whatever it was, it wasn't good news for Warwick. "I'm on it," Walker said, springing up from his chair and rushing past Ember as he pulled out his phone to dial Warwick.

"Areet, mate?"

"Are you still at the house?"

"Aye."

"You need to grab your gear and head out right now." He briefly explained what had happened. "Yates was here digging for intel on you this morning. We said we hadn't seen or heard from you, but safe to say he either thinks or already knows you're in the area. Thought you should know."

"Son of a bitch," Warwick muttered.

"Get out and head south. Keep your phone on so Ivy can track you. I'm going home to get her now. We'll contact you when we're on the road."

"Got it."

As soon as he hung up, he called Ivy. "Shit's going down with Warwick and Marley. I'm not sure what, but they're leaving town now as a precaution. I told him to keep his phone on."

"I'll start tracking him now," she said without missing a beat or any reaction whatsoever. "Are we heading out to rendezvous with them?"

Pride swelled in his chest. There were a hundred reasons why he loved Ivy, and a hundred more things he admired about her. This was one of them. An unknown and potentially dangerous situation was unfolding with a friend, and she reacted with the cool confidence of a seasoned operator, immediately ready to place herself in danger to help. "Yeah. I'm on my way now."

"See you in ten."

He already knew that by the time he pulled into the driveway she would be ready with their gear packed. Extra clothing, food, medical gear. As well as weapons and ammo. He hoped it wouldn't come to that. But if it did, they would be prepared.

He ran down the stairwell, the soles of his shoes on the

concrete steps echoing off the walls. In his vehicle, he called the sheriff to update him.

"Where are they going?" Noah asked.

"South. I'll get an update for them later. Can you send someone to find Teagan in the meantime? We need to find out what she knows and why she had Warwick's name and picture."

"I'll go right now. She's staying at The Breakers. I'll call you when I get there."

"Sounds good." He sped up the hill away from the waterfront, taking side streets to avoid traffic and lights as much as possible. As he drove, his brain turned over everything he knew about Warwick's situation. Trying to find the link between the recent events, Yates's sudden appearance and interest in Warwick, and Teagan.

The sheriff called back when Walker was three blocks from home. "Find her?" he asked.

"No. Front desk says she checked out over an hour ago, carrying the backpack she was given. She's gone."

TWENTY

"Marley."

She stopped stirring the soup she'd been heating on the stove and glanced back at Warwick, standing in the kitchen entryway. The grim look on his face made her stomach clench. "What?"

"We need to go. Now. Grab your stuff."

"What's going on?" she asked, shutting off the burner and hurrying toward him.

He turned away and strode down the hall toward the master bedroom. "Walker called. It seems there are multiple people in the area looking for me. We need to leave town."

Oh, shit...

She rushed to grab her bag from the closet. Jammed her clothes in it, her phone charger, then darted into the bathroom to toss in her toiletries. Warwick picked up the bag Ivy had brought them containing the weapons.

Marley took her holstered pistol from the bedside table and strapped it around her waist. "Ready."

He led the way to the back door while she shrugged into her

coat and shoved her feet into her shoes. "Stay here," he said in a low voice, then stepped outside to sweep the yard, pistol in hand. A few seconds later he came back into view and motioned for her to follow. "Hurry."

She shut the door behind her and darted into the backyard, across the narrow pathway to where his rental vehicle was parked on the little paved section hidden at the side of the house. A steady, cold rain was falling, the gusting wind tugging at her hair and blowing dead leaves across the ground. She jumped in the passenger seat, looking all around for any sign of danger, heart drumming fast.

Warwick fired up the engine and started down the steep driveway. The house was at the end of a dead-end road. There was only one way out. If someone cut them off… "How many people are we talking about?" she asked, staring straight ahead.

"At least two. Probably more."

"Who?"

"Trained agents," he answered, posture tense as he turned onto the road and sped away.

She glanced in the side mirror and caught a final glimpse of the house before it disappeared from view amongst the trees. Being stuck there hadn't been ideal, but it had been a refuge of sorts, and the intimacy she and Warwick had shared left an aching void in her chest. An ache that was rapidly being displaced by a rising tide of unease.

"Decker can provide backup," she said. "I can call him—or even Grady." They would both help them.

"Walker and Ivy are going to rendezvous with us once we're clear to the south."

"Where?"

"I don't know yet."

Thick forest whipped past on either side as he sped down

the road. It curved to the left up ahead, whatever lay beyond it hidden from their view. He eased up on the accelerator slightly as they neared the turn.

The moment the front of the vehicle rounded the corner, she gasped and went rigid in her seat. A pickup was parked sideways across the road up ahead, blocking it.

Warwick cursed and hit the brakes just as a figure emerged from behind the cab, aiming a rifle at them over the back of the bed.

"Get down," Warwick barked, burying a hand in her nape and shoving her downward. He jammed the transmission into reverse and hit the gas. She jumped as two bullets slammed through the center of the windshield, missing Warwick by inches.

"Hang on." He swerved, threw the car into neutral and swung the wheel hard. The back end of the car skidded around on the wet asphalt, throwing her sideways into the door as he straightened them out.

"Who was that?" Bent over at the waist, she stayed down, heart in her throat. Her hands itched to reach for the rifle stowed in the back but Warwick was already racing them in the opposite direction.

"Dunno," he muttered, speeding back the way they'd come.

Bang!

She jumped and swallowed a cry when the car suddenly careened to the right. Warwick was forced to take his foot off the accelerator and wrestle the wheel to keep control. "Tire's shot."

Bang!

The car veered left, another tire gone.

"Fuck," he snarled, the wheels grinding and wobbling under the slowing car. "All right." He turned the wheel hard just before the bend in the road, angling for the shoulder. "Listen to me."

She unstrapped her seatbelt and lunged between the front seats to yank the bag on the floor open and took out the rifle Ivy had brought them. It had been a damn long time since she'd fired one, but it felt good in her hands right now.

He brought the car to a sudden stop and took the rifle from her before she could sit back down. "We're gonna have to run for it. Wait here until I get out so I can cover you."

She reached a hand out for the rifle. "I can—"

"No. You're gonna run."

She bit back another argument and looked past him out the window at the thick forest lining the road. It was the only option for them. They couldn't stay here.

He jammed a magazine into the rifle and hit the bolt catch lever on the side. "As soon as I'm out, you run straight into the woods. Head north." He pointed toward the trees in front of them, then shoved his pistol into the holster on his right thigh. "When you reach the road on the other side, find the closest house and call for help. I'll find you."

She didn't want to split up. Didn't want him to stay here to lay down covering fire for her. "Warwick, no—"

He swung his head around to meet her eyes, the raging emotions there hitting her hard. "I love you. And I'm goin' to make sure nothin' happens to you."

Her insides went cold. Because that sounded *way* too much like a goodbye. As if he was planning to sacrifice himself to save her. "No, don't you dare—"

He was already throwing open his door and stepping out. "Go!"

"*No.*" There was no way she was leaving him behind to face this alone. She had a pistol to help him. There had to be another way. "I'm not—"

"*Now*, dammit!" he barked, raising the rifle to his shoulder. "Run, Marley."

He wasn't going to budge. And the longer she sat here and argued with him about it, the more at risk he would be.

Feeling like she was being torn in two, she cursed and flung open her door. The shoulder was soft and muddy from the rain, and immediately gave way to a deep ditch dividing her from the comparative safety of the woods.

She backed up a few yards and ran at it, putting all her strength into her right leg as her foot landed on the edge of the shoulder. Her arms lifted to balance her as she sailed across it.

Her left foot hit the other side. The sudden shift in momentum pitched her weight forward. She threw out her hands to break her fall, landing hard in the mud, the beckoning shadows of the woods only thirty or so feet away.

Picking herself up, she stole one glance over her shoulder at Warwick. The fleeting image seared itself into her brain. Him standing behind the open driver's door, rifle to his shoulder as he faced the man coming for them. Standing between her and the deadly threat to buy her time to escape.

Protecting her with his life.

He fired a three-round burst, the sharp cracks echoing through the rain.

The hair on the back of her neck stood up, her gaze tracking up the road. *Oh, shit, he's coming...*

She shoved to her feet and ran up the hill, scrambling along the slippery terrain and into the waiting trees. Moving through the dense underbrush, she ripped her phone from her pocket.

Her heart sank when she saw she had no service. She had to get to the other side of the woods and get help. Trying to cover him with her pistol against a trained rifleman would be useless unless she got up close.

Breathing fast, she paused in the shadows behind a thick

cedar tree to look back at the road below. Warwick was still there, behind the car now, rifle to his shoulder.

Three more shots echoed through the woods.

Her throat tightened, determination hardening inside her. *I love you back.*

So she made the only choice she could, and acted on it.

TWENTY-ONE

Ivy grabbed two go bags from the downstairs hall closet she always kept packed full of essential supplies and selected two Glock 19s from the gun safe, along with extra ammo.

This was her home now and she'd made certain modifications born from living a lifetime of uncertainty and danger. Living with a former Valkyrie couldn't be easy but Walker had let her do what she needed to in order to feel secure.

She was shoving a Glock into the back of her waistband when Shae came downstairs from her room looking half-asleep, eyes barely open, wearing oversize sweats and her hair thrown up in a messy bun at the top of her head.

She stopped at the bottom of the stairs when she saw Ivy, her eyes widening as she took in the bags and weapons. "What's going on?"

"A friend of ours is in trouble. We're heading out to meet up with them."

She raised one hand to grip the neck of her sweatshirt. "Where's Dad?"

"On his way to get me." Ivy tugged the hem of her black turtleneck over the butt of the pistol and slid her jacket on.

"We'll be fine, we're only backup if it becomes necessary." And it might, but she wanted to alleviate Shae's fears. "Keep your phone on you and we'll contact you once we know what's going on."

Shae nodded, still looking alarmed as Ivy picked up the bags and strode for the door. "Ivy."

She glanced back at Shae. Raised her eyebrows.

"Take care of him."

Ivy smiled, glad that Shae trusted her abilities so much. The bond between Walker and his daughter was a beautiful thing. And just one of the many reasons why she'd fallen in love with him. "Always."

She was standing at the end of the driveway when Walker pulled up a minute later. She tossed the gear into the backseat of the SUV and got in the front passenger seat, handing him a pistol. "Any update?"

"Nothing good," he said as he sped away. "Did you tell Shae?"

"Just now. I told her we'd update her when we know more. What's not good?"

"The woman Warwick pulled out of the water had a picture of him on her phone along with some coded messages. Noah went to question her at the hotel, but she'd already taken off and no one knows where she's gone."

"You're right. That's not good." She slid her phone from her pocket and accessed the app that let her track Warwick's location.

"You got a lock on him?"

The program took several frustrating moments to load. Cell service in and around Crimson Point was always spotty, but today it just pissed her off. Then a flashing dot appeared. She frowned.

"What?"

"He's at the side of the road just up from the house. Stationary."

Walker kept speeding down the road. Moments later the dot began moving.

Slow at first. Retreating toward the woods on the north side of the road. Then faster. But not anywhere near a road, and not moving fast enough to be in a vehicle.

Shit. Warwick was on the run on foot. "They're in trouble. We need to hurry."

SIMON INSTINCTIVELY DUCKED behind the bed of the pickup as James returned fire, allowing Marley to disappear into the trees and fighting to ignore the fire streaking through his left shoulder. But the current distance between them marked the rifle's end range and the rounds barely punched into the metal.

He was going to change that. Any second now James would jump the ditch and charge after her.

As if he'd willed it into happening, James did just that.

Simon hopped back in the truck. He wheeled the vehicle around in the opposite direction and raced to the next street a quarter mile up, then turned north. The thick band of forest on the right where James and Marley had disappeared into led to another street on the opposite side.

They wouldn't go back to the target house. But they would have at least tried to call for backup by now. He needed to end this before anyone else got here to interfere.

He whipped the pickup around the corner, braked hard in a rocking stop behind the wooded area and killed the engine. Rifle balanced in his hands, he climbed out and made his way through the rain into the woods. The drugs he'd taken earlier, combined with the surge of adrenaline, muting the pain in his shoulder.

Shadows and the sharp scent of cedar engulfed him. The tall mix of evergreens cut the force of the rain to a patter, their thick branches swaying and sighing in the strong wind gusts that rippled through the underbrush. He moved west, keeping parallel to the edge of the road, scanning the uneven terrain as he went.

Marley and James would want to get to this road and find help in one of the houses behind it. He had to cut them off before they made it past him.

It was perfect that they had been separated. If he could take Marley first, he could force James's hand. Lure him into range and use her as a shield until he could kill the bastard. There was no way James would endanger her by taking a shot with her in front of him.

The only thing Simon had to worry about was ensuring neither one made it to the road.

A sudden strong gust of wind whistled through the trees. A sharp crack rent the air.

He ducked behind a thick trunk to scan for where the single shot had come from, just as something crashed to the ground twenty yards away. A long, thick branch snapped from the canopy above.

Not a rifle shot. Just a fucking snapped tree branch.

Resuming the hunt, he snuck across a thin trail worn through the brush. The forested area they were in wasn't that big. Marley and James couldn't hide from him in here for long.

Another sharp gust of wind cut through the trees. He dropped to one knee behind a fallen log, watching the underbrush in front of him. The wind died away, the mix of evergreen ferns and brush settling. Then, to the left, a slight movement drew his attention.

Raising the butt of his weapon to his shoulder, he tracked it. Caught a faint hint of red emerging from the undergrowth.

Marley. She was maybe sixty yards away. She had smeared mud on her hands and face to camouflage her pale skin, and into her hair to dull it, but in this landscape the distinct color was still a dead giveaway when the faintest bit of light hit it.

He edged toward her, stalking her like a predator on the hunt. Then something to the right caught his attention. He stopped and dropped to one knee again, waiting. Scanning. Finger poised on the trigger while the wind moaned amongst the trees and the rain pattered the ground.

A clump of ferns quivered in the distance a little to the left of the spot he'd been watching. He remained motionless, controlling his breathing and the sharp rush of excitement in his veins.

Seconds later, he saw a shadow move between two trees in the same area.

James. Closer to him than Marley.

Simon glanced left to check her position. Saw the giveaway glow of deep red through the undergrowth, and hesitated.

He wanted to use her to force James's hand. To kill her in front of him. If he didn't go after her now or chose to engage James here, she could make it to the road and possibly call for help. But if he moved at all, he would be exposed.

He refocused back on James's current position, staring through the rifle sight where he'd seen the shadow move. James was gradually edging east toward Marley. Simon was almost certain James hadn't spotted him yet. But if he moved, James would have a bead on him.

The decision had been made for him.

Simon curled his finger around the trigger and locked on James's hiding spot, waiting for the shadow to move again. Willing it to so he could put a bullet through him.

TWENTY-TWO

Warwick hunkered down behind the flared base of the cedar trunk he was using for cover, peering through the dimness toward where he'd seen the momentary flash of red a few moments ago. Marley was a canny lass, and her training was evident in her actions.

She was being cautious and moving slowly to the road, using the landscape as camouflage. But her beautiful hair would give her away the moment she stepped out of the shadows.

The wind had picked up more in the past few minutes, making it harder to hide amongst the underbrush. His current position was less than ideal. He couldn't protect her and keep a lookout for the shooter if he stayed here, and the ravine behind him meant he had to keep moving either sideways or forward.

He needed to move closer to her, find a dip or hollow in the terrain and settle there so he could cover her better when she moved.

Just as he thought it, she moved. Edging slowly out from her hiding spot, body crouched. She'd rubbed dirt and mud on her hair, face and hands, but her clever thinking wasn't enough to conceal the auburn tint of her hair amongst the green, browns and rusts of the forest.

He rose to his feet, quickly scanned ahead, to either side and then behind him.

A shot ripped through the woods. He whipped around to see Marley drop to the ground, red cedar bark exploding right where she'd been a heartbeat before.

His heart stopped. "Marley!" He took a running step toward her.

She jumped up, appearing unhurt. *Thank you, God…*

He stopped, a wave of relief flooding him as he frantically searched for the shooter's position. *Where are you, you bastard?*

He leaned his upper body out from behind the tree to scan for the shooter. Noticed a slightly unnatural movement behind a thicket of dark green ferns to his eleven o'clock.

Warwick shifted his aim. Waited, sent up a prayer for her.

"Marley, run!" he shouted, and stepped out from behind cover to fire at the spot he'd picked out. The rounds plunged into the middle of the ferns, the report of the rifle echoing through the forest.

Marley darted off to the right like a deer, running flat out. Warwick began moving toward her, body angled to face where the shot had come from. Placing himself between her and the threat. He risked a glance right to check her position.

She was nearing the far edge of the trees. Almost to the road.

Another rifle shot cracked through the air.

A hot, searing pain ripped through the back of his right thigh.

He bit back a scream, grabbed the back of his leg and fell to one knee. Fire streaked through his leg, blood flowing freely from the wound.

Marley.

He struggled to his feet, gritting his teeth against a strangled roar and brought his weapon to his shoulder again. Took aim. Fired in the direction of the shooter he still couldn't see.

His leg gave out.

He stumbled. Threw a hand out to try and catch the closest tree for balance. But the edge of his left foot caught the lip of the ravine.

A wave of fear crashed over him as the muddy edge gave way. He pitched sideways to try and save himself, the rifle falling from his grip as he toppled backward.

He hit the side of the ravine on his injured side and tumbled over.

The world spun in a dizzying kaleidoscope of pain and confusion as he rolled down the steep side, bouncing off rocks, roots and branches. Near the bottom he went airborne for a second, then plunged face down in the pool of muddy water that had collected at the bottom.

Cold punched through him, momentarily cutting through the pain. He shot his hands out in front of him, frantically trying to find purchase on the slimy bottom. Finding it, he planted his left foot and shoved upward. He surfaced a heartbeat later and flung his head back, dragging in a breath of air.

His right leg was on fire, his ribs and back burning. He shoved his left foot down hard to stabilize himself, dragging his filthy hand across his muddy face to clear his eyes. He blinked the stinging water and mud away but more trickled in, and when he went to take a hobbling step, his left shoe stuck in the thick mud at the bottom of the pool.

Marley. Have to get to her.

His left foot kept sinking deeper in the mud. He cursed and threw himself forward to pull free, aiming for the end of a root sticking out a few feet above him.

The edge of his left hand brushed the bottom of it. He grabbed tight, threw his right arm up to bolster his grip and pulled with all his strength to drag himself out of the muck, pure determination driving him.

Marley was up there alone with a single pistol, facing a killer armed with a rifle. He would make it to the top no matter what it took.

The tree root stretched under the force of his weight as he pulled. Searing agony tore up and down the back of his right thigh, hazing his already impaired vision. He dug the toes of his left foot into the side of the ravine, sinking into the wet, sticky clay soil, and strained to heave his body upward.

The root snapped in his hands.

He hit the water on his back. It closed over his head, the momentum plunging him to the bottom again.

He swallowed a scream when his torn thigh hit something sharp. Shoved up grimly with his left foot. Managed to propel himself to the edge of the pond as he surfaced and grasp the edge of a large pointed rock sticking out.

Hurry. Have to get to Marley.

He fought his way out of the filthy pond, scrabbling in the dirt like a trapped animal. Dragged his body a few feet up the steep side.

A slight movement above him made him glance up. His chest constricted when a man suddenly appeared at the edge of the ravine holding a rifle, his face concealed by a black balaclava.

The same bastard who had attacked him before.

A howl of rage built in his throat. There was nowhere to go. Nothing to defend himself with.

He stayed where he was, clenching his back teeth together until he thought they would shatter and stared right at the bastard, refusing to look away or give him the satisfaction of showing any fear in the face of death. Expecting a bullet to rip through his skull at any second. Then it would be over.

And Marley would die.

A razor-sharp blade of grief pierced him. A hundred times more agonizing than anything he'd felt before. He'd failed her.

I'm sorry, pet. So fucking sorry…

The man raised the rifle. Slowly. Taunting him.

Warwick let out a feral snarl, but it was cut off when his enemy inexplicably tossed the rifle aside.

Then the man straightened and peeled off the balaclava.

Shock paralyzed him for an instant as his enemy smiled down at him. A cruel, triumphant smile in that hateful face he'd hoped to never see again.

"And now we finally finish this the right way," Simon sneered, drawing a blade from the sheath on his belt.

PURE ELATION SURGED through Simon in a drugging haze. James was trapped below him like an animal in a cage, wounded, unarmed, with nowhere to go and nothing to fight back with.

He watched the shock flicker across that face, nearly unrecognizable with mud, then recognition and felt a rush of satisfaction. And hatred.

Killing James with a bullet was weak. Way too quick. And would give him far too easy a death.

Nuh uh. Not after the humiliation he'd suffered because of James. Not after so many years of fantasizing about this moment.

He wanted revenge and now he had the chance to get it. Marley had run off somewhere. Even if she got help, it wouldn't get here in time to save James. Simon would deal with her later. Finishing James hand to hand was a gamble, but the payoff made it more than worth the risk.

This was going to be up close, personal…and as painful as Simon could make it.

James saw the blade and shoved back from the side of the ravine, turning his body as he slid back into the pool of water at the bottom. And Simon was done waiting.

Blade clutched tight in his hand, he charged, sliding down the rough side of the ravine and then launching off it near the bottom. Throwing himself at his trapped prey.

They collided in the deepest part of the pit, the impact driving them both through the water to hit hard against the bottom. Pain blazed through Simon's left arm like fire. He fought past it, falling back on his training. This was what he'd come here for. No amount of pain was stopping this.

There was zero visibility in the muddy water, but Simon didn't need it. His outstretched hand found James's shoulder. Locked on tight as he dragged his knife hand through the water, ready to strike the first painful blow.

Something sharp jabbed him in the face. He jerked his head back, choking back a curse of surprise as James ripped away from him. They both surfaced a moment later on opposite sides of the pool. Simon quickly dragged his right hand across his eyes, struggling to see through the mud clinging to him, his damaged shoulder screaming at him.

James was almost at the far side of the pit. Reaching for something above him.

With an enraged snarl, Simon dove at him. Grabbed the back of James's sodden jacket in his left hand and hauled him backward, fighting through the pain that ripped through his arm.

James spun and threw an elbow, slamming it into the side of

Simon's jaw. Simon stumbled back a step, briefly lost his grip on James, his feet slipping in the thick muck beneath the water.

He lunged again. His back boot plunged deep into the thick, sticky mud. Cursing, he fought to free his leg. Finally succeeded in yanking it out, but his boot remained embedded.

James was struggling to scrabble his way up the far side of the ravine. Simon went after him. His other boot sank deep.

Frustration roared through him. He was already panting for breath, the cold water and struggle to free himself from the mud blending with the punch of adrenaline coursing through him.

The stabbing in his shoulder hazed the edges of his mind. He refocused it, used the pain to center himself. Steeling himself against it for one final attack.

Unleashing a cry of fury, he dove at James's back.

James turned at the last instant, his hand flashing out to catch the wrist of Simon's knife hand, fingers clamping tight. Simon bared his teeth, forcing the blade closer to James's throat. Their arms shook as they each fought for control of the blade, eyes locked.

Rage pumped through him. Fueling him. Making him stronger.

"You always thought you were better than me," Simon snarled, determined to end this here and now. "Could never let anything go. Had to show me up and humiliate me to be the golden boy." He was breathing so hard and fast he could barely get the words out, rage all but choking him.

"Aye, because you're a reckless…criminal…piece of shite," James growled back, his grip on Simon's wrist still maddeningly strong despite the way he was shaking all over.

"You should've just gotten in line like the others. Should have shut your fucking mouth." He forced the blade another inch closer, the tip quivering just above James's jugular. The pain knifing through his shoulder was like fire, stealing his breath. "But now…you'll…pay."

"Fuck you," James bit out, shuddering from the cold. He'd be far colder in a minute.

"No. Fuck you, *mate*." With all his strength, he twisted sharply to the side, breaking free of James's hold.

The sudden shift in momentum threw James off balance. He lurched to the side. Let out a strangled cry of pain, his hands scrabbling for purchase on the side of the ravine.

Simon seized his moment.

Triumph swamped him as he threw himself forward, blade raised high. Ready to plunge it through the bastard's spine and twist it. Hungry for the scream of pain that would follow. To watch the life slowly fade out of James's eyes—

He jerked as two bullets punched through his side in rapid succession. Slamming into his right ribcage. Tearing through his lungs before exiting the other side.

He staggered and dropped the blade. Burning, white-hot agony filling his chest, eclipsing the agony in his shoulder. Blinding him. Sucking the air out of his lungs.

The report of the weapon echoed from above him as blood flooded his mouth. He choked, one hand going to the gaping exit wound in his left side. Panic seared his brain. He slumped over, his hand falling from James's shoulder as he fought for air.

James twisted and threw him off. Simon hit the edge of the pit and crumpled up in a ball, terror paralyzing him.

There was no air. Only pain and fear.

Blood continued to pour out of his nose and mouth. His eyes bulged. He rolled them upward. Stared in disbelief at the lone figure standing at the rim of the ravine.

Marley. Holding the rifle he'd discarded.

He sank into the freezing water waiting to swallow him, his strength draining away as fast as his blood. His eyes remained on Marley as his lids began to droop and his vision turned gray.

She'd fucking killed him.

TWENTY-THREE

Heart slamming against her ribs so hard it felt bruised, Marley hovered in position at the edge of the ravine, muzzle of the rifle trained on the asshole who'd shot Warwick. She'd seen him drop.

The shooter wasn't moving now but she held her aim and kept her finger on the trigger anyway, ready to hit him again if he so much as twitched in Warwick's direction.

Holy shit, she was scared. She hadn't fired a rifle in so long, but as she'd crept back to cover Warwick from above with her pistol, she'd seen the fallen rifle and grabbed it to give her better range and accuracy. Then the bastard had been about to plunge the knife into Warwick's back, forcing her to act.

She'd hit him with both rounds, but given the angle she'd been terrified of hitting Warwick too. A few inches on either side of where she'd aimed, and she would have killed Warwick.

Her breath hitched, muscles seizing. Chest constricting, making it hard to breathe.

Warwick shoved the man off him. The attacker lay slumped against the side of the pit, choking, blood flowing from his nose and mouth as he slowly slid down into the water.

She'd shattered his lungs. He must have dropped the knife because she couldn't see it in either of his hands.

"Mar…"

She tore her gaze from the man and focused on Warwick, her body rigid, a wave of numbness creeping in. He was covered in mud, shivering like hell, his voice raw and strained from exhaustion and the terrible pain he must be in.

Oh, God…

"I'm coming." She set the rifle down and ran around to the other side of the ravine on weak legs to get above him. There was no easy way down to him, and no way he could climb out of there on his own.

The way he was shivering scared her. He'd already been weakened from shock and blood loss before the fight. His body temperature must be low from being in the cold water, and his leg had to still be bleeding like hell.

"Don't move, I'm coming," she called out, starting to shake as she crouched down and eased one foot over the edge. This side of the ravine was less vertical than the other, but still steep.

She slid down carefully on her side, digging her boots into the soft, rain-soaked earth to slow her descent and keep her from tumbling down on top of him. When she reached the bottom, she found him holding onto a rock sticking out of the side a foot above his head. His head was down, eyes closed, muscles trembling and teeth chattering.

"Take my hand," she told him, reaching down for him. A few feet away the attacker was mostly submerged, only the top of his head visible above the waterline. It was quickly turning red around him, spreading out toward Warwick.

Her stomach twisted at the thought. She didn't want that evil sonofabitch's blood touching him. "Warwick. Look at me."

Shuddering, he raised his head. Blinked up at her through the sticky mud covering his face, his chest heaving. The pain in his face wrenched at her heart. "I'm sorry, Mar. So s-sorry…"

"There's nothing to be sorry for. Now take my hand." The muscles in her arm ached as she stretched it out, fingers straining.

He reached a shaking hand up to her. Their palms touched. She grabbed hold of him and they locked grips around each other's wrists. She glanced upward, more dread hitting her. From down here it was like climbing a small cliff.

Didn't matter. They were getting out of here. Together. "Okay, on three you're going to plant your good foot on the side and shove upward. Understand?"

He nodded, the vibrations of his shivering muscles traveling up her arm.

"One. Two." She tightened her grip, braced both feet. "Three."

She hauled upward with all her might. Teeth clenched. Muscles quivering.

His agonized cry cut at her but she refused to stop pulling, determined to get him out. There was no phone service out here, and she wasn't going to leave him behind while she ran around trying to find someone to call for help. "Push, Warwick!"

His fingers were clamped around her wrist so hard she felt her bones compress. He made a deep, animalistic sound of mingled pain and determination and strained upward. Struggling to pull free of the water.

Digging the heels of her shoes in, she angled her body and grabbed his wrist with her other hand, shoving with her feet, muscles burning with the effort. Somehow he found the strength to climb out of the water.

"That's it," she panted, focusing all her will into getting him to the top. "Little bit at a time. Come on."

She helped him a few feet before he collapsed against the side. She swallowed a cry as they started to slide back down, but he drove his left foot into the earth and stopped them both from ending up in the water.

"It's okay," she said, her voice breathless and not just from the exertion. The shock and adrenaline drop had hit her, making her tremble as much as him. "Bit by bit. Let's g-go."

She didn't know how long it took to climb out. They made slow progress. Moving up a few feet and then he'd have to stop to rest, breathing hard, his exhaustion heart-rending. Sometimes they would slip down before he managed to stop them.

Two steps forward, one step back. All the way up the steep side that crumbled under their hands and feet.

Marley glanced up. Saw the lip just above her. "Almost there," she gasped out, her muscles almost depleted. "Just a little m-more."

His grip on her wrist was weakening.

"Warwick, *no*." She put a whip-like edge in her voice. "Look at me."

His head lifted. He peered up at her hazily.

"One more push. One more and you're out of here. Now dig down and give me everything you have."

He closed his eyes, gathering himself. Then his grip firmed. He opened his eyes. Bared his teeth as he shoved upward, body straining.

Tears clogged her throat. She loved him so fucking much. This strong, brave, incredible man.

With a throttled cry, she forced her shaking legs to heave upward. Her searching hand touched the flat ground at the edge of the ravine.

She scrambled over it. Leaned back and hauled him up. Then fell back on level ground. Panting. Spent.

Warwick collapsed facedown next to her. Blood flowed out

of the back of his thigh, the wound hidden by the muck caking his pants.

But he was alive, and that was all that mattered.

Flipping into first-aid mode, she knelt beside him and slid his belt out of the loops. Quickly wrapped it around his thigh above the wound and cinched it tight, twisting it for good measure and ignoring his choked cry, the way his body arced.

"I have to," she told him, hardening her heart. There was no other way to slow the bleeding, and no other equipment to help him with.

After that she stripped off his sodden, muddy jacket and shirt, then ripped off her own jacket and put it on him. It was way too small and tight everywhere but at least it was mostly dry and would trap whatever body heat he was still generating against his skin. She couldn't get the zipper up but some of the snaps over top of it closed in spite of the way her fingers shook.

Warwick lay on his side throughout, eyes half-closed. "I'm areet," he rasped out.

Not even close. "We have to keep you moving," she told him, still trying to catch her breath. She was freezing now, probably mostly from shock. They had to get to the road and find help. "Come on. Up," she ordered, sliding an arm around him to help raise him up to a sitting position.

Getting him to stand was even harder. He was heavy as hell, forced to lean a large chunk of his weight on her just to stay upright, while balancing on his left foot. "This way," she said, steeling herself for the grueling trek ahead.

With grim determination, she started around the edge of the ravine, half-carrying him, half-dragging him while he hopped, every jarring motion tearing a hiss or a groan from between his clamped teeth. In this spot they were closer to the road they'd come from originally. It wasn't that far, but with every step draining what was left of his strength and making him bleed more, it felt like ten times the distance.

"Stop," he groaned after they'd gone about fifty yards. "Have to...rest."

She did, struggling to brace his weight and keep her knees from buckling. He was only a few inches taller than her but had to be at least two-twenty. His weight dug her holstered pistol into her hip but she wanted to keep it on her right side because it was her dominant hand and she was a better shot with it than the left.

She was able to catch her breath within a minute. But they had to keep going. There was no way she could carry or drag him out of here on her own. "Just a little farther, then I'll call for help." She forced him onward, leg and back muscles burning.

He struggled along, then tripped on something. They both went down hard, landing with a grunt. Marley muttered a low curse, got up and bent down to grab him. "You can do it," she told him, refusing to think about anything but getting him to the road so she could call for help. "Almost...there."

He groaned and fought to stand. Managed to get to his knees and start to rise, then a cold voice came from the shadows in front of them.

"Drop your weapon now, or you both die."

WARWICK STARED, CERTAIN for a moment that he must be hallucinating as Roland Yates stepped out from behind a thick stand of trees, aiming a pistol at them. Marley was frozen in place beside him, her whole body rigid.

"What the hell are you doin'?" Warwick blurted, the flood of adrenaline counteracting the exhaustion that had been sapping him only moments ago. Yates had been behind all this. For the love of God, *why*?

"You're a loose end I needed to tidy up," Yates said, taking another step toward them. "I'm not letting you destroy everything I've worked for."

The sound of Yates's voice triggered something. Warwick sucked in a breath as everything suddenly clicked into place in his mind.

He remembered. All of it.

Raw rage punched through him, making his heart pound.

The night of the op. When he'd heard his commander speaking to someone behind the building. It had been too dark to see who it was. But it was Yates's voice he'd been struggling to remember.

You and I are the only ones who know where Grey was the other night.

What about the bomb? Collingwood said.

Warwick hadn't understood what it meant at the time. Hadn't questioned it. Hadn't realized what would happen, or that he and his teammates were about to be sent into a death trap to cover Yates's and Collingwood's sins.

It doesn't matter, Yates responded. *Doesn't matter that we hid the intel. Nobody else will ever know, and now we'll be the ones to get him tonight. Trust me, it's all for the best.*

"It was you I heard," Warwick rasped out. "Talkin' to Collingwood that night."

Yates's face tightened. "You weren't supposed to hear any of it."

The rage turned deeper. Darker. Growing until it pulsed through him with every thud of his heart. "You set us up," he said in disbelief, his grip tightening around Marley. He was still shivering but not as much, the punch of anger counteracting the cold. "You knew where Grey was days before the op but you held off to make sure you would get the credit if we got him. And you knew about the bomb."

"You don't know what you're talking about," Yates snarled.

"Aye, I do." And it made his insides clench in revulsion. "And when you thought I might have overheard what you said, you panicked. Called in another team last minute and sent us to the original target *knowin'* Grey had planted the bomb and sent us in there without warning. All to cover your lyin' ass because telling us would have exposed you."

"Shut up," Yates snapped, jerking the pistol at Marley. "Drop it, *now*."

She had already drawn it from her holster, holding it by the butt. Held her other hand up beside her head in a gesture of surrender as she slowly bent her knees and crouched.

Once she set the weapon down, they would both die. Warwick could read the intention in Yates's face as Warwick stood there balancing on one foot, fury coiling deep in his gut.

And Yates might get away with it. Might get away with it all and return to the UK to cover his ass and resume the career and lifestyle he'd sacrificed hundreds of lives to achieve.

No. *Never*.

Making a split-second decision, he snatched the Glock from Marley's hand and shoved her down even as he rolled, then jackknifed up to take aim at Yates—

A shot rang out before he could squeeze the trigger. Yates dropped his weapon and lurched forward with a scream, an expression of surprised agony on his face as he toppled over and hit the ground, holding the back of his shoulder.

Warwick looked past him and trained the Glock on the source of the shot.

"Don't shoot," a calm female voice said while Yates writhed on the ground between them, swearing. "I'm alone. I'm going to step out and lower my weapon."

Moments later a woman emerged from the shadows. Another wave of shock blasted through him.

The woman he'd rescued from the beach.

She held her hands up on either side of her head, pistol held loosely in her right.

Warwick kept his aimed right at her. "Don't you dare move," he growled.

TWENTY-FOUR

Marley's mind was reeling as she lay on the ground on her belly watching all this unfold. Holy shit, what the hell was going on? How many more people were coming after them?

The unknown woman stood calmly in place, unmoving as she faced Warwick with her hands in the air, his pistol aimed at her the whole time. "I'm going to set this down," she said with that same stunning calm, then slowly bent and placed her pistol on the ground before rising again, watching Warwick steadily.

"Kick it over there," he ordered, her Glock rock steady in his grip.

She couldn't believe how quickly he'd reacted. Wouldn't have believed it was possible given how weak and worn out he'd been. But he was a fighter to the core. A survivor. And she believed with her whole heart that he would get them out of here.

The woman's foot swung and kicked the pistol out of reach, skidding to a stop in a pile of rust-colored cedar needles.

"Turn around."

She did, hands still on either side of her head. "I've got a blade strapped to my calf."

"Throw it the opposite way." Marley could hear the strain in his voice now. See the slight shake in his hand as he held the pistol.

The woman bent, the movement oddly elegant, almost dancer-like. The rip of Velcro came a second later, then she tossed the sheathed blade to her other side and lowered her hands. "I'm going to restrain him now," she said, taking a step toward the wounded man writhing on the ground.

He'd scrambled to his knees, one hand clamped to the back of his shoulder, watching the woman with a menacing glare. "You stupid bitch," he hissed. "You just ruined everything. Getting me arrested will only make the world a more dangerous place."

"I'll risk it."

Recovering from her shock, Marley pushed up and ran over to help her, but it was quickly apparent the woman didn't need it.

Before Marley got there the woman had the man flat on his face and a knee in the small of his back. She wrenched his uninjured arm behind him, secured his wrist with a zip tie produced from her coat pocket, then caught his other wrist as he let out another bellow of pain, swearing and twisting beneath her on the muddy ground.

"I'm good," the woman said, looking up at Marley. "You just worry about him." She nodded at Warwick.

Marley glanced back. He was struggling to stay upright on his left foot, his mud-caked face a mask of pain. "You were on the beach," he said to the woman, his voice raspy.

"Yes." She had both the man's hands secured behind him now, her knee still firmly planted in his spine. "Thank you for that, by the way. And for paying for my hotel. I'll pay you back."

"You've more than covered it already," he said, nodding at the man on the ground.

Marley rushed over to bolster him, wrapping an arm around his waist.

"Who are you?" he asked, leaning into her as he watched the woman.

"My name's Teagan," she answered in a no-nonsense manner. "And I was sent here to bring you in."

"By who?"

Teagan nodded at the man beneath her. "Him."

Marley shook her head. This was crazy. "Who is he?"

"Roland Yates," Warwick answered, his jaw tight as he stared at the man with utter loathing. "He's an MI6 intelligence officer." He shook his head, the rage pulsing off him palpable.

"Not for much longer," Teagan said, satisfaction lacing her voice.

"You son of a bitch," Warwick snarled at Yates. "Our men fuckin' died that night to cover up your dirty secrets. Not only that, Grey slipped the net and disappeared from the other target anyway. Then carried out more attacks and inspired a dozen more by others while we kept searching for him. It took over a fuckin' year to find him again and get him in Durham!"

"You knew the hazards of the job when you signed up," Yates snarled back. "Risk comes with the territory." He clenched his teeth, let out an enraged howl of pain when Teagan unceremoniously grabbed the elbow of his injured arm and hauled him to his feet. "You goddamn bitch!" he hissed, trying to wrench around. "You'll pay for this!"

"No, I won't. But you will." Holding his bound wrists, Teagan shoved him forward, pulling another yelp from Yates. "Now move before I lose my patience and decide to get rough."

Marley laughed, she couldn't help it. This whole scenario was too surreal, and what Teagan had just said seemed hilarious. Maybe she was in shock, she wasn't sure, but it was funny as hell to watch this woman coolly take down Yates as if she did it on a daily basis. "I like her," she murmured to Warwick.

"Aye. I think I like her too." He tucked the Glock into his waistband.

"Should I grab their weapons?"

"Nah. Leave them for the forensics team when they come." His voice was taut with pain, blood still flowing from the wound in his thigh even with the belt she'd twisted around in a sort of tourniquet.

"Come on. We need to get you to the road."

He nodded once, wrapped his arm tighter around her shoulders and tipped her chin up with his other hand to search her eyes. "Are you okay?"

His concern for her in spite of his own suffering hit her dead in the heart. "Yes, I'm fine, but I'll be a lot better once I know you're being taken care of. Now come on."

It took a while to get through the trees because they were forced to stop and let Warwick catch his breath. Meanwhile, Teagan frog-marched Yates past them. When the road finally came into view, Marley could see Teagan crouched next to Yates. He was once again facedown, on the wet pavement this time while the rain fell steadily and the wind gusted around them.

Just as she and Warwick finally neared the tree line an SUV roared up. Warwick let out a relieved breath. "It's Walker and Ivy."

She'd never been so excited to see a familiar face. "Over here!" she called out when they jumped from the vehicle. "Warwick's wounded."

She saw a streak of shoulder-length brown hair as Ivy flew

past her field of vision to meet Teagan and Yates. Then a tall, well-built man with a dark trimmed beard appeared just ahead of them, carrying a first-aid kit. Walker.

"What happened?" he asked, hurrying toward them.

"Yates hired a woman to bring me in, then must have changed his mind for some reason and tapped a former teammate of mine to take me out, and Marley too. He showed up here in person to make sure the job got done."

"Where's the hitter?"

"Marley took him out."

"Good." Walker rushed up to Warwick's other side. "I'll carry him."

"Nah, mate—"

"Save it," Walker said, then bent and put his shoulder to Warwick's middle. "Brace yourself."

Warwick nodded, bit back a scream when Walker straightened, levering him across his shoulders. He paused, adjusted Warwick's weight, then started back toward the road. Marley grabbed the first-aid kit and hurried after them.

"Sheriff's on the way," Walker said, his voice a bit strained as he carried Warwick over the uneven terrain. "Who's the woman?"

"Teagan. Yates hired her. She shot and restrained him when he was about to kill me."

Walker grunted. "She must want him brought in bad."

"Aye, and I do too," Warwick said through gritted teeth, his eyes clenched shut. "Could you not bounce me so much, ya tosser?"

"I'm doin' my best, man. Almost there. Hang on."

Warwick groaned, his body rigid. Blood dripped off the back of his thigh, down Walker's arm and onto the ground.

Marley shivered, her muscles starting to tremble again. She was cold but not from the wet or the weather. This was more intense. A bone-deep chill that came from knowing that she and Warwick had almost both died out here.

And she'd also killed a man. He'd deserved it, her conscience wasn't bothering her one bit, but it was still hard to process.

There was no ditch separating them from the road on this side of the woods. Walker finally stepped onto the edge of the pavement and eased Warwick down amidst a string of bit-off curses. She and Walker immediately laid him on his back.

Marley knelt behind him and set his head in her lap, leaning over to shield his face from the rain. She glanced up when an umbrella appeared above her.

Ivy angled it to protect them both. "How's he doing?"

"He's hanging in there." She wiped at the mud coating Warwick's face. Tried to stop shivering.

Ivy wrapped a blanket around her.

"Th-thanks," she whispered, suddenly short of breath.

Ivy patted her shoulder. "Yeah, no worries. Sheriff should be here any minute, and I already called for an ambulance."

Warwick opened pain-dazed eyes and peered up at her, reaching his hand up for hers. "Areet, pet?"

"Y-yes," she managed, trying to smile. She didn't fully understand what Warwick had said to Yates or what it all meant, but what she did infuriated her.

"How sure are you that there aren't any more threats in the area?" Ivy asked as Walker went to work on Warwick.

"Positive," Teagan called out from thirty feet behind Marley. "There's no one else."

Ivy glanced back at her, one side of her mouth kicking up. "Okay, then." But Marley saw the butt of a Glock sticking out of the back of Ivy's waistband, and from everything she'd heard about this legendary woman, knew Ivy wasn't letting her guard down yet.

Walker was busy cutting Warwick's pant leg off. The wound on the back of his thigh was ugly, the torn flesh filthy and still bleeding profusely. Walker adjusted the belt slightly. "The good news is, the artery appears to be intact or you would've been dead a while ago. But the impact might have fractured the femur, and the wound is full of mud."

Warwick closed his eyes, his hand tightening on hers. She focused on his face rather than on what Walker was doing, heart clenching when Warwick's expression twisted in agony and he bared his teeth against an animalistic roar.

"I know. Sorry, man, has to be done," Walker muttered, tightening the belt.

Warwick's cry died away and suddenly there was only the patter of rain on the asphalt, the wind rushing in the treetops… and distant sirens. Finally.

"Almost here," she said to him, shivering harder. He didn't answer, taking quick, shallow breaths through his nose, his lips compressed into a thin line. She cupped his muddy, scruffy cheek in her hand. "Warwick." She didn't care that Walker and Ivy were right here to bear witness to this. She had to tell him. Couldn't wait a moment longer.

He opened his eyes. Squinted up at her through the pain.

"I love you back."

He groaned and closed his eyes almost in relief, turning his cheek into her palm.

The sheriff's vehicle turned the corner and sped toward them, lights and sirens going. Four patrol cars were behind it.

Sheriff Buchanan stepped out and hurried toward them. "Ambulance is about three minutes behind us." His gaze narrowed on Teagan while his deputies ran past to her and Yates.

"The area's supposedly secure," Walker said. "One KIA at

the bottom of the ravine in there." He nodded into the woods. "And Teagan shot and apprehended the other shooter."

Noah let out a curse and got on his radio and started issuing orders to have the area searched and secured, then hooked it back onto his belt. "Marley, can you explain to me everything that happened?"

"Y-yes." But she didn't want to leave Warwick.

As if sensing her distress, he squeezed her hand then let it go. "It's all right, pet. Go talk to him."

The sheriff helped her to her feet and walked her away to his car to begin questioning her. She was shivering harder than ever, her teeth chattering. "S-sorry," she managed. "C-can't s-stop."

"It's okay. Here, get in the front with me." He helped her in, went around to the driver's side and turned the heating vents on her. "Go ahead and take a couple minutes. Close your eyes, just breathe."

She did as he said while he spoke on the radio again. When she opened her eyes, she noticed a picture on his dash. His wife, Poppy, holding their little son. And for some reason, the sight of that picture made her teary as hell. She thought of her own brothers. How much she loved them and the pain they would have suffered if she'd died today.

It took longer than she wanted for her nerves to settle. While the heat pumped at her, she organized her thoughts, then drew a breath and began. "Warwick and I were at the house when Walker called, telling us we needed to leave." Her voice sounded steady and she was feeling calmer.

She went through the sequence of events from start to finish. "I'm still fuzzy on exactly who Yates is and what happened leading up to today, but Warwick clearly blames him for what happened to him and his teammates during that op in the Lake District. And whoever the dead guy is, they were former teammates. I'm unclear whether Warwick meant SAS or MI6, but it has to be one of the two."

She swallowed, remembering how savage the fight had been. How intent the man had been. "From his position he could have easily killed Warwick with either the rifle or a pistol. But instead he dumped the rifle and jumped into that pit, going after him with a knife."

Buchanan was rapidly writing everything down and glanced up at the rearview mirror when another siren became audible. "Okay, ambulance is here. Stay put and keep warm while I talk to the medics and then talk to Teagan." His voice had an edge to it as he said her name. "Do you need to go to the hospital to get checked out too?"

"No, I'm okay." Not really, but as good as she could be under the circumstances.

He nodded. "Don't leave with Warwick when they take him. I need to talk to you again."

He got out as the ambulance sped up the road. Marley watched through her rain-streaked window as Walker kept tending to Warwick, now covered with another blanket. Buchanan spoke to the medics, who then rushed straight to Warwick.

She released a long breath and stepped out of the vehicle. Went over to hold Warwick's hand as they placed him on the stretcher and got ready to load him into the ambulance.

"I want to go with you, but the sheriff needs to talk to me again," she said. "But I'll come straight to the hospital as soon as I'm done, I promise."

A wry smile tugged at his mouth. "I'm not gonna die on ye, lass. Not after you finally admitted you love me."

She smiled back faintly, but her heart was breaking. The last thing she wanted was to be separated from him right now. She hated what had happened. What he'd gone through and was still suffering. Wished she could take it all away.

"It's all right." He squeezed her hand. Brought it to his lips to kiss it. "I'll see you soon."

"Okay." She stepped back, wrapped her arms around herself as they loaded him into the back. The sheriff was talking to Walker, Teagan and maybe Yates, who was finally sitting up now as the deputies applied pressure to the wound in his shoulder.

"You did well."

She glanced to her right as Ivy came to stand next to her, sheltering her with the umbrella. "With what?"

"Taking out the hitter with two shots center mass without hitting Warwick."

Oh, God, just thinking about it made her feel sick. "I was terrified I'd hit him too. I angled around behind them and to the side to try and get a clean shot, but…"

Ivy rubbed a soothing hand up and down her back. "You got the clean shot and you did what you had to do."

She blew out a breath. It wasn't something she felt like being praised for. "Yeah."

"Ah, there he is. Someone to see you." Ivy nudged her and nodded to the end of the row of vehicles now parked along the edge of the road.

Marley glanced up, confused, but then she saw Decker's head appear as he climbed out of his rental. "Deck!"

She took off running. His expression eased when he saw her. He stalked forward, opened his arms and she ran right into them.

"Jesus, Mar," he breathed as he caught her, hugging her tight in his steely arms. "You okay?"

She nodded, eyes flooding with tears. The hug was just

what she'd needed. "How did you get here?" she asked in a rough whisper.

"Ryder Locke called me. Walker alerted him and asked him to contact me."

Oh. That was so nice of him.

Decker squeezed her once more then took her by the shoulders and set her away from him a bit to study her with a critical eye. "What happened?"

She pushed closer, wound her arms around his waist and laid her head on his shoulder. "It's a long story. And you're not gonna like it."

By the time she was done, Decker was rigid. She looked up at him to find his jaw clamped tight and a fierce look in his eyes. "That him over there?" he asked, jerking his chin at where Yates was still on the ground. Another siren was coming their way, another ambulance to transport him to the hospital.

She was glad they had taken Warwick in separately. "Yes."

"And you said he's MI—" He stopped and sucked in a swift breath, his spine snapping taut.

Marley glanced over her shoulder. "What?"

"Is that Teagan?"

She blinked at him in surprise. "You know her?"

"We've met," he said in a dark voice. "Stay here." He seemed genuinely stunned as he started toward where Teagan was standing with Walker and the sheriff.

WHAT. The *hell*.

Decker kept his eyes pinned on Teagan as he strode over. If that was even her real name.

She was wearing the same rumpled, ill-fitting outfit he'd

seen her in before, her black hair pulled back in a ponytail. But now he was seeing her in a completely different light.

He'd misread and underestimated her before. Badly.

She wasn't a lost, confused woman on the run from an abusive guy, or a helpless victim. She was a pro. Had shot Yates, who had hired her to go after Warwick in the first place, and maybe Marley too.

He was really damn grateful for what she'd done, but she'd also lied right to his face about the amnesia earlier, and maybe even played him if she'd somehow known who he was. He'd even offered to help her, not realizing she'd been sent to hunt his sister and Warwick.

She stopped talking when she saw him coming. "Excuse me a minute," she said to the sheriff and the other guy, and started toward him. Head up, gaze locked with his. Zero awkwardness or apology in her expression. "What are you doing here?"

"What are *you* doing here?" he countered, stopping ten feet away to size her up. Looking for the signs he'd missed earlier.

He thought of the way she'd reacted when he'd startled her. Her knee-jerk reaction had been to throw a punch at him. A good one, too. If she'd connected with his throat, it would have put him on the ground. She'd seemed horrified that she'd done it.

He'd believed her story. His gut had believed her, and that was something he trusted after all the experience he'd acquired in sizing people up over the years as an MP. So had she been lying or not?

There was an obvious difference in her now, a cool confidence radiating from her. She was one hell of an actress, because he'd absolutely bought the lost-and-trying-to-hide-how-scared-she-was routine she'd put on before. "I came here to right a wrong," she said.

The half-answers weren't helping. "Who are you." A demand, not a question.

"Teagan."

"Teagan who?"

"Kim."

Uh huh. The most common Korean surname. An alias? "And who are you? Because it seems like your amnesia is gone all of a sudden."

Annoyance flashed in her deep, dark brown eyes. "I wasn't lying to you earlier. I really did have an accident, and I really couldn't remember anything except my first name when we met. You think I did this to myself?" She gestured to her face, gave him a pointed I-don't-think-so look. "I figured out the password to my phone. The things I found on it brought my memory back."

"Well, that's real convenient." This was nuts. "And what things?"

She maintained eye contact, unflinching even though the hard look he was giving her now had been known to shrivel the balls of combat-hardened Marines twice her size. "I can't tell you."

"You can. Because that's my sister over there," he said, nodding in Marley's direction, "so I want to know what the hell's going on."

She glanced past him, surprise flickering over her face. Either acting again, or she really hadn't known he and Marley were related. What kind of "accident" had she had? "Oh."

"Yeah. So who do you work for? FBI?" She had to be an agent of some sort.

"I'm not at liberty to say. But the FBI will be here soon enough if you want to talk to them personally, and they'll want to talk to your sister too."

"Ms. Kim, another word if you don't mind," the sheriff called out before Decker could open his mouth.

"I have to go," she said, then the hint of a smile tugged at the corner of her mouth, making him blink. He didn't see anything to smile about here. "But tell your sister from me that she's a badass." She turned abruptly and walked away, leaving him staring after her with a hundred more questions burning in his mind.

Along with a bone-deep certainty that their paths would be crossing again in the near future.

TWENTY-FIVE

Marley leaned over the hospital bed to hear him more clearly. "Pardon? I didn't catch that."

Henry scowled and grabbed at the oxygen mask strapped over his nose and mouth. "Fuckin' ridiculous thing. Makes me sound like Darth Vader."

She bit her lip to keep from laughing. "I'm glad to see you're still so salty."

"And I'm just glad to still be seeing at all. Especially when I've got a gorgeous lady to look at." He gave her an adoring wink, squeezed his fingers around her hand weakly.

"Henry, you're bad. You're lying there half-dead and you're still flirting with me." She looked a helluva lot better than she had a few hours ago though. After being released on scene, Ivy and Walker had taken her back to their place so she could clean up and change into fresh clothes.

He grimaced. "I know it. But I guess the devil isn't ready for this devil dog yet, because I'm not dying anymore." He looked over at Grady, busy writing in a chart on the other side of the room. "Ain't that right, Mendoza?"

"That's one-hundred percent accurate," Grady answered with a smile.

She'd found him soon after arriving at the hospital. Warwick was still being prepped for surgery and they wouldn't let her see him until he came out of recovery. She'd needed a distraction and been anxious about Henry. Grady had let her into the room for a short visit, providing Henry didn't get too tired.

"Good," she said, cheered by the dramatic change in his appearance and status. "Because this devil dog kinda makes my day every time I come into work, so he needs to get back there A-freaking-SAP."

His wrinkled cheeks flushed. Actually turned pink as he looked away, and she was ecstatic to see it. "Aw, go on."

"Nope. It's the truth."

He cleared his throat. Finally looked at her again. "So. Any news on the asshole?"

She huffed out a laugh. She hadn't planned to bring any of this up, but he was alert and obviously curious. "Oh, Henry, have I got a story for you."

His watery blue eyes widened. "What, tell me."

"It's long. And boring, you probably—"

"Young lady, you know damn well I've got nowhere to be, just like I know whatever you're holding back is juicy as hell. Now gimme the goods."

"All right. But don't say I didn't warn you." She glanced at Grady, who was watching her with interest, and told them everything that had happened, beginning with Walker's call.

"Holy *shit*balls," Henry said into the silence when she'd finished, looking stunned. "And you took the first asshole out with an M4?"

"Two shots, center mass." It still didn't seem real.

He squeezed her hand with surprising strength. "Every Marine is—"

"First and foremost a rifleman. Yeah. But Henry, you have no idea how scared I was. Not to shoot him, but scared of hitting Warwick." They both still had to meet with the FBI. Maybe the CIA too, along with whichever UK officials were going to be involved in the case. Everything was a tangled, confusing mess.

Marley didn't even want to think about any of that. Right now, she was focused solely on making sure Warwick was okay. Everything else would have to wait.

Henry frowned at her. "Of course you were scared. We're all scared in combat, don't let anyone shit you about that. But you used your training and got the job done. That's all that matters." His blue eyes glistened. "I'm proud of you, Marine."

"Aww, jeez, Henry," she whispered, a lump in her throat. He had sort of become the grandfather she'd never had.

"So," he said after a minute, watching her thoughtfully. "He's the one?"

"Yes. He's the one." She was done fighting it. There was no way she could walk away from him now.

"Okay. But he better treat you right, or he'll have to deal with a world of hurt from us. Right, Mendoza?"

"That's affirm," Grady answered, winking at her.

Henry sighed and relaxed against his pillow, closing his eyes. The visit had drained him visibly.

She glanced over at Grady, and he gave her a subtle nod toward the door. Time to go.

"You rest up now," she told Henry, leaning over to kiss his forehead. "I expect to see you sitting up and jabbering away at me next time I come through this door."

"Yes, ma'am," he murmured, a faint smile on his lips.

Grady walked her out. "There's a quiet waiting room down

on the second floor if you want to wait in there. Bit more private for you. Ev's on her way, FYI. Should be here in about twenty minutes or so."

He must have contacted her. "*Thank* you," she whispered, throwing her arms around him. He was so great. And it was beyond wonderful that her best friend was marrying someone so amazing.

"Yeah, of course," he said, giving her a quick hug and then stepping back. "I need to check on another patient, but I'll look in on you later to see how you're holding up."

"Okay. See you later."

She found the waiting room and reluctantly switched on her phone. As expected, a barrage of texts and voicemails lit up her screen. Decker and the twins, all demanding to know what was going on and if she was okay, whether she needed anything, what was happening with Warwick.

She answered Decker first. He'd volunteered to come with her to the hospital, but she'd wanted to decompress without his brooding intensity hovering over her. Especially when things were already so tense between him and Warwick. After that, she contacted both the twins, reassuring them she was okay, and promised to call when things settled down.

She had just sent the last message when Everleigh came through the door. Her bestie sailed over to engulf her in a warm, loving hug she felt all the way to the marrow of her bones. "I'm *so* glad you're okay."

"Me too. Thanks for coming."

"Of course."

They sat down, and though she was exhausted and tired of talking about it, she absolutely needed to fill Everleigh in.

Everleigh shook her head, face pale. No doubt the story had reminded her of what she'd gone through at the concert just a few months ago. "Mar, I'm so sorry."

She nudged her, frowning. "It's not *your* fault."

"I know, but... Any update on Warwick yet?"

"No, but Grady's going to let them know I'm in here so they can update me as soon as he's out of surgery." She counted her blessings that she wasn't sitting here waiting to find out whether he was going to make it or not. But he'd already been through so damn much pain and trauma. She didn't want him to have to live with permanent damage to his leg on top of everything else.

"Good." Ev blew out a breath and leaned her head back against the wall. Then looked over at her. "So you and he are..."

"In love. Yeah."

A big grin lit up Everleigh's face. "Yes! Oh, I just *knew* it. Who said it first?"

"He did."

"Called it."

Marley raised an eyebrow. "Oh, did you?"

"Yep." She gave her a dry look. "Mar, the man came halfway across the globe just to catch a glimpse of you from afar without intending to ever let you know." She snorted. "Please, it was so obvious."

She laughed and it felt so good. All of this did. Having Everleigh beside her. Her brother nearby. The threat all over. And Warwick in good hands on the operating table right now.

They talked a while more, then she fell asleep for a bit, her head resting on Everleigh's shoulder. Her bestie's hair smelled like green apples and she made a mental note to find out what brand of shampoo it was as she drifted off.

She snapped awake when someone else came in the room. Blinked in confusion at the nurse standing there. Light brown skin, tight dark brown curls and amazing sea-green eyes. "Hi, Ev. Marley? I'm Molly, Grady told me where to find you. Just wanted to let you know that the surgery went well and Mr. James is awake and in recovery."

She expelled the breath she'd been holding, relief hitting her hard enough that she suddenly felt weak. "Thank you."

"You're very welcome. He'll be brought up to the third floor in about forty minutes. You can visit him then."

"Perfect." She'd already waited well over a year for him. She supposed she could handle another forty minutes.

WARWICK LAY in the hospital bed sorting through his thoughts while a line dripped pain medication and antibiotics into his veins. His thigh still burned like fire but the bullet had missed the bone, and more importantly, the femoral artery.

The surgeon had told him he had a partial hairline fracture of the shaft of the femur from the shockwave of the bullet. And that he would possibly suffer permanent loss of strength and nerve damage there.

It was a far cheerier outcome than he'd been expecting. And he'd been through much worse before during his recovery after the explosion.

Yates's and Collingwood's betrayal cut deep. All he could hope was that they would both receive the maximum sentences for their crimes.

The door opened. He glanced over, a tidal wave of emotions crashing over him when Marley walked in.

She gave him a wobbly smile that tugged at his heart, and hurried toward him. "Hey."

He reached up. Wrapped his arms around her as she bent down to hug him, and held her close. "Hi, pet."

She squeezed him hard, shoved her face into the curve of his neck and drew in an unsteady breath. Her shoulders jerked.

He closed his eyes, his throat tightening as he drew her closer. "I'm alright. We're both alright. It's all goin' to be okay now."

She nodded, struggled to get control, her grip around him almost bruising, making his bashed ribs burn.

"It's alright, pet," he whispered. "Christ, I love you."

"L-love you too." She eased back, wiped away the tears on her cheeks to peer down at him with concerned brown eyes. "How do you feel?"

"Lucky to be alive." He reached for her hand. Curled his fingers around it. "You saved my life, Mar."

She broke eye contact, started to shake her head.

"Aye, pet, you did." She amazed him. The courage and strength it had taken for her to do what she'd done…

"I was terrified that I had hit you too. For a moment there, I thought I had. Until you threw him off you, I couldn't tell." She put a hand to her chest, blew out a breath.

"You were incredible. And I'm still breathing right now because of it."

She shifted to set her hip on the edge of his bed, clearing her throat. "Who the hell were those guys?"

He sighed, knowing how confused she must be about everything. "The first one was Simon Ellard, a former SAS teammate of mine. He was a fuckup and a criminal, even back then. We crossed swords several times when we were deployed in the Middle East together. He was always cuttin' corners, taking the easy way instead of the right way, and had no discipline. Always talkin' shite and corrupting blokes around him.

"When I caught him tryin' to smuggle civilian contraband into his barracks that he and a few of his men had stolen on a mission, I refused to let it go. I reported him and his unit, provided a statement used to prosecute him later. There was bad blood between us after that." Although he hadn't realized just how bad until today.

"And the second guy?"

"Roland Yates. MI6 intelligence officer who worked closely with my commandin' officer, Collingwood. It was them I overheard the night of the op."

Anger hardened in her eyes. "What did they say?"

"They were talkin' about Grey. I heard enough to make me suspicious that they'd both known where he was two days before informing anyone else. Time that would have allowed us to act and catch him off guard."

"Instead, he planted the bomb that nearly killed you."

"No, it's worse than that."

"Worse?"

"Yates was worried that I'd overheard too much of his conversation with Collingwood. He made up a shite story about getting last-minute intel on Grey at a different location than our original target. He called in another team to send over there, and sent mine to the original, knowing full well that Grey might have planted a bomb there. Knowing full well that I would be the first through the door and that it would cover his ass if I died during the breach."

"Oh my God." Horror and outrage flooded her expression. "That son of a bitch!" She drew a breath to calm herself. "So if he was hoping you would die, why wait until now to come after you? Why not right after you came out of the coma?"

He'd been thinking about that too. "They must have been tryin' to figure out what I'd heard or how much, and whether I remembered after I regained consciousness. They both questioned me at length about everythin' that night leading up to the explosion. But at that point I didn't remember shite about what they'd said. There was just this…feelin' at the back of my mind that somethin' wasn't right."

He shook his head. "Yates must have been suspicious all along, maybe thought I was lyin'. He finally decided to have me watched, then at some point he wanted to make sure I couldn't reveal their secret. Maybe even Collingwood was in on all this too. Time will tell." It sickened him.

She shook her head, looking distressed. "So they were both in on all this? Trying to find and kill you here, outside of the UK because it what, might make it look less suspicious?"

"Looks that way right now. Easier to wash their hands of it like that." He rubbed his thumb over the back of her hand. How the hell had he ever imagined he could live without her? There was no way. It would have killed him in the end. "I gave my official statement to the sheriff already. Shite's going down at MI6 and the Home Office right now, I'll wager."

"It better be. And what about the threat? Are you sure it's over and no one else is out there gunning for you?"

He nodded. "It was over the moment Teagan shot Yates. No one else involved will want to take more heat than they already are now that word's out. MI6 will be movin' to arrest Collingwood as we speak."

"Then what about the drive-by at my place? Do you think it's connected?"

"I don't know, to be honest." He frowned. "I thought the suspect car was the same one I'd seen earlier in town that night, but... I don't know." Maybe it hadn't been the same car. Maybe feeling like he'd been followed and the shooting weren't connected at all. Hell, he hoped the investigation would piece all that together.

She rubbed her temple, looking tired. "I just can't take it all in. It's too much. How are you so calm about it?"

"Because I know they'll get what's comin' to them." He reached up to take her face in his hands. Gazed up into her beautiful brown eyes. "I meant what I said before. I love ye, my canny lass. Always will."

She swallowed, blinked fast. "I love you too. So much."

"I know I broke your heart and your trust before, and—"

"Stop. You don't have to keep apologizing. I believe you now about the danger you felt before." She gave him a wry smile. "Obviously. So I understand why you stayed away."

He grinned for a second, then got serious again. It was important he say this aloud, make sure she understood he wasn't leaving her ever again. "I want to stay here with you. I never had family. Not really. Never felt like I belonged anywhere. But I know I belong with you. I want to make a life together, if you'll still have me with me gammy face and leg."

She leaned her cheek into his palm and grasped his wrist, her eyes as soft as her smile. "I want that too. And yeah, I'll still have you. I'm pretty fond of your face, gammy or not, and I guess I'll learn to tolerate the leg."

Every muscle in his body eased. Chest loosening, limbs relaxing. He felt like he was floating. And it wasn't from the medication, even though it was definitely working because the pain in his leg was down to a hot throb instead of a five-alarm fire. It was all Marley. "Thank you."

"You're welcome." She bent forward, brushed a kiss across his lips and straightened. "So, what's the plan after you get out of here?"

"You. You're my plan." For the rest of his life.

TWENTY-SIX

Marley tipped her head back as a low groan escaped, let the blissful sensations wash through her as she planted her hands on Warwick's bare, sculpted chest and rode him to her heart's content. The deep teal chiffon of her maid of honor gown dumped over the dresser was just visible in the corner of the room as her eyes fell closed, a long, liquid moan coming from her.

They really didn't have time for this, she was supposed to be at the church in thirty minutes, but when Warwick had walked out of the bedroom doing up the cufflinks on his tux, she hadn't been able to control herself. She'd had him stripped and toppled backward on the bed in under ten seconds, his low, sexy laugh revving her libido even higher.

"Ah, pet, I love watchin' you ride me," he said in a deep, rumbling voice drenched with pleasure.

"And I love…riding you," she gasped out. He was so hard and thick inside her, filling her completely and stroking all her hidden nerve endings that shivered to life at the decadent friction.

Warwick half sat up, the glorious display of his abs and chest flexing. His big hands splayed across her back, his mouth finding and closing around a tight, sensitive nipple while she stroked her clit.

Every single pleasure point in her body lit up, ecstasy flowing through her veins like warm honey. She slowed the rocking motion of her hips. Savored the upward spiral, the way the feeling expanded, her core clenching around him.

"Oh, yeah, *more…*" Her cry filled the room as her climax hit, pure and sweet and powerful.

He lay back down, his hands sliding down to grip her hips. She sighed as the beautiful ripples gradually faded, opened her eyes to look down at him. His dark eyes blazed with desire, the muscles in his arms and chest standing out in sharp relief.

She planted her palms on his pecs, reveled in his strength and the way he surrendered to her, allowing her complete control.

It had been five weeks since the attack, but she wasn't worried about hurting him anymore. The wound in his thigh had healed but he didn't have full strength in it, probably never would again, and the back of his leg was still partly numb. She loved it when he took control in bed, but she also loved it when he relinquished it to her like this.

She kept the motion of her body slow, hungrily drinking in every shift in his expression while she rode him. The tension in his jaw. The way his breathing turned rough.

His fingers bit into her hips. She picked up her rhythm. Smiled at his low growl that turned into a helpless groan. "Does it feel good?" she whispered, enjoying making him lose control.

"Aye. Christ, *aye*," he gasped out, then arched beneath her with an expression of ecstasy so intense it bordered on pain and started to come.

She stilled, allowing them both to fully absorb the moment together, the feel of him flexing inside her. When he collapsed back against the pillow with another groan, she bent over him, resting her weight on her forearms on either side of his head so she could kiss him.

A slow, intimate kiss filled with love and awe.

These past few weeks together had been hard in a lot of ways, yet in others even better than what they'd had last year. Their relationship had been strengthened by what they'd been through, and because he'd finally been honest with her about his past and who he was. Every morning she woke up beside him, she fell in love with him all over again.

Warwick slid his hands up and down her spine in a soothing rhythm that made her want to curl up on him right here and fall asleep. "Was it the tux?"

She grinned. "Yep. You're lucky I didn't rip it stripping it off you."

"Huh. Guess I'll be lookin' for more black-tie events in the area to attend on a regular basis, then."

She laughed softly. "You don't have to go to events in it. You can just wear it around the house. Or just put on the pants and shirt but don't button it up, so I can see all these incredibly sexy muscles under here." She stroked a hand over his chest, down his flat stomach. He'd lost weight initially after the attack but was putting it back on now.

"Ah, but then I'd miss out on the chance to seduce you in it. Make you wait while we're out together, let the anticipation build until you can get me alone again."

"Okay, I can't argue with that logic." She dropped a kiss on his lips, sat up with a sigh and shoved her hair back. "I need to get ready. Again." Hopefully her hair was still intact. She'd spent forty minutes with the curling iron getting everything the way she wanted it.

"Worth it."

"Absolutely." She scrambled off him and scurried to the bathroom to clean up. "Hurry. We leave in seven minutes."

"Got it."

The moment she saw Everleigh in the anteroom at the back of the church, Marley put a hand to her chest and blinked back tears. "You look like a fairy princess," she whispered roughly.

Everleigh smiled, her white-blond hair pulled up into an elegant coif with soft, artful ringlets framing her face and neck. The filmy white veil cascaded down to her hips, embroidered with delicate little lace roses. "You've seen me in this before. You were there when I first tried it on, remember?"

"I know, but it's different now." She handed her the pretty bridal bouquet made of white and pink roses interspersed with sprays of white and green fillers.

The wedding was a tear-jerker. Grady stood at the front in his dress uniform next to his best man, Travis, another PJ in his unit. The moment Everleigh appeared at the end of the aisle with her father, the smile on Grady's face was a sight to see, and then he clearly struggled to contain his emotions and Marley almost lost it.

She glanced over at Warwick, sitting next to Walker and Ivy near the front, and her heart turned over when she saw he was looking at her instead of the bride and groom. His smile made her heart swell until her chest felt impossibly tight. She was so damn lucky.

Everleigh and Grady exchanged vows and rings. And when the minister pronounced them man and wife, a loud, raucous cry went up from all the military guys in the church.

Everything after that was a joyous whirlwind, from greeting the guests to posing for pictures, and then the reception that followed at a golf and country club up on the hill with a view of the ocean. When the guests flooded out to hit the dance floor,

Marley walked over to where Warwick sat at a table near the front and slid into his lap.

"Hi." She nuzzled his smooth-shaven cheek, her lips brushing his scar.

He looped an arm around her, cuddling her close. "Sorry about me gammy leg," he murmured against her temple. "Though I'm not much of a dancer with two good ones, to be honest."

"I doubt that, given the way you move in bed. But this is better than dancing anyway." She laid her head on his solid shoulder, content to watch the others.

A sense of deep peace settled over her. They'd both suffered a lot of trauma, but they were dealing with it and he was a patient listener when she wanted to talk about it. She was back to work now, which helped keep her mind busy, and with Henry back in his room, she looked forward to going in every day.

As for Warwick, he was officially retired and dealing with the ensuing investigation and legal process unfolding both here and in the UK, while working on his physical rehab. He could walk on his own without crutches or a cane, albeit with a pronounced limp for now, and saw Everleigh at the physio clinic four times a week.

The legal process was moving along, though way too slowly for her liking. Roland Yates was in prison in the UK awaiting trial. Warwick had to travel to London next week to meet with more officials from MI6 and the Home Office.

The local investigation here in Crimson Point had cleared up a few things too. The FBI had verified that the shooting at her house had been meant to target the drug dealers next door. But Warwick had been correct, the first car he'd seen near the waterfront had been following him.

Yates had hired a private investigator from Seattle to follow Warwick and keep tabs on him from the moment he'd landed in

Portland. When he'd lost the trail, he'd started following Sheriff Buchanan around in the hopes of getting a lead. That's how Yates and Ellard had found their location at the house in the woods.

Yates had then hired Teagan, though even Warwick still wasn't certain what her story was or who she'd been working for. When she'd dropped off the radar after being injured on "another job" no one in any of the government agencies would admit to sanctioning, Yates had brought Ellard in to hunt Warwick down. And Marley along with him.

She hated them all for what they'd done—except Teagan, of course. Hated everything she and Warwick had been through. Although without it, she would never have seen Warwick again and they wouldn't be together right now.

He didn't say much about it, but she knew this whole thing had been incredibly hard on him. Finding out that an MI6 officer and his former commander—Collingwood was also now in jail awaiting trial—had sat on critical intel regarding Isaac Grey in order to further their careers, and then purposely sending Warwick and his team into a deadly situation to cover their tracks, was an unforgivable betrayal.

A breach of trust and duty that had nearly killed Warwick and cost the lives of not only two of his team members, but the hundreds of innocent people killed and wounded in subsequent attacks by Grey prior to his own death in Durham this fall.

She ran her fingers through the back of his hair. "I'm gonna miss you when you go next week."

He made a low rumbling sound. "Been thinkin' about that."

"Thinking what?"

"That you should come with me."

She lifted her head to look into his face. "Really? To England?"

"Aye. I don't know how long it'll take, but you could

always meet me there after for a holiday. You said you wanted to see Newcastle."

She wanted to see where he was from, to know that part of him. "And Durham and Edinburgh," she said as a surge of excitement hit her. Although she really didn't think it was going to work out right now. She'd only just gone back to work and doubted she could get the time off on such short notice.

"Aye, those too." He toyed with a curl hanging in front of her ear, expression thoughtful. "I was thinkin' maybe we could extend it into a honeymoon."

She went completely still, staring at him. "I…honeymoon?" They'd talked briefly about getting married one day, but she'd never expected him to want to do it this soon, especially with them dealing with so much already.

He met her gaze. Smiled. "We could get married either here or there, and then honeymoon afterward."

Her heart beat faster. "You'd need to propose properly first," she said crisply, putting a teasing note into her voice. "On one knee, the whole works, gammy leg or not."

"Aye, and I will."

Will?

Three frosted mugs of beer appeared as someone put them on the table beside them. She looked up at Decker, gave him a smile. "You bought us a round?"

"Yep." He handed them each a glass, then held up his own. "Cheers, y'all."

They touched glasses, and Decker shot Warwick a smile as he sat down to join them. Marley was happy to see it, but also startled. He and Warwick had gotten off to a really rocky start as far as introductions went. But apparently they had smoothed things over now?

"Oh," she said, putting it together. "Did you guys meet up

the other night and not tell me?" Warwick had said something about meeting up for dinner with someone in town. She'd assumed he'd meant Walker.

"Aye," Warwick said, taking a sip of beer. He made a face. "This is absolute shite compared to good old Newcastle brown ale back home."

"But it's free, so just enjoy it," Decker said with a smirk that told her they might actually *like* each other. It was such a huge relief.

"Why didn't you tell me?" she said, looking back and forth between them.

"We had private things to discuss between us lads," Warwick said.

Marley glanced at her brother for clarification but he only grinned and took another sip of beer. "Not sayin' a word, so don't even bother."

She looked back at Warwick, read the satisfaction in his expression, and gasped. Oh my God. He'd not only smoothed things over with Decker, he'd actually asked for her hand. Had planned this all out because he was intent on proposing before he left.

"Oh my God, I love you so much," she whispered, and threw her arms around him.

His chuckle reverberated in his chest, his heavy arms sliding around her. "Love ye too, pet. Forever."

WEDDINGS WEREN'T HIS THING. Dancing was even less his thing. So by the time he'd finished his second beer and the guests began to trickle out of the reception, Decker said goodbye to his sister and Warwick and headed out to the parking lot. Not like they would notice his absence the way they were making eyes at each other.

It was pretty clear Warwick intended to pop the question later tonight. And equally clear that his sister would say an enthusiastic yes.

He hadn't expected to like the guy, especially not after the crazy shit that had happened and what he'd done to Marley last year, but since then he'd seen the way he'd treated Marley over the past few weeks. He'd also heard about what Warwick had done to protect her. And after sitting down and spending a few hours with him alone the other night, listening to what he had to say, there was no doubt in Decker's mind that he loved Marley and would treat her right.

So while he normally had a hard time changing his opinion of people once he'd made his mind up about them, he'd decided that Warwick was a good guy after all, and that he could do worse in terms of a brother-in-law.

Not only that, this place wasn't a bad spot to make a home in, either. He'd moved all his stuff from Kentucky to Crimson Point two weeks ago and was enjoying the town.

His Jeep was parked near the back of the lot. He stepped past a group of people talking in the middle of it, then stopped for a car as it passed him heading for the exit. Then stopped dead again when he saw the woman leaning against his driver's-side door.

Teagan. Dressed in a dark blue pantsuit, her hair pulled up into an elegant bun at the back of her head.

So he'd been right about their paths crossing again. He just hadn't expected it to happen here of all places. Had she been a guest and he just hadn't noticed her?

No way, he chided himself. There was no way he wouldn't have seen her.

She watched him approach, glossy pink lips curving in a half-smile as she waited for him to come over.

"Hi," he said, stopping in front of her. The bruising on her face was gone. She looked good. Beautiful in an elegant, untouchable way.

"Hi." She ran her gaze over him, the hint of interest there capturing his full attention. But he could also see a hint of fatigue in her eyes, and maybe some shadows as well. "Wow, you clean up nice."

"So do you." He'd thought about her too many times since the day she had saved Marley and Warwick. Wondered what her real story was and what she'd been up to. About who had beaten her up and hoping they'd been caught and prosecuted.

She laughed, and it transformed her to stunning. He was staring. Couldn't help it. "Well, anything would be an improvement from the last time you saw me." She nodded toward the country club. "Friend of the bride or groom?"

"The bride's my sister's best friend. What are you doing here?"

"I was in town for meetings and heard you guys were all at the wedding." She nodded at the building. "Warwick and Marley still in there?"

"Yeah. Do you need to talk to him about something related to the hearings next week?" It was the only reason he could think of for her coming here.

A mischievous smile curved her lips as she refocused on him. "Nope." Her deep brown eyes twinkled up at him. Teasing, but there was definite female interest there too. And she wasn't trying to hide it.

Taken aback, he blinked at her even as an answering wave of attraction rolled through him. He was surprised she'd wanted to see him that much, but flattered. "If you wanted to see me, you could've just gotten my number and called."

"I thought this would be better."

He sure as hell wasn't complaining about seeing her in person again. This was definitely a new kind of flirting for him, but he was down with it, and he'd be lying if he said he wasn't attracted to her. "How long are you in town for?"

"A few days. But after the hearing in London next week, I'll be coming back again to handle some unfinished business I need to take care of."

That sounded intriguing and made him more curious than ever. What agency was she with? She had training. Had to be some kind of agent, though even Warwick swore he still didn't know for sure. "By the way, I never got the chance to thank you."

She frowned slightly. "For what?"

"For saving my sister."

The corners of her mouth quirked in amusement. "Believe me, it was my absolute pleasure." Her gaze flitted over him again, this time sending a pulse of heat straight into his gut. She cocked her head. "Feel like going for a drink?"

He'd already consumed his alcohol limit for the night, but there was no way he was turning that offer down. "Sure, where do you wanna go? The Sea Hag's still open."

"No, I was thinking more like…back at my rental." The flare of desire in her stare was like a match strike to his libido. "That work?"

A hot bolt of lust shot through him at the invitation in her dark eyes. It had been a while for him, but there was no misunderstanding her meaning. Anticipation pulsed through him. "Yeah, that works."

She smiled, looking so gorgeous and sexy his whole body tightened. "Good." She straightened and sauntered away, aiming her key fob at a sleek Lexus parked in the row across from his. "Follow me."

He stared after her for a moment, taking in the shape of her slender curves, unable to believe his luck at this sudden turn of events. When she pulled out of her parking spot he was right behind her, ready and willing to follow her wherever she led.

TWENTY-SEVEN

Christmas Day

"Can I open my eyes now?"

"No, not yet. I'll tell you when." Marley grasped Warwick's hands and backed through the doorway. They'd literally just arrived home from the airport. His luggage was still in the trunk.

"Where are you takin' me, lass?" A bemused smirk tugged at his mouth as he followed her, his limp less pronounced than it had been weeks ago.

"You'll see." She led him into the living room of the house they'd bought together and moved into three weeks earlier.

He'd still been in England when the deal closed. She hadn't been able to go with him because of work, but buying this house was the culmination of a lifelong dream for them both. It was on a hill at the north end of town, with ocean views from the backyard and upper floor.

She'd never imagined owning a home like this, and it wouldn't have happened except when they'd sat down to look at their finances together, it turned out Warwick had a lot more money than she'd expected. As a single guy with no family to support, he'd been saving everything and investing it wisely.

Over the years, it had turned into enough money that they'd not only been able to afford this house outright—they could live off it comfortably for many years to come.

She wasn't willing to quit her job, however. She loved her work. Loved Henry and a few other residents who had stolen their way into her heart.

"Now?" he asked.

So impatient. "You hate surprises, don't you?" she said with a laugh. He had to be tired, having just landed in Portland two hours ago after yet another trip to London to deal with more hearings in the aftermath of everything that had happened. But he'd been determined to spend their first Christmas together in their new place and it was the best gift she could have received.

"Never really had any good ones," he answered, and she sobered.

"Well, that all changes today." He'd told her he'd never had a real Christmas. Not once in his whole life. That was too unbearably sad to even contemplate, so she'd gone all out this year to show him what it was all about.

"Okay," she said once she had him in the center of the room and facing the tree, her diamond engagement ring sparkling in the lights she'd strung up.

He'd dropped down on one knee and proposed on a hill overlooking the ocean the night of Everleigh and Grady's wedding. They'd decided to wait to get married at the same resort they'd stayed at last year, and now there was less than a week to go.

"Open up," she commanded.

He opened his eyes. Stared at the transformation she'd

coerced Decker and Everleigh into helping her with two days ago. "Wow," he said in awe, looking all around.

"I made Decker and Everleigh help me after we got off our video call the other night." She wrapped her arms around him, grinning from ear to ear. "Well? What do you think?"

"It's champion," he said, his captivated smile filling her with warmth.

"I'm glad." She'd added little touches all over the house, but this main living area looked especially cozy and festive.

"Where did you find a tree that size?"

"At a lot in town." She'd seen the seven-foot blue spruce as she was driving by and immediately stopped to buy it. "I made Decker help me haul it home and set it up."

After pizza and beer, the two of them had smothered it with multicolored lights and decorations, half of which were sentimental things she'd saved from Christmases with her brothers over the years. Garland and lights twinkled around all the window frames and doorways.

Christmas pillows and a cheery red-and-white patchwork quilt were nestled on the sofa, waiting for someone to cuddle up there. A large, tiered platter of homemade Christmas cookies sat in the center of the coffee table. And under the tree, brightly wrapped gifts spilled out all over the rug placed on the hardwood floor in the corner of the living room.

Warwick stepped over to the blazing fireplace where the stockings were hung, bulging with the things Santa had filled them with late last night. "You got me a stockin'."

"I made it."

He looked over at her, raised his eyebrows. "Made it?"

"Mmhmm. Everleigh signed us up for a class at the quilting shop in town while you were gone." She'd sewn the stocking and then cross-stitched his name across the top to match the ones for her, Decker and the twins, even though the younger boys couldn't be here.

She was still hoping they might be able to come down to the wedding next week, but she hadn't heard yet if they could get time away. Decker, Everleigh and Grady were coming though. "You like it?"

He shook his head. "I love it." He dropped a kiss on her lips. "This is amazin', pet. Thank you."

"You're welcome. I'm so glad to have you home." She kissed him again. Deepened it.

The clearing of a throat from the doorway broke them apart. "I can leave if you guys need a minute. Or more," Decker offered, having driven over from his condo across town. She'd been so engrossed in Warwick she hadn't heard the door open.

She laughed. "Don't be silly, get in here." She went over to hug him. "Merry Christmas, Deck."

"Merry Christmas," he answered, returning the hug. He was getting so much better at it. Easier with talking, too, even smiling, and she loved to see it. He seemed happy here. Less serious and grim. And he was enjoying working for Crimson Point Security, along with the training he got to do.

"Okay!" She stepped back, rubbed her hands together. "I'll go pour us some coffee, and we can enjoy the treats I made while we open our stockings."

"Did you make the peanut butter reindeer?" Decker asked, already seating himself on the sofa.

"Please, you know I did." She'd started making them for the twins when they were young. Round peanut butter cookies with a red M&M candy for a nose, and little eyes and antlers drawn on with melted chocolate. "Make yourselves comfy. I'll be right back."

She turned on music with her phone, hummed to herself as

she padded into the kitchen to get the coffee ready. She added peppermint creamer to hers and Decker's, and left Warwick's black because he thought flavored creamers were "ghastly."

In the midst of pulling a serving tray with handles from the cabinet next to the stove, she thought she heard footsteps and glanced behind her. Decker and Warwick were both sitting on the couch eating the cookies she'd put out. She smiled at the sight and quickly set the mugs on the tray.

"All right, who's ready for stockings—" She froze in the kitchen entryway, gaping.

The twins were both standing next to the tree, grinning at her.

"Oh my God," she cried, and just about dropped the tray in her haste to get rid of it so she could hug them.

Tristan laughed and wrapped her up in his arms. "Hey, Mar."

"Oh my *God*," she repeated, then let him go and grabbed hold of Gavin, who grunted at the force of her hug.

"Hi, Mar." He patted her on the back, his chin resting on her shoulder.

"What are you both doing here? I thought you said you couldn't get the time," she accused, easing back to look at them both. They were twenty-nine and pretty much the same size as Decker, but had her coloring, though their hair was a lighter shade of auburn.

It made her eyes sting to see how much they'd changed since she'd last seen them. Almost a year this time. Way too damn long.

"We wanted to surprise you. And we thought we'd better meet our future brother-in-law before you marry him," Tristan said.

"We're coming to the wedding, by the way," added Gavin.

"Oh!" She flung an arm around each of them, squeezed hard. "This is the best day *ever*. But how did you set this up?"

The twins smiled slightly and looked past her. She glanced over her shoulder, found Decker and Warwick both looking extremely pleased with themselves. "You guys did this?"

"Maybe," Decker said with a shrug, and polished off the last part of the cookie.

Tristan gasped. "Are those peanut butter reindeer?" He rushed for the table but Gavin beat him there and grabbed the remaining three for himself. "Hey!"

"You snooze, you lose." Gavin took a bite, rolled his eyes at the dark look Tristan was giving him and talked around it as he chewed. "Oh, fine, I guess it is Christmas," he muttered, handing one to his twin.

"Relax, I've got a whole other batch waiting in the kitchen," she told them, shaking her head. "Because I knew this would happen." Some things never changed. They'd fought over these cookies every year since forever.

They both gave her innocent looks that she didn't find the least convincing. She knew better.

Bubbling with excitement, she pushed past them and plopped down on the sofa between Decker and Warwick. "Thank you both. This was the best present ever."

She leaned into Warwick's side as he wrapped an arm around her. "And you. How did you manage to pull this off without me guessing?"

He gave her a funny look. "I used to be a spy."

She laughed. "Fair point." She shook her head. "You sneaky thing."

He shrugged. "Well, aye."

This was so like him. She'd done all this to give Warwick a Christmas to make up for all the ones he'd missed out on. Instead, he'd turned the tables on her and made her heart overflow by giving her the family Christmas she'd dreamed about for so long.

Warwick's grin turned her inside out. He pulled her into his lap, his dark eyes promising more surprises later once they were alone in their bed. "Happy Christmas, pet."

—The End—

Dear reader,

Thank you for reading ***Lethal Reprisal***. If you'd like to stay in touch with me and be the first to learn about new releases you can:

Join my newsletter at:
http://kayleacross.com/v2/newsletter/
Find me on Facebook:
https://www.facebook.com/KayleaCrossAuthor/
Follow me on Twitter:
https://twitter.com/kayleacross
Follow me on Instagram:
https://www.instagram.com/kaylea_cross_author/

Also, please consider leaving a review at your favorite online book retailer. It helps other readers discover new books.

Happy reading,
Kaylea

GUARDING TEAGAN
CRIMSON POINT SECURITY SERIES

By Kaylea Cross
Copyright © 2023 Kaylea Cross

PROLOGUE

Teagan finished scooping out the guts of her second pumpkin onto the newspaper she'd spread out on her kitchen table and wiped her hands on a rag, then paused to glance up as Disney's *The Legend of Sleepy Hollow* played on her TV across the living room. Poor Ichabod was starting his lonely, midnight trek home after the party at the Van Tassel farm, with no clue about what he was in for.

It was a classic for a reason. Every time that trumpet blared as the headless horseman's mount reared on its hind legs, its rider brandishing its sword, she got chills.

She picked up the sharp paring knife and began cutting a triangular eye into the pumpkin flesh, feeling like a kid again. Halloween was still almost a week away but you wouldn't know it from the state of her Pacific Heights neighborhood. Almost everyone on her block already had their Victorian porches all decked out with spooky witches and ghosts and bats, spiders and cobwebs hanging from the railings along with strands of orange and purple lights. San Fran did up Halloween right.

Once the eyes were done she checked her phone for the

time and saw that her cousin should be on her way over soon. She and Lily had carved pumpkins together ever since they were little, but Lily had picked up an extra shift on a research boat today and told Teagan to start without her.

She loved this time of year, the weather turning cool and crisp, leaves changing into their brilliant autumn colors. Having a whole Saturday to herself was a luxury she planned to make the most of. In anticipation of Lily's arrival she had a crockpot full of homemade spiced apple cider ready to go on the kitchen counter along with a tray of cupcakes frosted with purple and green icing.

Once Lily got here they'd decorate them with little spiders on top made of chocolate wafer cookie bodies, slices of marshmallows and mini chocolate chips for eyes, and thin black licorice strings for legs. Their rule was, calories didn't count at Halloween, Christmas or Easter.

Just as she picked the paring knife back up to start the jagged outline of her grinning jack-o-lantern mouth, her phone rang. She hit the TV remote to pause the movie, then answered Lily's call. "Hey, you all done down there? I'm just carving my pumpkin face now, and—"

"I'm hiding in a boat and I'm scared," her cousin said in an urgent whisper.

She tensed. "What's wrong?"

"Remember how you told me to keep my eyes and ears open for anything suspicious?"

Oh no. "Yeah, why?"

"I saw a couple guys acting suspiciously on a boat moored next to us. It was already dark and they didn't know I was there so I moved in closer until I could hear them. I overheard their conversation. It was about something bad. Then he saw me and stopped. I left in a hurry."

This didn't sound good, and Lily was still whispering. She set the knife down, pulse accelerating. "Where are you?"

"Still at the marina. My car's parked out back."

"Did they try to confront or follow you?"

"No. Well, I'm not sure, actually."

"What did they say?"

"Some things about avoiding certain checkpoints to get the shipment through tonight. And other stuff, but it was enough for me to tell they were definitely talking about smuggling."

Unease built in the pit of Teagan's stomach. There had been a large uptick in drug smuggling and related crime all along this part of the coast in recent months. She'd been briefed about it again the other day, including chatter about exactly the kind of thing Lily had just described. "You're sure they saw you?"

"Yes, they both went dead still and stared at me in a creepy way. I turned away and pretended to keep working on deck as though I hadn't heard anything alarming."

She stood, ready to head for the door. "Do you feel unsafe?"

"Yes, and I don't know what to do. They definitely suspect I heard them. I know you have contacts, so I'll tell you everything when it's safe. I don't want to say more over the phone in case anyone overhears me, because that's how people die in the movies."

Not just in the movies. Teagan was genuinely concerned about her cousin's safety. "Hang up and call the cops."

"No, I don't want to involve the cops yet. I want to talk to you first and see if you think I'm right."

"You need to get somewhere safe." She rushed for the back door. Dammit. She'd been the one to put Lily in this position by asking her to keep an eye out for anything suspicious when she was at the marina. "Where are you at the marina?"

"Hiding below deck in another boat. I was too scared to go

to my car in case they're waiting for me in the parking lot or something."

"I'm coming to get you," she said, grabbing her keys as she shoved her feet into her boots. It was completely dark out, making it easier for someone to attack or follow Lily.

"No, just wait and stay on the line with me. I'm going up on deck now to take a look around."

Teagan bit back an argument, not liking the feel of this at all. She had military training. Lily was a civilian. A marine biology student working on her Masters degree and making a bit of extra money by picking up shifts on research vessels on the weekends. "Be careful."

"I will." A full minute passed before Lily spoke again. "Okay, I think they're gone. Don't see anyone else around. But I'm going to ask someone at the office to escort me to my car just in case."

Good. "Are you sure you don't want me to come get you? It's no problem, I can be there in twenty minutes." With a weapon.

"No, I'm good," she said at normal volume, clearly feeling less afraid. "I was just spooked, that's all."

"Never ignore your intuition. It was warning you for a reason." Women dismissed that inner danger detector way too often.

"Okay."

"I'll stay on the phone with you while you go to the office."

"All right. I'm up on the dock now." Hollow footsteps sounded in the background as Lily hurried along the wooden planks. Then a door squeaked open. "Hey, Bob. Would you mind walking me to my car?"

"Sure," a male voice answered. "Everything okay?"

"Yes. I'd just feel better with an escort."

"No problem."

"Don't hang up," Teagan told her, the sharp edge of anxiety easing slightly now that Lily had someone with her. If the men from the boat were watching her, they were less likely to try anything in front of a witness.

"It's okay, Bob's taking me to my car now," Lily said.

"You know him? Enough to trust him right now?"

"Yes."

Teagan would still have preferred to come get her herself. "You still want to come over? Or you want me to meet you somewhere?"

"Actually... Can you come over to my place instead?"

"Yeah, of course. I'll leave right now."

"Thanks," Lily said on a relieved sigh. "I'll fill you in on everything when you get there."

"Okay, but call if anything feels off. Anything at all. Promise?"

"Yeah, promise."

"Love you."

"Love you too. See you in a bit."

Teagan shrugged her coat on drove to Lily's place over in the Marina District. Road construction and detour traffic delayed her by ten minutes and when she arrived at the townhouse complex Lily's little black car was already sitting out front at the end of her walkway. Her cousin's front porch light was on, and so was the one in Lily's bedroom in the second floor front window.

She rang the bell and waited but there was no answer. She tried knocking. Then texted, thinking maybe Lily was in the shower.

Hey, I'm at the front door.

But after several minutes, there was still no response. It was cold out and a light rain was starting to fall so she decided to get the spare key and let herself in.

She went around to the side of the townhouse and through the wooden gate into the tiny backyard. Lily kept the key hidden in a faux rock set in the little garden off the back patio. She picked it up, slid the top portion to the side and took out the key in the slot before heading back around to the front again.

"Hello?" she called as she stepped inside, locking the door and taking off her boots on the mat in the entry. "Lil?"

Still nothing.

She jogged up the stairs to the lower landing, paused. She didn't hear the shower running upstairs. "Lil?"

Frowning, she kept going to the second floor and stopped outside the master bedroom door. Knocked. "Lily, I'm here." She knocked again. "Hey, are you okay?"

When her cousin didn't answer she tried the doorknob. It was locked.

"Lily, I'm getting worried," she called out in a louder voice. "Are you in there? Just answer me."

She waited another ten seconds, then went to the hall closet and took out a coat hanger, anxiety buzzing in her gut. She straightened out the hook and stuck it into the hole in the lock, jimmied it around while turning the knob and pushing it in.

It snicked open. She shoved it wide and barged in, only to freeze in horror.

Lily lay sprawled facedown on the carpet beside her bed. Her head was turned toward the door. Eyes open, her lips blue.

"Lily!" She raced forward, knelt beside her cousin and cupped her face in her hands. "Lily, can you hear me? Come on, wake up." She checked her carotid pulse. Felt only the tiniest flutter, and Lily's chest wasn't moving.

Swearing, she rolled Lily to her back, quickly checked her airway for a blockage and then began chest compressions with one hand as she whipped out her phone with the other and put in on speaker to call 911. The instant the operator answered,

Teagan cut her off to list the address and explain what was going on. She kept up with the compressions all the while, frantic to keep Lily's heart beating.

"Come on, Lil," she choked out, own heart hammering. Tears blurred her vision. This wasn't happening. Couldn't be.

But Lily wasn't responding to anything. Her lips were turning purple now, the rest of her face an awful, ashen grey, her half-closed eyes staring at nothing.

"Paramedics and the police have been dispatched," the operator's voice said through the phone.

Teagan didn't answer, busy tipping Lily's head back to give her a breath and then jumping back into the compressions. Knowing her cousin was dying right in front of her and determined to stop it from happening. *No, no, no…*

Something fell out of Lily's right hand as her fingers relaxed. A small plastic bag. Tiny multicolored pills spilled out onto the carpet.

Teagan stared at them, ice trickling up her spine. She knew what they were instantly.

Rainbow fentanyl. A deadly opiate lethal in even the smallest doses.

Except Lily had never taken an illicit drug in her life.

This was a setup.

Her cousin had just been murdered. And Teagan knew it had been the men from the marina.

End Excerpt

ABOUT THE AUTHOR

NY Times and USA Today Bestselling author Kaylea Cross writes edge-of-your-seat military romantic suspense. Her work has won many awards, including the Daphne du Maurier Award of Excellence, and has been nominated multiple times for the National Readers' Choice Awards. A Registered Massage Therapist by trade, Kaylea is also an avid gardener, artist, Civil War buff, Special Ops aficionado, belly dance enthusiast and former nationally-carded softball pitcher. She lives in Vancouver, BC with her husband and family.

You can visit Kaylea at www.kayleacross.com. If you would like to be notified of future releases, please join her newsletter.

Direct link: http://kayleacross.com/v2/newsletter/

COMPLETE BOOKLIST

ROMANTIC SUSPENSE

Crimson Point Security Series
GUARDING TEAGAN (Decker and Teagan)

Crimson Point Protectors Series
FALLING HARD (Travis and Kerrigan)
CORNERED (Brandon and Jaia)
SUDDEN IMPACT (Asher and Mia)
UNSANCTIONED (Callum and Nadia)
PROTECTIVE IMPULSE (Donovan and Anaya)
FINAL SHOT (Grady and Everleigh)
FATAL FALLOUT (Walker and Ivy)
LETHAL REPRISAL (Warwick and Marley)

Crimson Point Series
FRACTURED HONOR (Beckett and Sierra)
BURIED LIES (Noah and Poppy)
SHATTERED VOWS (Jase and Molly)
ROCKY GROUND (Aidan and Tiana)
BROKEN BONDS (ensemble)
DEADLY VALOR (Ryder and Danae)
DANGEROUS SURVIVOR (Boyd and Ember)

Kill Devil Hills Series

UNDERCURRENT (Bowie and Aspen)
SUBMERGED (Jared and Harper)
ADRIFT (Chase and Becca)

Rifle Creek Series
LETHAL EDGE (Tate and Nina)
LETHAL TEMPTATION (Mason and Avery)
LETHAL PROTECTOR (Braxton and Tala)

Vengeance Series
STEALING VENGEANCE (Tyler and Megan)
COVERT VENGEANCE (Jesse and Amber)
EXPLOSIVE VENGEANCE (Heath and Chloe)
TOXIC VENGEANCE (Zack and Eden)
BEAUTIFUL VENGEANCE (Marcus and Kiyomi)
TAKING VENGEANCE (ensemble)

DEA FAST Series
FALLING FAST (Jamie and Charlie)
FAST KILL (Logan and Taylor)
STAND FAST (Zaid and Jaliya)
STRIKE FAST (Reid and Tess)
FAST FURY (Kai and Abby)
FAST JUSTICE (Malcolm and Rowan)
FAST VENGEANCE (Brock and Victoria)

Colebrook Siblings Trilogy
BRODY'S VOW (Brody and Trinity)
WYATT'S STAND (Wyatt and Austen)

EASTON'S CLAIM (Easton and Piper)

Hostage Rescue Team Series
MARKED (Jake and Rachel)
TARGETED (Tucker and Celida)
HUNTED (Bauer and Zoe)
DISAVOWED (DeLuca and Briar)
AVENGED (Schroder and Taya)
EXPOSED (Ethan and Marisol)
SEIZED (Sawyer and Carmela)
WANTED (Bauer and Zoe)
BETRAYED (Bautista and Georgia)
RECLAIMED (Adam and Summer)
SHATTERED (Schroder and Taya)
GUARDED (DeLuca and Briar)

Titanium Security Series
IGNITED (Hunter and Khalia)
SINGED (Gage and Claire)
BURNED (Sean and Zahra)
EXTINGUISHED (Blake and Jordyn)
REKINDLED (Alex and Grace)
BLINDSIDED: A TITANIUM CHRISTMAST NOVELLA (ensemble)

Bagram Special Ops Series
DEADLY DESCENT (Cam and Devon)
TACTICAL STRIKE (Ryan and Candace)
LETHAL PURSUIT (Jackson and Maya)

DANGER CLOSE (Wade and Erin)

COLLATERAL DAMAGE (Liam and Honor)

NEVER SURRENDER (A MACKENZIE FAMILY NOVELLA) (ensemble)

Suspense Series

OUT OF HER LEAGUE (Rayne and Christa)

COVER OF DARKNESS (Dec and Bryn)

NO TURNING BACK (Ben and Samarra)

RELENTLESS (Rhys and Neveah)

ABSOLUTION (Luke and Emily)

SILENT NIGHT, DEADLY NIGHT (ensemble)

PARANORMAL ROMANCE

Empowered Series

DARKEST CARESS (Daegan and Olivia)

HISTORICAL ROMANCE

THE VACANT CHAIR (Justin and Brianna)

EROTIC ROMANCE (writing as ***Callie Croix***)

DEACON'S TOUCH

DILLON'S CLAIM

NO HOLDS BARRED

TOUCH ME

LET ME IN

COVERT SEDUCTION

Printed in Great Britain
by Amazon